JAN COFFEY

THE
PUPPET MASTER

MIRA®

Recycling programs for this product may not exist in your area.

ISBN-13: 978-0-7783-2610-6
ISBN-10:   0-7783-2610-1

THE PUPPET MASTER

Copyright © 2009 by Nikoo K. and James A. McGoldrick.

MIRA and the Star Colophon are trademarks used under license and registered in Australia, New Zealand, Philippines, United States Patent and Trademark Office and in other countries.

www.MIRABooks.com

Printed in U.S.A.

To our Taft "children"

Hilary Andrysick, Isaac Bamgbose, Yara Benjamin, Mina Blossom, Mathieu Bogrand, Zach Brazo, Amy Brownstein, Pat Clare, Kathy Demmon, Grace Dishongh, Lindsay Dittman, Jack Dowling, Cyrus Eslami, Julie Foote, Ches Fowler, Mackenzie Holland, Bo Jones, Allyson Kane, Alex Kendall, Paul Kiernan, Holly Lagasse, Dan Lima, John Lombard, Bobby Manfreda, Alexis McNamee, Catie Moore, Liesl Morris, Austin Paley, Chelsea Ross, Patrick Salazar, Will Sayre, Max Scheifele, Ben Slowik, Ryan Uljua, Katie Van Dorsten, Bob Vulfov, Annie Ziesing... and Sam McGoldrick.

And to the entire
Taft '09 Graduating Class

May God give you...
For every storm, a rainbow,
For every tear, a smile,
For every care, a promise,
And a blessing in each trial.
For every problem life sends,
A faithful friend to share,
For every sigh, a sweet song,
And an answer for each prayer.
                              —An Irish Prayer

BOOK 1

Whether 'tis nobler in the mind to suffer
The slings and arrows of outrageous fortune,
Or to take arms against a sea of troubles,
And by opposing end them? To die: to sleep;
No more; and by a sleep to say we end
The heart-ache...

—*Hamlet*

1

FEAR

Kapali Carsi, the Grand Bazaar
Istanbul, Turkey

Kapali Carsi, Istanbul's largest covered market. A rabbit warren of over four thousand shops, restaurants, public or private rooms. Nothing existed under the sun that you couldn't buy or sell under the gold, blue and white tiled arches and painted domes. Turkish carpets, tiles and pottery, copper and brassware, leather apparel, cotton and wool, meerschaum pipes, alabaster bookends and ashtrays...along with opium harvests and shipments of semiautomatic weapons, if you knew who to talk to. Anything a buyer could want, so long as he had euros or dollars to offer as payment.

Though Kapali Carsi was becoming more of a tourist attraction than a local market, amongst the crowded stalls a person could still find Turks of every walk of life brushing shoulders with people of every nationality.

Everyone. And in the streets around the bazaar, the stalls and shops were as crowded.

In the daytime, that is.

Nathan Galvin was enjoying Istanbul. After twenty days in the city and many walking tours through it, he was feeling very at ease here. He was even using the Turkish he'd studied for the six months prior to coming here from the United States. He no longer took cabs, preferring to walk or take a tram to get around. He now haggled and never paid full price for anything. And that included food and even the price of his new hotel room.

Nathan looked out the tram window at the orange setting sun as it flashed between the buildings. He was dressed in jeans and old sneakers and a gray down jacket that kept out the cutting January wind. With his Mediterranean complexion, short hair and stubble of beard, he knew he didn't look much different than most of the natives. He liked that. He preferred to move about freely. He liked to eat where the locals ate and live the way they did. He wanted to weave himself seamlessly into the tapestry of Istanbul. Simple as that.

Nathan picked up his backpack off the floor of the tram and got out at Carsikapi stop. One of the south entrances of the Grand Bazaar loomed ahead of him. It was near sundown. The air was growing colder. He zipped up the jacket to his chin. The smell of spices and kebabs from various restaurants permeated the air. His stomach began to protest in hunger, but he ignored it. The streets were already nearly empty of shoppers and tourists. The storekeepers he passed were beginning to close for the night, taking in the merchandise hanging out on poles for display.

He walked up the slight incline to the nearest arched doorway. A group of young men and women who looked to be university students stood at each side of the door, passing out flyers as people made their way out of the bazaar. Nathan noticed that he was one of the only ones going in. A dark-eyed beauty turned and handed him a flyer. He took it with a nod and looked down at the Turkish words as he entered the bazaar. His command of reading and writing hadn't caught up to his conversational Turkish.

Inside, the air was much warmer, and Nathan dropped the paper into a nearby barrel. The place was nearly deserted. He hadn't been here before at this time of day, but as he walked by the stalls, it occurred to him that he recognized the smells of the place. The scent of wool from rugs stacked up in the nearest shop. The smell of saffron and other spices from the next stall. Each store seemed to offer its own distinct scent. Since arriving in Turkey, he realized, he was so much more attuned to his senses. Smells, tastes, the bright colors. At twenty-three, he didn't think he'd ever been so aware of these things.

The rug seller was pulling sheets of plastic over his inventory. He gave Nathan a cursory glance but found him unworthy of his time.

Nathan unzipped his jacket and took out a small notebook from his pocket. He stared down at the directions written on it: name, place, time. The shop mentioned wasn't one that he'd visited before, nor did he remember going by it on his other visits to the bazaar. He had some walking to do to get there.

He adjusted the backpack on his shoulder and made his way straight into the belly of the building. Following a major concourse, he looked down shop-lined alleys bleeding off to the left and right. Most of the shops this far into the bazaar were already closed, their wooden shutters bolted and the owners gone to their suppers and their hookahs and their tea. Almost no one was going in the direction he was going now.

Unexpectedly, a cold sliver of fear slid upward along Nathan's spine.

Shaking it off, he went over in his head what he was supposed to say. Digging his hand into the front pocket of his jeans, he touched the flash drive that he needed to exchange when he arrived at the shop. The instructions were simple. What he needed to say was brief. He'd practiced it enough times that he could do it in his sleep. Still, he could feel the anxiety building. He was still new at this, and he wanted to be done with the job. There were even fewer people when he took a left down a narrower alley. All the stores were closed, except one near the end. In the darkness beyond it, Nathan could see a closed wooden double door, just large enough for bringing in merchandise. It was barred, and on the other side, he decided, lay one of the alleyways surrounding the bazaar.

Two men were talking loudly about soccer as they refilled bins with dried fruit from burlap sacks.

Nathan saw someone materialize in the darkness by the door. The man was smoking a cigarette, his eyes intent on Nathan.

The cell phone in his pocket vibrated to life. He

reached for it. He knew it would be his parents. He'd been playing phone tag with them for the past few days. He knew he shouldn't answer it now.

Part of his instructions had been to have no personal items on him today. No cell phone. No passport. Nathan had made an exception with the phone.

The phone vibrated again. He actually considered answering it. He glanced at his watch. It was around 8:00 a.m. back on the East Coast in the U.S. There would be no short conversation with them. He could call them after he was done with this job. He noticed that the man by the door had disappeared. Nathan's parents made the decision for him. The cell phone stopped vibrating.

Nathan nodded to the two dried-fruit sellers as he passed them. When he reached the end of the row, he peered in the dim light at the notebook in his hand. He was to turn right and take the next left, where another concourse crossed. A woman wearing a black chador and dragging a toddler by the hand behind her was the only person in this stretch of shops. She steered a wide path around Nathan and hurried on.

Without the lights of the shops, it was now quite dark. He saw a shadow by the next archway. Nathan thought it must be the same man who'd been watching him before. Dark leather jacket. The glow of a cigarette cupped in his hand.

Nathan's scalp prickled and he slowed down. He'd been told this would be a clean, in-and-out job. Simple. A chance for him to meet a local contact. He was sent here alone. It should be easy, but still, doubt nagged at Nathan as he reached the archway. He glanced down at the directions again. He was close to the meeting place. The smell of cigarette smoke hung in the air. The alley ahead was one dark shadow. The man with the cigarette had certainly moved through here only seconds before. He had to be the contact.

An unexpected breeze touched his cheek. He looked up. A small window high in the archway was open, and Nathan could see a white moon in the dark sky. It was beautiful. Forcing himself to be calm, he made a mental note to walk by the river before going back to his hotel tonight. Istanbul had its dangers, but it was a civilized city. A city of beauty. Paris of the Middle East. He filled his lungs with the fresh air and made up his mind. He stepped through the arch into the darkness.

"Merhaba," a voice whispered. The man was ahead and to the right.

The tip of the cigarette glowed, and Nathan zeroed in on him before stepping forward and repeating the greeting. *"Merhaba."*

"Nasilsiniz?" the man asked. *How are you?*

"Iyiyim," Nathan answered, suddenly uncomfortable with the small talk.

He knew this wasn't the final destination. He'd been told he would meet his contact at a shop.

"Isminiz nedir?" Nathan asked. It wouldn't hurt to ask the other man's name. He wanted to be sure he had the right person.

"Arkada."

Nathan had to repeat the name a couple of times in his head before the meaning dawned on him. It wasn't a name. The word meant "friend." He was saying he was a friend. Nathan stopped a few feet away from him. The man was leaning against the wall. He was wearing a black leather jacket over a dark shirt and black pants. In the darkness, his face was obscured. The cigarette in his hand hung at his side.

"Isminiz nedir?" Nathan repeated. He wanted a name.

The man dropped the cigarette, crushed it beneath his boot. He shifted against the wall, and his face came into view. Uncontrollably, Nathan took a half step back.

"It…is not…matter," the man said in broken English.

Nathan stared. The man's upper lip was marked with a scar that started on the right side of his nose and ran down on a diagonal through his thick mustache. A short white line from the same cut scarred his lower lip. His black eyes showed nothing.

The man's hand slipped into his jacket pocket and Nathan's body tensed.

"You here…want this," the man said, taking his hand out of the pocket. Within the palm Nathan saw the small flash drive.

Nathan nodded, a head jerk intended to be friendly, and pulled the flash drive from his own pocket.

"Yes. Everything you need is here. This was easy." He realized he was speaking too quickly. He never thought the job would go like this. He didn't like it.

Nathan extended his hand, holding out the flash drive. He couldn't wait to get out of here.

At that moment the cell phone came to life again in his pocket. Its soft buzz echoed in the silence of the dark.

"Here it is…I have to go."

"Wait." The man looked at Nathan's pocket. "Not go."

"It's nothing. We've made our—" From behind, the hood snapped over his head even as a light flashed brilliantly behind his eyes. Voices murmured for only a moment in muffled Turkish as Nathan felt himself falling from a great height.

And the rest was silence…

2

LOSS

NASA Ames Research Center,
Moffett Field, California

The day the Loma Prieta earthquake rocked the Bay Area in October of 1989, Alanna Mendes had been working for NASA at Moffett Field for exactly one month. At the very moment the quake began, she was on her way home to Mountain View when the roadway suddenly shuddered and then buckled beneath the shuttle bus. She helped others out of the vehicle, waited with them for rescue vehicles to arrive and eventually made her way home on foot.

The next morning, Alanna was on time for work, as she would be every morning for the next nineteen years. Rain, wind, fog, good weather, bad weather, earthquakes…it made no difference. One thing that never changed was Alanna Mendes. She was punctual, precise, dedicated to her job. She was a creature of habit.

And after what had happened these past few months, she needed that in her life.

Each morning was the same. Leaving her apartment at 6:20, she would board the shuttle bus one block away at precisely 6:29. She sat in the second to last seat on the exit-door side of the bus. She said very little to others who got on the bus after her. The shuttle would make one more pickup stop in Mountain View and then four stops at various buildings once it entered the complex of facilities at Moffett Field. She would have between seventeen to nineteen minutes before reaching her destination at Building 23 of the NASA Research Park. Alanna would be at her desk between six forty-five and six-fifty.

She liked beginning the day this way. The precision and the predictability of it appealed to the engineer in her. The time on the bus was her prep time, her focus period, and her chance to immerse herself in work. She loved her job. She was good at it. But doing what she did required a clear head, a focused mind. The commute gave her a chance to shake out the cobwebs…and leave her personal life behind. Like every other morning, she spent the minutes going over her schedule for the day on her BlackBerry and reading e-mail that had been sent to her overnight and that she'd downloaded this morning while her coffee brewed. She took the indispensable electronic device from her bag now.

Other NASA workers who rode the bus kept their distance. Her seniority and rank gave her clout, and they all knew what she'd endured this past fall. Everyone respected her desire for privacy.

"Mind if I sit here, Dr. Mendes?"

Almost everyone, Alanna thought, looking up. A new hire. She'd been introduced to the young engineer right before the holidays. She'd also seen her on her floor twice during the days between Christmas and New Year's, when just a skeleton crew had been working. There were over a hundred and fifty people who worked in her group. It was a miracle that Alanna remembered the engineer at all. She looked up at the round, cheerful face and decided she didn't care to remember her name.

Alanna motioned vaguely at the four unoccupied rows of seats in front of her and looked back down at her BlackBerry screen. "There are plenty of seats."

"You probably don't remember me," the engineer said, dropping her briefcase and lunch pack on the seat in front of Alanna. She didn't sit down, though, and Alanna was forced to look up again.

Some of the other riders were directing surprised looks back at them.

"I'm Jill Goldman," the young woman continued, extending her hand. "I'm working with Phil Evans, who works for you. He's been telling me so much about you and all your work on STEREO project. I've read every one of your publications. And when I was interviewed by NASA, I was astounded to think that I would actually be able to work beside you and—"

"I remember you," Alanna interrupted, deciding there was no point in being an absolute bitch. She shook the woman's hand briefly. "Look, Ms. Goldman, I have to get this done before we arrive at Building 23."

She moved her briefcase from the floor to the seat beside her. She snapped it open and took out a pen, hoping that would make her point about the seat not being available.

"Sure, sure…I understand." Jill slipped into the seat in front of her.

Alanna made a mental note to talk to Phil today. He could explain some ground rules to the young woman.

Jill turned around in her seat. "Did you have a nice New Year's Eve?"

Alanna decided to write an e-mail to Phil, instead. Right now.

"This was the first New Year's Eve my husband and I spent as a married couple," Jill said, leaning her head back against the glass. She was staring into space, caught up for a moment in her own little world, not even realizing that her question had gone unanswered. She refocused her attention on Alanna. "We were married the weekend before I started working here at Moffett. The Friday of Thanksgiving weekend. We had a small ceremony at my parents' house. The immediate family and a handful of friends came over. It was just perfect. Just the way we both wanted it to be."

As much as Alanna wanted to brush her off, the tone of the young woman's voice and the date tugged a string deep inside. She stared down at the BlackBerry. A haze covered her vision.

That was supposed to be Alanna's wedding weekend, too. Ray and Alanna had planned to be married the day after Thanksgiving. A small ceremony. Just a handful of friends and her grandmother. She hadn't wanted to wear a wedding dress, just a suit. Ray had talked her into choosing a white suit.

The rush of emotions tore at the facade she forced herself to maintain. Alanna closed her eyes, remembering how on the same Friday night this Jill Goldman had been married, she had checked into the hotel in Carmel where she and Ray had planned to spend their wedding weekend. Locked up in that suite, she'd shed so many tears, rehashed it all. Guilt. Denial. More guilt. *Why* had she encouraged him to go on that trip?

It wasn't her fault. A freak explosion, the police had said. An accident.

Alanna felt a single tear squeeze past her eyelids. She brushed it away.

"Oh my God," Jill whispered. "It was you they were talking about. I'm so sorry. I heard half a conversation— I didn't know…I never realized it was you. It was *your* fiancé who died on that boating thing this past fall just before the STEREO satellite launch. How horrible that must have been! I am *so* sorry."

A lump the size of a basketball had lodged itself in Alanna's throat, but it didn't matter. She felt the bus pull away from the first stop at Moffett Field, the Microsoft facility. She didn't want to talk about this. She shoved her things into the briefcase and closed the top.

Jill's voice was hushed. She was apologizing again, but Alanna couldn't hear it. She'd thought she was done with these sharp, slashing cuts of emotion. The antidepressants she'd been given by her doctor before Christmas had been helping. Until now. She needed air. She needed to walk. She needed to screw her head on straight before she arrived at work.

Alanna pushed to her feet.

"Are you okay?" Jill placed a hand on her sleeve.

"I'm fine," Alanna managed to say. She started toward the front of the bus. She could feel the curious glances of a few of the riders as she passed.

"You getting off at the next stop, Alanna?" a voice asked. It was another project manager in Building 23.

She nodded and walked past him, too. The shuttle slowed down at the stop. Alanna cleared her voice, tried to paste on a fake smile. She pulled on her sunglasses, despite the fact that the day was overcast. Too many people were getting out at this stop. She knew some of them. She would have no privacy.

At the last moment, she dropped into a vacated seat. She slid to the window and stared out at the departing riders and the commuters. Men and women, casually dressed, juggled coffees and briefcases and purses as they made their way along the sidewalks. Engineers, researchers, clerical workers, technical types. They were so young, she thought. They seemed to be getting younger every year.

The bus door swung closed, and they pulled away from the curb. Two stops more, she told herself. She could manage two stops.

Alanna froze.

She saw him on the sidewalk. Only for an instant, but she couldn't be mistaken. He was walking toward the bus stop they'd just left. He was wearing a blue blazer and carrying a leather briefcase. His hair was longer, curlier. She stared at his face as the bus flashed past him, her breath crushed from her chest. She whirled in her seat, staring at his back for only a second, and then he was gone.

It was Ray.

Stunned, she sat still, unable to grasp what had just happened.

It couldn't have been Ray. He was dead. It was a freak accident. He was gone.

Alanna was on her feet in an instant.

"Stop!" She scrambled toward the door. "Stop the bus!"

3

DESPAIR

Brooklyn, New York

His hand shook. The stack of mail slipped to the floor and scattered around his feet. David Collier read the letter from the insurance company for the second time.

> *At present, no recognized studies provide evidence that the aforementioned treatment is viable. We regret to inform you...*

They were rejecting his daughter.

"Daddy...is everything okay?"

We regret to inform you...

David bent down to pick up the pieces of mail. He tried to pull himself together.

"Absolutely, honey," he said quietly. "Why wouldn't it be?"

He put the bag of groceries he'd brought in on the kitchen counter and dumped the mail next to it.

The small apartment smelled like a hospital. David couldn't bring himself to look up at Leah. The eight-year-old was lying in the rented hospital bed they kept where a dining table should be. His little girl was halfway through the day's peritoneal dialysis. The visiting nurse put aside the magazine she was reading and changed one of the plastic bags on the elaborate setup.

"How is it going?" he asked her.

The dour woman gave a firm nod and leaned back in her seat, once again lost in her reading.

The home treatment was one that David's wife, Nicole, had been trained in last year. As far as time and Leah's comfort, this was so superior to what the child had gone through in the clinics and hospitals since the first time the doctors discovered the rare kidney disease.

This method used the lining of Leah's abdominal cavity, the peritoneum, as a filter. David knew all the specifics. All the details. A catheter was placed in Leah's belly to pour a solution containing dextrose into the abdominal cavity. While the solution was there, it pulled wastes and extra fluid from the blood. Later, the solution was drained from the belly, along with the wastes and extra fluid. The cavity was then refilled, and the cleaning process continued.

Not pleasant to think about, but it was keeping his daughter alive.

The dialysis could be done at home, usually while Leah slept, without a health professional present. Since Nicole's death, though, there'd been a change in schedule. David wasn't trained in the procedure. A visiting nurse had to come to the house to set up and monitor it. And this had to be done during the day, which meant for those two days every week, Leah was not going to school. But that wasn't the extent of it. David had met with Leah's doctors yesterday. They were planning to increase the dialysis. Starting next week, it would be every day. Her kidney function was rapidly failing. David had guessed at a need for change in treatments before he was told. Every day, he could see the steady decline in her health. She was losing weight again and she had no energy.

David hadn't been able to get up his courage to tell the eight-year-old the bad news, though.

"Any mail for me?" Leah asked, stretching a hand toward him.

David knew what his daughter wanted. She wanted to have him sit on the edge of the bed and wait with her until they were done. Leah wasn't too keen on this specific nurse. They'd had her in a couple of times before. David went through a large visiting-nurse agency that accepted their insurance. Liking a specific person seemed to be the kiss of death. They never came back. On the other hand, the sour ones were always repeats.

This one hadn't said more than two words to him. He had a feeling she hadn't been any more talkative with her patient.

Leah smiled when David sat down on the bed beside her. "So, anything good?" she asked, some of the strain gone from her pale face.

David gave a cursory glance at the mail he'd dropped on the counter. The insurance denial topped bills and bills and bills. There was no end to it. They were breaking him. And the letter today threatened to destroy what he had left of his family. Leah had been through a kidney transplant once already. Her body had its way of rejecting the organ. The doctors had predicted it would happen within a six-month to a one-year window. They were almost at ten months, and it was happening.

Then, the last time they were at the hospital, one of the doctors had told David about the research that was going on in Germany. They were cloning a person's kidney. He thought Leah would be a perfect candidate for the study.

An endeavor like that cost a lot of money, though, and David had gone through everything he had. He looked over at the mail again. With the rejection by the insurance company, he didn't know where else he could turn.

"Anything good, Daddy?"

David caressed Leah's soft brown hair. He shook his head. "Sorry, love. Nothing good."

He reached down, picked up the morning newspaper off the floor and glanced at the headlines he'd already read earlier in the day. He couldn't trust his emotions right now.

"It'll be okay," Leah whispered to him.

David was shaken by the tone, by the gentleness and love that it conveyed. There was so much of Nicole in their daughter. There had been so many times over these past four years that David had been on the verge of a breakdown—of doing something stupid. The world was against them. Everything that could go wrong had gone wrong. His job, Nicole's and Leah's health, the financial strains, the legal troubles that had dogged him. Nicole had held him together, though. She'd been able to keep him in one piece and standing straight, facing life's challenges each day. Her enthusiasm for life and her optimism had been contagious.

But now Nicole was gone, and he had to be as strong as his wife…for Leah's sake.

"Is there anything in that bag that is going to melt?" the eight-year-old asked, once again filling the shoes of the adult in their life.

He chuckled and ruffled her short hair as he got up. "Yes, there is."

"Popsicles?" she asked brightly, a child again.

He nodded. "Popsicles."

As Leah's kidney functions were dropping almost daily, she was having difficulty with urination. As a result, she couldn't drink like healthy children. Chewing ice cubes was one way David got liquids into her. Popsicles were a treat that they splurged on every now and then.

In the adjoining kitchen, he opened a drawer and shoved the delinquent notices from the counter into it. He'd go through them when Leah was sleeping.

"Tell your father about the phone call."

David and Leah both stared at the nurse, surprised that she had spoken.

"What phone call?"

"I'm sorry, Dad, I know you always tell me not to answer it and let the machine pick up. But the phone was right here and I picked it up without thinking." She held up the phone that was lying on the bed.

David didn't even answer the calls himself. These days every one of them was from some collection agency. He definitely didn't want to expose his daughter to their practiced rudeness.

"That's fine, honey," he said. He picked up another handset from the counter in the kitchen and checked the ID on the last incoming call. It showed as unknown.

"The man didn't leave a name or phone number. But I told him that you'd be back in half an hour, and he said he'll call again."

David made a mental note to make sure the call went directly to his answering machine. Whenever possible, he avoided speaking with creditors when Leah was awake. He went back to putting away the groceries. The box of Popsicles looked lost in the spacious empty freezer.

"He said the call was about a job offer."

A jolt ran through David. He turned to his daughter.

"A job offer?" he repeated.

A job offer.

Four years ago, David had been the CFO of a hot new international banking consortium. Heady stuff. A guest interview with Lou Dobbs. Even a glowing article in the *Wall Street Journal* about the management team. Good things never seem to last, though, David thought. Not in his life.

The title, the paycheck, the perks, the future had all come crashing down on him when his boss had embezzled a hundred and eighty million dollars before disappearing—but not before arranging everything to look as if David was behind it all. He was to be the fall guy…caught in the act, it appeared.

After months of spending his own money on lawyers, David had been lucky to walk away free, but that had been the end of any possibility of working in finance. Now he didn't have enough to cover all his family's monthly expenses, never mind Leah's medical bills.

"Is that what he said?"

Leah shrugged. "I think so."

David tried to remember who might still be looking at his résumé. It didn't matter. People make mistakes. All they had to do was look him up on Google, and that résumé would go in the round file. There was still enough inaccurate information out there to bury him twice over.

The phone rang. He looked at the display. Unknown.

"I told you he'd call back," Leah said, giving him the thumbs-up as he disappeared into the bedroom.

Already knowing the end result of this call, he answered the phone anyway. No sense leaving the poor guy hanging.

4

FEAR

Greenwich, Connecticut

Kei Galvin couldn't sleep. She couldn't eat. She couldn't sit for more than a few minutes at a time. She was restless, worried, a total mess.

The African violet on the coffee table lay dead, the vibrant purple flowers only a memory against the drooping green leaves. She couldn't bring herself to touch them. She hadn't checked the greenhouse for two days. The spring bulbs she'd started there in pots three weeks ago needed watering, but she couldn't rouse herself to spend time on them. She'd stopped taking her morning walk with her neighbor. She'd missed two doctor's appointments yesterday. She couldn't focus.

"I think we've waited long enough," she told her husband when he came back into their sitting room, carrying a cup of tea for her.

"I didn't know we'd been waiting."

At any other time she would have appreciated his

sense of humor. But not now. "He hasn't gone back to his hotel room. He doesn't answer his cell phone. He hasn't called."

"We don't know if he's gone back to his room or not. The two different desk people I spoke to on the phone just didn't know. We only know that at the time of our calls, he hasn't been there," Steven said reasonably. "And you know how it goes with the cell phone. He's not in New York City, with reception everywhere he goes. He's twenty-three years old, sweetheart. We don't have to hear from him every day. You have to—"

She whirled to face her husband. "Don't do this to me. I know my child. He knows me. He knows when I'm worried about him, and it doesn't matter where he's traveling or what time it is. He always calls or e-mails or somehow lets me know he's okay."

"And he will this time, too," Steven said softly. He put the cup down on the coffee table and placed both hands on Kei's shoulders, pushing her to sit down. "It's only been four days since he called."

"Eight days since I spoke to him," Kei corrected.

"Four days ago…he left a message."

She was back on her feet again, resuming her pacing. "Do we know anyone in Istanbul?" She didn't wait for an answer. "You have to know someone. Your company—"

"I sold my business, honey. It's been two years. I don't have the contacts I used to have."

"Did you have offices in Turkey?"

Steven ran a hand through his hair. Her mind ran on one track. She wouldn't hear reason. Waiting was out of the question. They'd been married nearly thirty years.

He knew Kei better than she knew herself. She was all love, emotions, affection. Kei wouldn't rest until they heard from Nathan. This had been the way their marriage had gone since the day Nathan was born. Their son always came first. Steven didn't begrudge him that, of course. He was certainly not neglected. And Nathan was their only child. For all the years that Steven had been building his company and living and breathing the air that was trapped inside those concrete walls, Kei had played the part of both parents. There was no denying it, the result was a bond between Kei and Nathan that ran deeper than the father-son relationship Steven had with him.

"Please, Steven." She took his hand. "Believe me… or just humor me. But do something. Get me some news of him. I know you can. Please, love."

Steven looked at Kei's teary eyes and gathered her in his arms. They'd become so much closer since he'd sold his company. They'd rediscovered what it was that had brought them together in the first place. More than best friends, they were soul mates. He loved her more than ever. He appreciated who she was.

"Okay, my love. I'll find that monster today. You'll hear his voice. I promise you."

5

STIGMA

Boston

For the hundredth time, Jay Alexei scraped his knuckle on the sharp edge of the narrow mailbox.

"Dammit!" he muttered, looking at the piece of hanging skin.

Shaking his head at the row of chrome-colored mail-boxes, he carefully slid his hand back in and tugged at the manila envelope, trying to free it. Apartment-building mailboxes suck, he thought as the corner of the envelope tore. The letter carrier had shoved the envelope all the way to the back, with all kinds of junk mail stuffed in front of it. That didn't help, of course.

He'd rented the studio apartment on the fifth floor of this building in South Boston last September. That had been right after he and Padma had decided to go to the courthouse in Pawtucket and get married. Neither of their parents had shown up for the wedding. She'd been eighteen and already four months pregnant. They'd moved up to Boston right after that, and he'd gotten a job in a warehouse six blocks away.

The place wasn't great, but it was convenient. For now, at least.

It'd been a hard four months for Padma, though, living here. For him, it wasn't bad, but he wasn't pregnant.

No, this was a lot better than Jay had seen in the past. Jail, for instance. That had been no picnic.

Until hooking up with him, though, Padma had never had to worry about heat or phone bills or where they were going to get the money to pay this month's rent. She'd been an only child. Just as her name denoted, Padma had been the lotus, the goddess Lakshmi, in her parents' eyes. They were first-generation immigrants from Mohali, India. Her father had come to this country for an engineering degree, gone back, married, and then returned to Rhode Island to stay. Her mother had spent her life taking Padma to piano lessons and ballet and all kinds of other extracurricular activities. They adored and spoiled her. That is, until she'd gotten knocked up by Jay. Then, she'd been given a choice. Lose the baby and forget Jay…or stay with him and they'd disown her.

Luckily for him, she'd taken Door Number Two.

Deciding he needed to use two hands, Jay put the open box containing the computer on the floor to get a better grip on everything that was stuffed in the mailbox.

The thing that twisted his heart day in and day out, however, was that she never complained. Sick as a dog during the whole pregnancy, she always had a smile for him. It didn't matter that her bathroom back home had been bigger than the entire apartment they were renting.

She greeted him every night as if she were welcoming the king to his castle. And every morning, she sent him away, telling him that she was the happiest woman in the world.

He didn't deserve her.

The envelope came out with more junk, and he threw the ads and flyers into a trash can next to the door. He stared at the manila envelope and smiled bitterly at the word *Mr.* printed before his name. He checked the sender. It was from his old high school back in Rhode Island. He tore it open. It was his high-school diploma.

"So I get a piece of paper after all." He shoved the diploma inside the computer box and picked it up.

Jay had skipped the graduation last June. There had been no point in going. At the time, he'd been a month away from turning twenty-one. He'd been too old to go to classes during the day, but the night classes had given him enough credits. Granted, the kids all knew him. He was famous in town, but everyone was too afraid of him or too embarrassed to say anything about his jail time. No, there'd been no point in going. It wasn't as if anyone in his family was going to be there, celebrating with him. That night, Jay and Padma had taken off for Newport to celebrate on their own. They'd spent the night huddled up in a blanket on the beach.

He slid his key into the metal inner door of the apartment building. If he knew then what he knew now, he wouldn't have bothered to go back for this stupid degree after getting out of jail. He'd thought it would be more meaningful than just getting a GED while he was in the slammer. But this piece of paper hadn't made a bit of difference. No one wanted to talk to him. No colleges had been standing in line. It didn't matter that he'd scored perfect on his SATs in seventh grade and how, from the time he'd been four feet tall, the gifted teachers in the public schools drooled all over him. They called him a prodigy, a genius. He had a photographic memory. He was getting letters from MIT and Johns Hopkins when he was still in middle school. Now he couldn't even get a job as a techie at a local computer store.

He couldn't make a decent living to support his wife and the baby that was on the way.

Jay took a breather on the third-floor landing. He didn't know how Padma handled these steps every day. She worked four hours a day at a deli around the corner. When they'd first moved in, she was doing eight hours a day. But she couldn't spend so much time on her feet. In fact, the doctor at the free clinic they'd gone to last week together told her that she should stop working entirely until after the baby was born. She hadn't gained enough weight, and there were times when Jay thought the little bundle in Padma's stomach weighed almost as much as the rest of her. Even so, Padma wasn't hearing what she was being told.

As he stood there, that flash of heat washed through him, just as it did every time he thought too much about their situation. They had a baby coming. How in God's name were they going to pay for it all?

Jay switched the box from one arm to the other and started up toward the fourth-floor landing. Odd jobs. Keep working. Keep scratching for every penny.

The computer under his arm belonged to one of the guys he worked with. He'd been having trouble with the thing, so Jay had offered to fix it up for fifty bucks. There were other jobs he'd done at work for free, but it was time to start charging. People he worked with knew he was good at this stuff.

Even though this was the first paying job, Jay hoped that maybe the word going around would get him other jobs like this. He had to make more money. There was so much that he wanted to do…no, *needed* to do…for Padma.

Just last night, the two of them had gone shopping for a crib for their baby. They went to the Goodwill store. The only problem was that they didn't have any cribs available…they should check back again next week. Padma hadn't complained, but he could look at her and see right into her soul. She was sad, disappointed.

As he plodded up the last remaining steps, he wondered for the thousandth time whether he was staying on the right side of the fence for nothing. For every guy in the pen, he knew there were a hundred on the outside… making it.

Jay had made one mistake in high school. Other kids made them all the time. But he was much smarter than other kids. So, of course, his crime had been that much more serious. The punishment more devastating. Well, he'd paid. He was still paying.

In spite of it all, he didn't want to be Padma's one mistake, even though her parents were certain he was.

At the top of the steps, he stopped and looked at the number on that pale green door to their apartment. Just thinking of her on the other side sent a burst of energy through him. That was all he needed. *She* was all he needed.

Still, as he fished in his pocket for the key, he wished he was carrying a bouquet of flowers or a box of chocolate instead of a busted computer.

At that moment the door opened. Padma, phone cradled against one ear, motioned excitedly to him to come in.

Jay was surprised. No one called them. They didn't have any friends. They only had the phone since that was his way of getting onto the Internet. He spent a lot of time on that. Also, having the phone gave him the peace of mind that she could call him at work if there was an emergency. She gestured that the call was for him.

Jay walked in, gently laying the box down inside the door.

"Hold on. You can talk to him yourself. He just walked in. Okay, thanks." She covered the mouthpiece and held out the phone to him.

He took it out of her hand and tossed it onto their sofa. She looked pale, and there were dark circles under her eyes. Her face had lost its sweet roundness, growing more drawn all the time. Every day, she looked as if she was shifting weight from her own body to the body growing in her rapidly expanding belly. He kissed her, ignoring the look of shock in her face at his cavalier treatment of the phone.

The phone was immediately forgotten, and Padma nestled into his arms, pressing her face against his chest.

"Group hug," she said, smiling as she placed his hand against her hard stomach.

"I missed you," he whispered against her silky hair. "Both of you."

"We missed you, too." She rose on her tiptoes and kissed his lips. She motioned to the handset on the sofa. "I think you might want to talk to him."

"Who is it?" Jay asked.

"I don't know."

"But you think I should talk to him," he said with a chuckle.

She shrugged. "It's a guy. He sounds pretty nice. He knew we're expecting our first baby. He said he was calling with news of an employment opportunity."

"An *employment opportunity?*" he repeated, curious. The people he knew these days talked about *jobs,* not *employment opportunities.* Usually, they meant heavy labor–type work. Somebody moving or buying something and needing an extra hand to take it somewhere. Well, the people he was working for at the warehouse knew Padma was pregnant. Jay suspected that this person had been referred by them.

She shrugged again and looked up at him in that cute way that made her look like an imp. "I didn't make it up. That's what he said."

A dozen things ran through Jay's mind as he went over and picked up the phone. He'd stuck a résumé up on a Monster job board and on Craigslist last summer… just to test the waters. Nothing serious had come of it. He tried not to build his hopes up.

"Hello. Can I help you?" he asked.

"Mr. Alexei?"

Mister! This was the second time today. Jeez, they'd be calling him *sir* next.

"Yes?"

"I'm calling on behalf of a client. We'd like to set up an interview with you, sir."

Okay, what the hell was going on?

Padma was standing so close, trying to hear what was going on, that Jay figured the guy could probably hear her breathing into the phone. Jay gently pushed her down on the sofa. He knew it would take her at least ten minutes to find her balance and get up again.

"Who's your client, if I may ask?" Jay asked.

"A private computer firm. You wouldn't know the name."

For the first time, Jay's attention zeroed in on the caller. In two and half years in jail, he'd met plenty of guys running scams. They sounded just like this guy. "Okay. Well, what kind of a…job…is it that your employer wants to interview me for?"

"It is for a programmer position."

"A programmer," he repeated, not believing his ears. Now he knew it couldn't be legit. The résumé he'd posted online was clear that he only had a high-school degree. What legit company would want an entry-level programmer that had no degree or real work experience?

"That's right. I can tell you that the position comes with a standard benefits package that will cover you and your family. I am also permitted to tell you that the annual salary is in the $150,000 to $180,000 range, with additional bonus incentives. This position requires relocation, but my employer will take care of the moving costs and all the smaller details. Would this kind of arrangement interest you, Mr. Alexei?"

Jay sank down next to Padma on the sofa. He

couldn't catch his breath for a couple of seconds. Legit or not, this was music to his ears.

"Are you there, sir?"

He cleared his throat. "I am…I am. Are you sure you have the right…the right person?"

"Oh, yes. I'm quite certain of that."

"Mr.… Mr.… What was your name again?"

"My apologies, Mr. Alexei," he said from the other end. "I never introduced myself to you. My name is Mr. Diarte. Hank Diarte."

"Mr. Diarte," Jay started. "I have to tell you, I think you must be mistaken about whoever it is you think I am. I only have a high-school education, and I—"

"I know more about you than you think, Mr. Alexei." Jay could hear a touch of European accent in the guy's voice. "Your name is Jay Alexei. Twenty-one years of age. Birthday? July 21. Born in Providence Women and Infants Hospital at 2:47 a.m. Your mother has been a music teacher at the Saint Cecilia School in Pawtucket, Rhode Island, for the past twenty-three years. A devout Catholic. Your father was a computer technician. He has been unemployed for the past three years. He has a problem with alcohol, I'm sorry to say. Your parents are presently separated, and you're not on speaking terms with either of them. No siblings. Do I have the right Jay Alexei?"

Jay leaned back. This wasn't exactly Google material. Padma snuggled next to him, looking curiously up into his face. "Keep going."

"My client believes you are an exceptionally bright young man. 'A genius with computers,' were his exact words, sir. To date, you are the only person who has ever been able to hack into NASA's central mainframe. And at the time you did it, you were only seventeen. You served two and half years in the Federal Correctional Institution in Otisville, New York."

"Look, I only poked my head into their site and looked around. No damage was done. No data was stolen. I made that mistake once, and I paid the price," Jay said thinly, planting his elbows on his knees. "I'm not interested in going that route again."

"Yes, sir. My client…Mr. Lyons…understands that entirely. He—"

"I have a family of my own now."

"My client knows that, sir. You need not have any fear on that account. You should know that Mr. Lyons is a man who believes in second chances. He also believes in his ability to find exceptional…albeit unconventional… talent."

"Go on."

"He knows that you are lacking in a few formal programming skills. Two and a half years is a long time to be out of the field. Still, if you decide to take the interview and you are offered the job, then my client will make every arrangement to provide any necessary training. Mr. Lyons is offering you something you will be hard pressed to find elsewhere, Mr. Alexei. He is offering you a fresh start."

Jay looked at Padma. She'd been listening to most of the conversation since he sat down. She was pressed up against him. She looked as wary of the whole thing as he was.

"What do you say, Mr. Alexei? Would you like to schedule an interview?"

Just as he started to answer, Jay felt a sharp kick from the baby against his side.

"Yes, Mr. Diarte," Jay said, having come to a decision. "I'll talk to you."

6

LOSS

Apparently, you had to be Bill Gates or the director of NASA to get permission to look at surveillance-camera tapes of the parking lots at Moffett Field.

Alanna stood in the security office and looked at the line of monitors behind the security guard. In several of them she could see the noon lunch traffic going by.

Well, she thought, a person at least needed to sound reasonably sane. *I thought I saw someone who looked like my dead fiancé* clearly hadn't sounded sane to anyone. Not to Moffett Field security. Not to the police detective who'd investigated Ray's accident last fall. Not even to the handful of people she and Ray called friends. Even the woman in the Division of Human Relations who'd brought Ray in as a contractor a year ago had listened to her question with barely concealed skepticism. The records showed that Ray Savoy was deceased.

Aside from the HR representative, everyone had obviously felt sorry for her, of course. Alanna had heard the note of sympathy over and over again.

And that was really about to drive her crazy.

She didn't want sympathy. She lived in the world of real, hard, quantifiable data. Yes, she had been distraught after Ray's death. She was still distressed. But she wasn't crazy. Or, at least, she didn't think so. If hallucinations now had to be added to her troubles, though, she'd go right down and have herself committed.

She hated this uncertainty. She hated doubting herself. Either Ray had been here or he hadn't. The answer was simple enough to find out.

"Ready?"

"Are you sure you aren't going to get into any trouble for this?" She knew the security guard was bending the rules to help her. Juan's grandmother was a good friend of Alanna's own *abuela*. She'd known the young man since he was a teenager and, in fact, had been a reference for him when he'd been hired a couple of years earlier.

"No," he replied. "Seriously. No trouble at all."

She still hesitated. She understood Juan thought of her almost like family. She shouldn't have asked him, Alanna thought. She didn't want him risking his position here. His wife had given birth to their first child just before Christmas, and Alanna knew that Juan was the only wage earner in his household at the moment.

Alanna realized she was talking herself out of accepting the offer.

"It's no problem, Dr. Mendes," he said, looking at her meaningfully. "You said someone hit your car in the parking lot. It's a very common situation. People come and ask to do this all the time."

Because it was lunchtime, the two of them were the

only ones in the security office at the moment. The other security personnel were out enjoying their break. She looked down at the line of monitors again and saw herself in one of them. A camera mounted high in the corner monitored those who did the monitoring.

Alanna decided that the lie would be hers. "Yes, a scratch. They didn't leave a business card or anything."

Juan motioned to her to come around the counter. "Why don't you have a seat by that monitor, and we'll see if we got anything useful."

Alanna hadn't told him over the phone anything about having seen her dead fiancé. She'd only asked if she could see the tapes of the parking lots and the bus stop for that particular morning. Juan hadn't asked any questions. He didn't need any further explanation, and Alanna hadn't offered any. He knew she was no spy. He knew she had no plan to sell the layout of the parking lots to either North Korea or Wal-Mart. What he didn't know was that she was only testing her sanity.

The fact that he knew she rarely drove her car to work was unimportant. Actually, since seeing Ray, Alanna *had* driven to work every day.

Juan sat at another computer, and Alanna turned her attention to the screen in front of her.

"Four days ago, you said?" he asked.

"January 3. The day everyone got back from the New Year's holiday." She looked at the screen, realizing what Juan was doing. He was already on the right date, and he had eight videos running on a split screen in fast motion. They showed each stop inside the complex along her bus route and several views of parking lots.

Concurrent military times showed in the lower corner of each video.

The only video clips that really interested her were the two on the lower left. The stop where she'd seen him, and the parking lot across the street.

"Am I going too fast?" Juan asked.

Alanna shook her head. She stuffed her ice-cold fingers between her knees. Her throat was dry, and she could feel her heart pounding. She wanted to know the truth, but at the same time, whatever was or wasn't going to appear on that screen terrified her.

Another security guard came into the office carrying his lunch. He nodded to Alanna and held up the bag for Juan. "They were out of the fried-egg sandwiches, so I got you a scrambled egg and bacon."

"Jeez," Juan said. "That's the second time this week he's run out of my sandwich."

The other guard shrugged and went to another desk.

"This is close to the time," she managed to croak. "When I…uh, parked."

She had parked in this very lot the next day. She'd arrived an hour earlier, pacing the parking lot, waiting at the shuttle stop, hoping to see Ray.

"Can we just look at two of those views?" she asked, pointing.

"Sure." Juan froze the frames and enlarged them so that only the two views were on her screen. She leaned in closer, looking at the people lined up at the bus stop first. Ray wasn't there.

"Can you take it forward? And would you zoom in on the specific areas?" she asked.

"Sure. Tell you what, Dr. Mendes, how about if you sit here and look at what you want?" Juan suggested. "I'll just grab my lunch and I'll be here if you need me. But I know working these computers is a piece of cake for you."

"Are you certain that would be all right?" Alanna glanced at the other guard, who was opening a newspaper to the sports section.

"Sure, it is. Right, Mo?"

"Why not," the other guard said, his mouth full.

Alanna moved to the monitor as Juan vacated his seat. A moment later, he was retrieving his lunch from his coworker's desk.

She turned her attention to the monitor. The parking-lot view might as well have been a satellite image. Methodically, she went through every square inch on the screen. Nothing.

She looked at the bus stop and zoomed in. The camera didn't go out as far as the area on the sidewalk where she'd seen Ray, but he had been walking toward the stop. He would certainly come into the picture a moment after the bus left the stop. Then, carefully, she advanced the video until she saw the shuttle arrive, stop and depart. She continued.

Frame by frame she advanced the video. The people who got off the bus went out of the picture. She waited. He should have shown up. Others came along the sidewalk into the picture and passed by. But not Ray.

Not Ray.

Alanna backed it up and ran through the video again. The third time through, she stared at the time notation, looking for gaps. Nothing.

No one on the screen resembled Ray. Those few seconds trapped in her memory weren't on that screen. She rechecked the time and the date again. She went to the split screen again, advanced the video, and saw herself getting out in front of Building 23.

She looked like a zombie getting off the bus. Alanna saw herself standing at the stop for a long time after the shuttle had left. She was just standing there alone on the sidewalk, staring down the road, looking lost.

Oh, yes. This was the right day.

Still in denial, she rewound the videos and went through every step again, checking every nearby parking lot for the two hours after the time she'd seen him. Nothing.

"Did you see anything?" Juan asked.

Alanna realized she'd been sitting there for some time, staring at nothing. She took her fingers off the keyboard. The two men were done with their lunch. She slowly stood up, summoning all her strength and trying to keep her composure.

"Nothing," she managed to say.

"I think you can file insurance paperwork with Moffett for the damage to your car, even though it doesn't show up on the security tapes," the other guard started telling her. "You were parked inside the facility gates, so they might just cover you…"

Alanna nodded, not completely hearing everything that was being said to her. The guard handed her some papers he dug out of a file drawer. She thanked both of them and left.

There were two people waiting to get on the elevator,

so she took the stairs down the two levels instead. Walking along the line of parked cars, she filled her lungs with the sharp, cool breeze. As she passed a bus stop, she stopped and sat down on the empty bench. Alanna considered going home, but she knew that was a bad idea. Their presentation to the committee from Washington was coming up. Her team depended on Alanna to justify and keep their jobs. There was also the question of what she would do at home.

This week, especially the time she'd spent at her apartment, had been hell. All she did was cry. She only slept with the help of sleeping pills.

A shuttle bus stopped in front of her. She shook her head at the driver.

She needed to go back to her office. She needed to walk back to her building and bury herself in her work. That was the only answer. The only remedy that she knew would be sure to help.

What else did she have?

Alanna pushed herself to her feet and started walking.

As she walked, she suddenly felt embarrassed about the phone calls she'd made earlier in the week. She was almost sorry she'd asked Juan to show her those security videos. She now understood how transparent she'd been—how desperate she must have looked to everyone around her. Her only relief was that she hadn't said a word of this to her grandmother, who was fighting a cold and hadn't come over.

Her *abuela,* Lucia, would have told her exactly what was going on with a frankness that her grandmother was famous for. *Chica loca,* Alanna could hear her saying it.

She walked on, thinking of her grandmother and their life together. Her *abuela* had worked hard to give her a solid, sane life. Working as a cleaning lady, Lucia had struggled as most illegal immigrants do to stay healthy and keep food on the table. Alanna's mother had not been around very much. She'd been pregnant with Alanna when she first walked across the border from Mexico. Actually, it was a miracle that she'd found a clinic in San Diego where she could safely deliver her baby before depositing Alanna into Lucia's arms.

Miracles usually come with a price, though.

Alanna could count on her fingers the number of times she'd seen her mother while she was growing up. She'd never known her father. Home to her was whatever room her grandmother's current employers gave them to sleep in. As a child, Alanna was small and plain. She was shy. She didn't socialize very much. The only thing that she felt she had going for her was her brain.

Alanna had always been smart. She liked to read and study and work hard. Her *abuela* hadn't even gotten through grade school. Despite that—or perhaps because of it—Lucia made sure that Alanna made the most out of what she considered a gift from God. She had supported her granddaughter every step of the way. Alanna would be forever grateful for that.

And as the years went by, she had come to believe that her intelligence, her education, her doctoral research and her career would be enough to make her feel complete.

She'd thought so until she met Ray.

Love, passion, "happily ever after" had always seemed to be the stuff of books. She'd never thought she would fall in love. Even having a steady boyfriend had never held a great attraction for her. Marriage wasn't for her. Having children was a pipe dream. But then, suddenly, Ray had made her believe that all of it could be hers. He'd made her think that she could have everything she secretly wanted in life but had been too afraid to even hope for.

And she had been utterly happy, for those few months that they'd been together. Happily ever after… almost.

Alanna stabbed away a tear as she turned up the sidewalk in front of Building 23. She'd lived a life in those few months that most people couldn't experience in a hundred years. This was what she had to tell herself. And no more dreaming. No more imagining that Ray was coming back.

He simply hadn't been there on the sidewalk that crazy morning. Jill Goldman, with the talk of her marriage, had tipped Alanna momentarily over the edge. But that was over now. Alanna was back on track, back on schedule.

She decided against the elevator and climbed the stairs to her floor. Walking into the soft office noise of computers and people was comforting. This was home to her now. It had been her life for a long time and it would continue to be.

Before she could get back to her office, she was stopped with questions from two of her project managers. Even one of the interns asked her to look over a report he'd been preparing. By the time she got to her desk, she was focused. Work was the only thing on her mind. Disappointment was locked away…for the time being.

She sat at her desk and started checking her phone messages and e-mail. A message from another program manager about a five o'clock meeting that was canceled. Alanna was checking the second voice mail when her phone beeped, telling her of an incoming call. She looked at the display. The caller ID was blocked. She was surprised by that. She was under the impression that NASA didn't allow a blocked ID call to go through. Better to let it go to voice mail, she decided.

She opened her schedule for the afternoon. It was packed with meetings and presentations. She was also interviewing a potential hire at four. The phone rang again. She looked at the display. Again, no caller ID.

She reached for the phone but didn't answer it. A couple of minutes later, she saw that, whoever it was, they hadn't left a message. She tried to focus again on what she needed to do this afternoon, but she was distracted.

Less than five minutes later, her phone rang again. Same blank caller ID. She didn't hesitate to pick it up. "Mendes."

"Dr. Mendes?"

Alanna grasped the table with her free hand. With the phone pressed to one ear, she held her breath. She knew the voice. But it couldn't be. This past hour had confirmed it. Her imagination was playing cruel, vicious tricks. She remained silent, determined not to make a fool of herself for some stranger.

"Dr. Mendes?" the voice repeated her name, this time softer.

"Yes, this is she. Can I help you?"

"Ali," he whispered.

Alanna's head sank back against her chair. Tears rolled down her cheeks. He was the only one who ever called her by that name. "Who…who is this?"

"I need to see you, Ali."

7

TERROR

Antwerp, Belgium

"A little to the left, darling," Finn breathed. "Better. No, a little more…or we'll be getting it on yourself and that pretty yellow dress."

In a moment, it wouldn't matter. Dress or no dress, this was the time to hit his mark. As he stared through the long-range lens on the modified TRG-41, Finn saw the young woman turn and the chauffeur's attention shift as well toward the door of the DurerBank's Antwerp offices on Pelikaanstraat.

One last time, the sniper considered the variables and recalculated the bullet's trajectory in his head. Still no breeze, though that was hardly a factor. The Lapua .338 cartridge was designed for minimum wind drift. At 582 meters, a schoolboy would be able to hit this mark. Finn would fire as the banker moved between the door and his limousine.

Finn relaxed his shoulders and waited. He knew

almost nothing about Bernard Kuipers, the man who was about to leave the bank. But this was the way he did business. Address, city, country, date, time, name, pictures. He required a number of recent pictures. No sense hitting the wrong target. Other than these essentials, he required eighty percent of his money upfront, in cash. Fifteen years of operating in this business with perfect hit record had earned him the high percentage upfront. No one complained. He was reasonable, efficient and he had his own particular code of ethics. No children and no close-range hits. He was a sniper, not a murderer.

The woman in the yellow dress walked toward the bank door with open arms. Finn saw his mark come out, all smiles. Kuipers embraced the woman. Finn focused the scope on the face. It was him.

"Right on."

The two walked toward the open door of the car. They slowed and the woman started to climb in the car. Finn focused on his mark, the man's head, and squeezed. The target went down.

He laid the stock of the TRG-41 on the floor and eased the window shut.

"Ninety-seven," Finn whispered. He'd promised his wife that he'd retire after his hundredth hit.

Three to go.

8

DESPAIR

Brooklyn, New York

He had to rework the knot on the necktie twice before he got it right. He used to do this in his sleep.

Small wonder, he thought. The last time David Collier had worn a tie had been for his wife's funeral. He looked at the picture of her that he'd hung between the mirror and the doorway. Nicole's smiling face was, as always, so full of hope. He wanted her here beside him, brushing some imaginary lint off the shoulder of his suit. He wanted to hear her soft voice, her encouraging words, telling him how much she loved him and how nothing else mattered. God, he missed her.

He turned away and took a couple of deep breaths. "I need this. We need this."

His old briefcase lay open on the bed. The folder with his updated résumé lay on top. At least there would be no surprises. The gentleman who called him already had his complete CV, in addition to transcripts and findings of the court proceedings exonerating him. And they *still* wanted to talk to him. An absolute miracle.

He wasn't told the name of the company or his specific responsibilities. They were conducting first-round interviews. David's qualifications matched their opening. The salary range was comparable to what he'd been paid four years ago as a CFO. Another absolute miracle.

David closed the briefcase and turned toward the door.

"Wish me luck, honey," he whispered to his wife's image. As he passed it, David touched the picture like it was a mezuzah.

The TV volume was a little too loud. The sitter, fourteen-year-old Megan, who lived with her parents in the apartment on the first floor, was on her cell phone. David found his daughter on the sofa, the blanket pulled up to her nose. Leah looked to be asleep. He picked up the remote and muted the TV.

"I have to go. I'll call you back later," Megan told whoever she was speaking with.

David glanced at her as he put the remote on the coffee table.

"You have my cell-phone number on the pad in the kitchen. Also, the pediatrician's and hospital's numbers are on the same list. Leah's dinner is in the fridge. You have to pop it in the microwave for two minutes. She can't snack or have anything to drink. But she can have one of the Popsicles in the freezer after dinner if she feels like it."

Megan nodded cheerfully. "This isn't the first time you've left Leah with me, Mr. Collier."

"I know."

An hour ago, he'd let the teenager take Leah to the

playground at the end of their block. The eight-year-old needed fresh air. She'd been home from school all week and had cabin fever. Still, he didn't want to tell the young sitter that every day there seemed to be more complications with Leah's health.

"I should be gone no more than three hours." He was meeting the gentleman who'd called at Ulysses', a bar near Wall Street, at six o'clock. There'd been no mention of having dinner. He was sure he'd be out of there in a couple of hours tops.

"Take your time," Megan encouraged.

David sat on the edge of the sofa to say goodbye to his daughter. He caressed her short dark hair. "That fresh air tuckered you out, didn't it?"

She made a soft noise in her sleep.

Megan came over from the kitchen. "We had such a good time. She had to try every one of the swings and even the tall slide."

"I'm going now, sleepyhead." He leaned down and kissed her brow. Her skin felt clammy. "Are you feeling okay, honey?"

Leah was normally a light sleeper, but she seemed to be struggling to open her eyes. David saw her small fingers creep out from under the blanket in search of his and he noticed her hand. It was swollen. He moved to her feet and pushed back the blanket. Leah's feet and legs had swollen like balloons.

"Leah, wake up, honey," he said, trying to sound calm as panic flashed through him.

The eight-year-old opened her eyes and murmured, "It hurts. It hurts, Daddy."

"What hurts, honey?"

"My back…" She closed her eyes again.

David wrapped up his daughter in the blanket and picked her up. He turned to Megan. "Call the doctor's office. Tell whoever answers that we have an emergency and that I'm taking Leah to the hospital. Tell them I'm taking her to New York Presbyterian right now."

"What's wrong with her?" the teenager asked shakily.

"Tell them she's having kidney failure."

9

FEAR

Istanbul, Turkey

A cold, wet droplet hit him squarely in the center of the forehead, startling him awake.

His head felt as if it was about to burst, and a dark haze surrounded him. He blinked and decided the problem was with his eyes. His vision was blurred. His hands were tied behind his back, and his left arm was asleep. It took some effort to get his fingers moving. As he worked them, pain shot up his arms from gashes on his wrists from the cords that bound him.

He rolled and tried to wipe his face on the filthy fragment of carpet they'd dumped him on. Dried, crusted blood came away on the rough wool. He knew the blood was from several wounds on his head. They seemed to enjoy using his head as a punching bag. He blinked a few times to clear his vision.

Another drop of cold water hit him, this time in the shoulder. He was in a very small room, an unused storeroom perhaps. Ancient rusted pipes emerged from one wall, ran the length of the dark ceiling and disappeared into the opposite wall. A dim bulb hanging at the end of a thin wire was the only source of light in the room. There were no windows. Nathan didn't know how many days he'd been here.

His memory was foggy, and he only had a vague recollection of a man asking him the same questions… again and again. The one question that seemed to tip them over the edge every time had to do with his name. They didn't like his answer, for some reason. He kept telling him he was Nathan Galvin and that he was a tourist. That answer seemed to draw the most cracks to the head. He vaguely recalled, in an insane moment, being tempted to tell them he was Hillary Clinton, but he hadn't known what that would do to them. The other questions Nathan couldn't really remember. He'd been hit too hard and too often on the head.

He looked around the room. The piece of rug he slept on smelled of urine and vomit, but it was the only thing that separated him from the dirty concrete floor, stained with dark spots. Nathan didn't want to think about what had caused the stains.

There was a table near the door. A wooden folding chair sat in the middle of the floor. He remembered sitting on that chair as they continued to question him.

He pushed himself to a sitting position. His head hurt so much that he thought it might split in half. It took a few moments to stop the room from spinning. He tried to think back to his last clear memory. He was supposed to swap a flash drive with a local contact. Simple, he'd been told.

He'd asked what was on the drive. The answer had been vague, as well. Names. Just names. He'd asked what was on the drive he was getting from his contact. Again, just names.

Nathan felt cheated. Actually, he felt stupid for not asking more questions. His parents had raised an analytical son. He had always been encouraged to go through life with his eyes open, to experience things firsthand, not to accept anything at face value. All their advice had been thrown out the window the moment Nathan had accepted this job. A job that his parents knew nothing of. As far as they were concerned, he was spending the year following his graduation from college traveling—seeing the world.

He was in serious trouble, maybe even a dead man, and they wouldn't even know where to look for him.

10

STIGMA

Boston

Jay's only pair of khakis was the one he'd worn to the courthouse when he and Padma had gotten married. He wore those and a gray cardigan sweater his wife had found on her trip to the Goodwill store the day before.

Both of them had left home with a suitcase and what was on their backs. What little furnishings they had in their apartment they'd been able to gather from yard sales and thrift shops and Dumpsters in the area. The two of them were actually proud of what they had put together.

Six months ago, Jay would have looked in the mirror and said, "Good enough." At the time, he wouldn't have cared to work for an employer who was going to judge him based on how he dressed. Today, however, he was nervous. He wished Padma didn't know anything about this. He'd seen the excitement in her face, the hope. He was used to disappointment. He knew how to handle it. She didn't. He really wanted this job…for her.

For the first time in his life, he was worried that the lack of a tie or jacket or even dress shoes might make a bad impression on whoever was interviewing him.

"It's too late to think about that now," he muttered, crossing the busy street.

The Boston wind was damp and cold, and it cut right through him. His hair was still wet from rushing home and taking a quick shower before coming out. He hadn't worn a baseball cap as he usually did. His hair was getting long, but Padma liked it.

They were meeting at the hotel next to the convention center on the waterfront. He was supposed to go to the bar. Jay was relieved to have turned twenty-one. Boston was big on asking for ID, and he wasn't about to violate one item of his parole by printing himself up a fake one. Three times since being up here, he'd taken Padma out for dinner. She didn't drink. She was too careful for the baby's sake. He'd been asked to show ID every time.

Jay didn't have to try to act tough. He was tough. But he also knew he looked young. It was the baby face that he'd inherited from his father. He wondered if that would turn these people off.

He walked into the lobby of the hotel and looked around. He must have looked confused because a bell-hop approached him and directed him toward the bar.

Jay couldn't remember the last time he'd been this nervous. His first day in the slammer in Otisville, probably. He took off his jacket and frowned at his reflection in a mirrored wall as he passed. The work boots didn't seem quite right in this setting.

There was a restaurant beyond the lounge, and as Jay walked past the hostess's station, he could see there was a pretty good dinner crowd. The food smelled good, but he forced himself to forget the fact that he hadn't had anything to eat. There'd been no time for it. He hoped Padma was eating something.

He took a couple of deep breaths and went into the amber-lit lounge. Tables and comfortable chairs were scattered around the place. Half of the tables were taken, and two women who looked as if they were still in college were giving him the eye. Ignoring them, he moved toward the bar. A couple of large-screen TVs mounted on the walls had some sports channel on with the sound off.

It occurred to him that he had no idea what the guy who was supposed to interview him even looked like. Mr. Diarte probably didn't know what Jay looked like, either.

He glanced around. A couple dozen customers, more or less, were standing and sitting at the bar. Two bartenders were working nonstop. The crowd was mostly businesspeople, the men in ties and dress shirts, and the women still wearing office clothes. Most of the men's jackets were draped on the backs of the chairs.

Jay didn't have to find Mr. Diarte. A short, round-faced man with a very slick comb-over and tinted glasses approached him. He was wearing a dark gray suit, white shirt and a tie.

"Mr. Alexei." It wasn't a question.

Jay shook the outstretched hand. From the slight

accent, he knew this was the same man he'd spoken to on the phone. "Mr. Diarte."

Diarte motioned to him to follow.

Jay moved his jacket from one arm to the other and followed the man to the far corner. An L-shaped room branched off from the main bar. He noticed that fewer people were seated in this section. There were no TVs, and the music coming over the speakers was muffled.

As Jay followed Diarte, he noticed a trim, middle-aged man at the far table looking their way. He was wearing a tie and sport jacket. Jay figured that must be the potential employer. A thick folder sat in front of the man, next to an untouched drink, and a briefcase was on the floor beside his chair.

Jay's palms started sweating. He hoped they weren't going to quiz him on anything important. He'd told them that he only had a high-school degree, but they knew that. Actually, they knew a lot about him.

He wiped his right hand on his pants before he shook the waiting man's hand. Diarte introduced him as Mr. Lyons. No first name.

Lyons was all business. No small talk. No BS. No offer of a drink or something to eat. He pointed to the seat across the table and immediately got down to business.

"My goal, Mr. Alexei, is to assemble a team of quality individuals together under one roof for a short period of intense training before our project takes off."

Jay never had a chance to ask questions as Lyons continued without a pause.

"This team will consist of only one person for each particular position required for the project. No backups.

No one drops out once the project is set in motion. Right now, we are considering more than twenty candidates for your specific position."

Jay thought he had no chance, but Padma's face was in his mind's eye. He had to give it all he had. "May I ask what the project is about?"

"There are confidentiality issues in play," Lyons told him. "I won't be disclosing any information until I know you're our chosen candidate."

Beggars can't be choosers, Jay thought. Whatever the job was, it was better than what he was doing now. And it certainly paid much better. Even so, he wasn't ready to join the dark side.

"You know that I served time in prison. I won't get myself into a situation that could put me back behind bars."

Lyons stared at him for a moment. "Fair enough, Mr. Alexei. If I decide that you are the man for us, I'll make sure that you are not put in any position that would jeopardize your future."

"Okay."

Lyons nodded and tapped his finger on the manila folder in front of him. "As I'm sure Mr. Diarte has already told you, we know quite a lot about your past. About your family. And about your present situation. So let's get to what we don't know."

Jay wondered if there was anything that they didn't know. He saw the man open the folder and take out a yellow pad with notes scribbled all over it. Some of the words were circled. Others were underlined, sometimes a couple of times for emphasis. Jay was good at reading upside down, but the dim light and the poor handwriting put him at a disadvantage. One thing was for sure, they'd done some homework getting ready for this interview.

Lyons opened an intricately folded pair of reading glasses and positioned them low on his nose. His thin face and the glasses reminded Jay of the public defender that he had used during his trial. The lawyer hadn't thought much of him. He hoped this man would have a different opinion.

Jay saw Diarte speak softly to a waitress who approached their table. She nodded and went off.

"Authentication factor." Lyons looked up from the file. "What can you tell me about it?"

Jay focused on the man. They were starting easy on him. "It's a piece of information used to verify a person's identity for security purposes."

"Two-factor authentication?" he asked next.

"A system where two different methods are used to verify. This way you have a higher level of authentication assurance." Jay had no degrees to flash at any potential employer. He had to dazzle them with knowledge he'd picked up along the way. "Using this method, the user has to have a physical token, such as a card, and something that is memorized, like a password. The rule of thumb is…something you have and something you know."

"But that's a piece of cake to crack, isn't it?" Mr. Lyons tapped his pen on the pad of paper. That was a habit his lawyer had also had.

The man, the question, the pen tapping were all reminders of Jay's past. He looked around as an uncomfortable feeling settled in the pit of his stomach. He'd done jail time for this. But this kind of information was available on the Internet for anyone to access. He told himself it was okay to talk about it. That was what he was doing now, just talking.

Jay nodded. "Two-factor authentication won't defend against phishing. It won't stop identity theft. Sure, it solves the security problems we had ten years ago, but doesn't address our problems today."

"And why is that?" Lyons asked.

Diarte was taking notes. He held the legal pad on his lap. Jay couldn't see any of the information that was being taken down. He wondered if they were recording him, as well.

Jay thought carefully about his answer before he started explaining. "The nature of attacks has changed over this past decade. Back then, the threats were passive…eavesdropping, offline password guessing. Today's threats might include phishing and Trojan horses."

Jay spent a minimum four or five hours a night on the computer. Padma couldn't keep her eyes open past nine. Jay stayed up. His mind was like a black hole, sucking in everything. The Internet was one giant universe. He had to learn. Not to break the law, but to expand his world.

"Tell me more," Lyons encouraged.

"There are two active attacks that are more common than others," Jay started. "The first one is a man-in-the-middle attack, where the attacker puts up a fake bank Web site page or an eBay page or some type of page that has the capability of accessing an account once personal banking information is supplied. The attacker entices the user to the page. Now, as soon as the user types in his or her password, the attacker uses it to access the site's real Web site and makes whatever illegal transactions he wants. Done right, the user will never realize that he isn't at the bank's Web site."

"And the second method?"

"Easier than the first method," Jay told them. "The attacker installs a Trojan horse on a user's computer. When the user logs into his bank's Web site, the attacker piggybacks on that session via the Trojan horse to make any fraudulent transaction he wants."

"Listening to you, I am amazed that anyone's personal information is safe."

Jay shrugged. "Banks are hot on coming up with new security techniques, but the hackers are right behind them, making adjustments. Sometimes, they're actually ahead of them."

Lyons looked down at his notepad. He put a check mark next to a line. "Two-channel authentication?"

"Yes…something recent. They use two different communication paths," Jay told him. "One bank sends a challenge to the user's cell phone via SMS and expects a reply via SMS."

"What's SMS?"

The waitress put a tall glass of water and a straw in front of Jay on the table. She left as quickly as she'd arrived.

"SMS stands for Short Message Service. It lets cell phones send and receive text messages," Jay explained, taking a big swallow of water. He hadn't realized until now that his throat was very dry.

"But all customers may not have cell phones."

"Exactly," Jay agreed. "But even if they all had cell phones, in this new world of active attacks, no one cares. The man-in-the-middle attacker is happy to have the user deal with the SMS portion of the log-in, since he can't do it himself. And a Trojan attacker doesn't care since he's piggybacking on the user anyway."

Lyons sat back in his chair. "So if I understand you correctly, you are saying that two-factor authentication is useless."

"Not necessarily," Jay told him. "It works fine for a local log-in…users working inside corporate networks. But it's definitely not safe for remote authentication over the Internet."

There was a pause in the questioning. Jay drank half the glass of water. Diarte appeared to be the silent observer—the court recorder. Mr. Lyons was leafing through the folder. He took out a piece of paper about ten sheets into the file. Jay immediately recognized MIT letterhead. A long time ago, Jay's dream had been to go to school there. Before Lyons pulled the letter away, Jay read his interviewer's name. The letter was addressed to him.

"Multifactor authentication?" Lyons asked, pushing the chair away from the table. The letter and the pad of paper went with him.

"What you know, what you have, what you are," Jay told him. "The password is what you know. A token or an ATM card is what you have. A biometric measure is what you are…like a fingerprint or the iris of your eye."

"And that is safe? Hacker-proof?" Lyons asked.

Jay shook his head. "*Anything* can be beaten. Any system can be cracked. Just like the Minotaur's labyrinth, any mystery devised by a human mind can be unraveled by a human mind." Jay hoped he didn't come across as arrogant, but he truly believed that. "Security systems are only puzzles waiting to be solved."

"Has biometrics been beaten?"

"I've heard that facial-recognition scanners can be cracked by showing the camera a short HD video of the person's face. The same thing goes for the iris scanner. All you need is the photograph of an iris printed on a high-resolution color laser printer. Even fingerprints aren't safe. Fingerprints can be pressed into gelatin mold similar to the type used to make Gummi Bears."

"Voice recognition?" Lyons asked.

"People don't like using it. It became obsolete practically right after getting released."

"And why is that?" his interviewer asked.

"What happens if you wake up with a bad cold or you're hoarse from yelling too much at last night's baseball game?" Jay took another sip of water. He felt as if he was about to lose his own voice.

"So is there anything out there that works?"

Jay shrugged. He thought about his answer. He glanced at Diarte. He'd stopped taking notes and was waiting for an answer, too.

"Things are changing every day. I mentioned before about puzzles. It's in our nature to want to climb the highest wall, the highest mountain. To go faster than anyone else…or even just the guy sitting next to us at the stoplight. New security methods only introduce new challenges. Everything can be hacked, though."

After making his little speech, Jay realized that he'd made no reference to the law and its dim view of hackers. That had been the problem when he was seventeen. He was too consumed with breaking codes to pay attention to the legality of what he was doing. He wondered if he was still too much like that. Too consumed with the mystery of the labyrinth…too little concerned with the monster at the center of it.

"And you, Mr. Alexei," Lyons said, clearly reading his mind. "I believe you are a man who likes a good puzzle."

11

LOSS

Meet me, Ali. Don't tell anyone. My life depends on it.

Alanna couldn't remember what excuse she'd used for leaving work in such a rush. She couldn't remember a thing about her afternoon's schedule. It didn't matter. Her people had to be getting accustomed to her mental instability these days.

Ray's words, though, she had no trouble remembering. *Don't tell anyone. My life depends on it.*

He was alive, she told herself as she drove like a maniac back to Mountain View. He was meeting her at her apartment.

Alanna didn't bother to pull around to her assigned parking spot. Instead, she pulled into the visitors' lot of her building. The eight-story Avalon Towers on the Peninsula, with views all the way from the mountains to the bay, was one of the prime neighborhoods to live for young workaholics on the move. Alanna had the distinction of being one of the first people to buy a unit…and was about the only one of the original owners who was still living there eight years later.

The security guard inside looked surprised to see Alanna this early in the afternoon. "Is everything okay, Dr. Mendes?"

Alanna tried to look calm. She forced herself not to ask if he'd seen Ray. She'd introduced her fiancé to everyone who worked at the desk. He had his own key. They all knew that he was dead.

Supposedly dead, she told herself again and again. NOT dead. Alive.

"Everything is fine, thanks. Any visitors?" she asked, deciding that Ray must have taken the access door from the back parking lot upstairs. Her apartment key also unlocked that door.

"The mail is in. Would you like me to get it for you?"

"Sure," she said vacantly as she continued toward the elevator.

"Dr. Mendes…you want your mail?"

She glanced back, realizing her actions were contradicting her answer.

"Oh! Never mind," she called back to him as the elevator doors opened. "I'll get it later. Thanks."

In her rush, Alanna blocked a couple trying to get out. Backing up with a quick apology, she let them exit first.

This was crazy. She didn't want to think of the disappointment she'd felt in not finding him on the security videos. She was certain she would see Ray in them. But she'd made up her mind that she had simply been mistaken…until the phone call.

But what if she'd imagined that, too. Maybe she *was* crazy.

Alanna was glad she was the only one in the elevator. She didn't need anyone watching her right now. For the first time since Ray's phone call, she saw herself reflected in the doors of the elevator. She'd lost weight since Ray had been gone. The gray suit hung loosely on her shoulders. Her hair was pulled back in a severe knot on the top of her head…just as she used to wear it before she'd met him. There were strands of gray visible in the front. But her cheeks were flushed. Her dark eyes could barely hide her excitement.

She looked alive.

Alanna pressed the seventh-floor button again and again. The elevator seemed to be crawling upward more slowly than she could ever remember.

On her floor, no one was waiting. Alanna stumbled leaving the elevator. She found herself smiling, actually talking to herself and making fun of her clumsiness.

It wasn't until she reached the door to her apartment that Alanna realized what she'd done. Her keys were still in the ignition of the car.

Acting on impulse, wanting to believe in her dreams, she pressed the doorbell to her apartment and waited. There was silence.

She pressed her cheek against the door and wrapped softly. She waited. There was nothing. No noise. No one looking through the peephole. No footsteps. Her heart sank. The pendulum that had swung her to such a high detached from its locus and dropped her into hell. She didn't have to wait for the tears to begin. They were already falling.

Leaning back against the wall beside her door, she slid down until she was sitting on her heels. Lost in her misery, she almost didn't hear the lock on the door when it turned.

She was on her feet in an instant, her hand against the door. He reached out and took hold of her wrist and pulled her inside.

Ray.

She opened her mouth but nothing came out. She felt herself beginning to shake. Her tears were now tears of joy. It was Ray. The same handsome face. His eyes caressed her, just as they always did. He made her feel beautiful. No one made her feel this way but him.

Finally, the words emerged. "Is this real? Ray, please tell me this is real."

He closed the door and pressed her against it. "I'm real. We're real. I'm here with you, Ali."

She looked into the blue eyes and wanted to believe. But her tears wouldn't stop. She didn't know if her dreams were making a fool of her again. She touched his face. She ran her fingers through his hair, felt the contours of the muscles of his shoulders and back. She hugged him hard and pressed her wet cheeks against his chest. She could hear the beating of his heart.

"You're dead," she choked out. "You died when the boat blew up. You were gone. You *are* gone. I saw you… but I didn't see you at Moffett Field this week. You didn't call me today. You're not here. I'm not holding you."

He bent his head and silenced her argument with a

kiss. Alanna lost herself to him as she remembered what being alive felt like.

She had a million questions, but she didn't ask them. He told her there was so much explaining he needed to do, but she wanted him, not explanations. Starved for what they'd had, for what they'd missed, she pulled him toward her bedroom.

Some time later, she was lying in his arms, finally sure that he was real, when the phone rang.

"Don't answer it," he told her.

Her call went to the answering machine. It was her office, one of her group technicians. He mentioned that he'd try her cell phone again.

"Don't answer that one, either. Throw it out of the window," Ray told her, nuzzling her neck.

"I can't. It's in the car…with my keys and my brief-case." Alanna rolled toward him, running her fingers through his hair. She forced his face up until his eyes met hers. "I still can't believe it."

A smile creased his handsome face. "Do you want a repeat performance?"

It would have been so easy to forget everything else and let him take her to oblivion again. He knew her body so well. He knew her weaknesses, what made her soar. He knew how to make her forget everything…to become one in mind and body with him alone.

"I thought I was losing my mind." Her emotions were beginning to overwhelm her again.

"This week?"

"Earlier than that. For the entire time you were gone. I died inside when I thought you were dead," she whispered. "What happened? Where did you go? Why did you say on the phone that no one can know? What do you mean, your life depends on it? If you're in danger, I need to know. What do we need to do? You aren't going away again…?"

He placed a finger on her lips. "My beautiful inquisitor, my precious Ali. You worry too much."

Nobody had ever called her beautiful except Ray.

"Please," she begged. "Tell me what happened. *Make* me not worry."

This had been the way their relationship had been when he was around. By nature, she was tense, focused, organized. She didn't make a decision without doing a risk analysis and figuring out the safety factor. He was the opposite. Carefree, happy, relaxed. At age thirty-six and with an engineering degree, he had yet to work for a company more than a couple of years at a time. He was proud of being a contractor, finding jobs through technical-temp agencies and word of mouth. He only worked when he needed money. They were opposites in so many ways…and yet they were so perfect for each other. She lectured him on responsibility. He listened cheerfully and then did what he wanted. He made her happy.

His eyes did not reflect any carefree attitude now, though.

"They staged my death," he finally said.

"Who staged your death?" she asked, raising herself on an elbow.

"I can't tell you too much, for your own safety… and mine."

"You haven't said anything yet."

He rolled onto his back, staring at the ceiling. She took hold of his chin and forced him to look at her again.

"Ray, tell me what's going on. Please."

He hesitated a few moments longer. His gaze searched her face. He reached up and combed his fingers through her hair. The elastic and the pins holding her hair had fallen away at the same time as her clothes.

"I've been in a witness protection program."

She couldn't remember any trials he'd been involved with—none that he'd told her about. He'd never acted nervous. He'd never seemed afraid. "Why? How?"

"It had to do with a job I had some time ago…before I ever met you. I was a witness to…to some irregular business dealings."

She opened her mouth to ask questions. He shook his head. "Don't, Ali. I can't say anything about it. I had no choice. If I were to survive, I had to change my identity and disappear…or they would have dragged you into it, too. The people I was testifying against aren't good people. They would have come after you to get to me."

Alanna tried to remember what she knew of the jobs Ray had held before they'd met. Not much. She only knew what he was doing as a contractor at Moffett Field.

"Where did they send you?" she asked.

He shook his head. "I can't tell you that."

"But you're back. Isn't it still dangerous?"

"It is, but no more dangerous than where I was. My identification and location got out."

"Got out to whom? To the people who were after

you?" she asked. "What kind of protection is that? What happened? What are you going to do now?"

He pulled himself up and sat back against the headboard. "There are plans being made as we speak. I should have some answers soon."

"Who's making the plans? The Justice Department?"

"Please, Ali."

Alanna was frustrated. She didn't want to go through losing him again. Not if she could do something. Seeing him today had made her remember everything that she'd forgotten about what was good in life.

"Do these new plans include me?" she asked quietly.

Affection filled his eyes. He leaned over and caressed her cheek. "That's why I'm here. This time I have to make it work for the two of us. I have to find a way where the life they give us can make you happy."

"I am happy when I'm with you. Nothing else matters. Tell me what you can."

12

FEAR

Steven Galvin was tired of not getting answers. And being six thousand miles away put a person at one helluva disadvantage.

The distance, the time difference, the language difficulties were only some of the obstacles. Although he tried to retain a calm demeanor, his inner frustration now matched Kei's.

It wasn't like Nathan to just disappear without sending them word.

Galvin wanted his wife to stay in Connecticut as he flew to Istanbul, but she wouldn't have anything to do with that. He would have had to lock her in a closet to keep her from coming.

Nathan had his own accounts and credit cards. Privacy policies blocked Steven from checking those accounts. He only wanted to know the last charge date, or the last time Nathan had withdrawn any money.

He had to file a missing person report with the local police department in Connecticut, as well as with the

U.S. Consulate in Ankara before the bank would consider releasing the information. But after a full day of total madness on the phone, he had enough documentation for the bank and the credit-card companies to release the information to him. Nathan hadn't charged anything or withdrawn any money since they'd heard from him. In fact, there was no record of any activity for the three days prior to when they'd last heard his voice. And even the last withdrawal that showed up had been minuscule.

Their son seemed to live very frugally. A quality, Steven thought, that he'd developed only since graduating from college. Unfortunately, that actually complicated things since there wasn't any credit-charge trail to follow. Also, Nathan had never bothered to register with the U.S. Consulate when he'd arrived in Turkey. Most tourists didn't. But that had just added to the red tape in dealing with the consulate.

Steven and Kei took a direct flight from JFK to Istanbul. Money hadn't been an issue with them for years. Through his old connections, Galvin hired a Turkish translator and a driver ready at the airport for their arrival. He had been told by his old associates in Turkey not to file a police report with the Istanbul police until he and Kei arrived in the country. The process was not the same as it was in the U.S. Dealing with the police face-to-face provided a much greater opportunity for "priority treatment." Galvin understood that to mean that American dollars provided the best incentive for action.

Well, he was prepared to pay off whomever it took and with whatever amount was required…with interest.

"Can I get you tea or coffee, sir?" a flight attendant asked softly.

Steven glanced at his wife. Thanks to the mega-strength sleeping pills their doctor had prescribed a couple of days ago, Kei had been knocked out about five minutes after they'd boarded.

He ordered another Scotch. The book he'd brought along on the flight sat on the tray untouched. He couldn't concentrate on anything but Nathan. He couldn't eat, but the thought of one more drink sounded good. He'd be drinking plenty of tea and coffee once they arrived in Turkey.

In his mind, he'd rehearsed over and over again the reprimand he was going to give Nathan when they found him. After selling his company, Steven had more money than Midas. Nathan wouldn't actually have to work a day in his life. So, when their son had told them that that he was going to travel around for a year after graduating from college, he and Kei had thought it a brilliant idea. But they were wrong. They wouldn't be in this situation today if they'd talked Nathan out of it.

"Something else, sir?"

He hadn't even realized that the flight attendant was back with his drink. He shook his head.

Little kids present little problems, big kids present big ones. Steven remembered one of his first partners telling him that years ago. Those were the days when he was upset about missing Nathan's childhood because of the hours he had to spend at work. His friend had reminded him that by the time those big problems rolled around, he'd have enough money to retire. He downed half of his stiff drink and glanced at his watch.

"How much longer?"

He was surprised to see Kei watching him. "I thought you were sleeping."

"You've been talking to yourself."

"I'm sorry I woke you up," he said, pulling the blanket higher on Kei's shoulders.

She shook her head. "How much time is left before we land?"

"We get in at 10:15 a.m., so we still have a couple of hours," he replied. "I'm glad you got some sleep. You needed it."

She still looked groggy. "Nathan was in my dream."

"Please tell me he was on some beach with a group of gorgeous girls around him."

She didn't answer. She didn't smile. Kei turned her face to the window and opened the shade to bright morning light. He took another sip of his drink.

"A little early to be drinking, don't you think?" she said, glancing back over her shoulder.

"I'm still on New York time, which makes it a little after midnight."

Kei nodded and looked back at the window.

Steven was worried about Nathan, but he also was worried about his wife. From the day that the first seeds of worry were planted in her mind, Kei had been on a steady decline. Her sleep, her eating habits, her behavior. He'd insisted on her seeing their doctor. He'd taken her to the office himself.

She refused antianxiety pills. She didn't want to be

numb. She wasn't fighting clinical depression. She'd agreed to a prescription to help her sleep, though. That was something, at least.

He saw her trace Nathan's name on the window. "What did you dream?"

She turned to him and Steven saw tears in her beautiful brown eyes. "He was a little boy again."

He reached up and wiped a tear off her silky skin. "And?"

"Do you remember when he was four, and we took a trip to Morocco?"

Steven remembered. Nathan had had too much energy and was too young to be interested in any sightseeing. He nodded.

"In my dream we were back in that beautiful mosque in Casablanca. Do you remember it?"

"The Hassan II Mosque. The one right on the ocean's edge. I remember. It was huge."

Steven recalled their tour guide telling them that, after Mecca, the building was the largest religious monument in the world. Inside, there was room for twenty-five thousand pilgrims, and the grounds surrounding the mosque could hold another eighty thousand people or so.

"That was the only stop where Nathan was actually happy," Steven said. "Thousands of people, all praying in a language that he couldn't understand, and he was mesmerized."

"In my dream he was at the very top of the minaret," Kei whispered. "He was standing right on the ledge where the muezzin used to call out the prayers."

Their tour guide had told them that the minaret was

the tallest in the world. While in Casablanca, Steven recalled, you could see it night and day from miles away.

He reached over and laid his hand on her arm. "He kept asking about going up in the minaret when we were there. He wanted to climb the steps. Maybe that's why you were dreaming about it."

"Except that in my dream he was in danger. He was scared. But I couldn't get to him. I couldn't move. That huge open space in front of the mosque was jammed with people. The crowds were pressing against me from every side. I kept screaming, but my voice was drowned out by the noise."

Steven reminded himself that there was no point in trying to analyze her dream. Kei was worried about Nathan and, awake or asleep, the worry wouldn't go away until she actually saw him.

She closed her eyes and another tear squeezed out onto her cheek.

"You're supposed to sleep so you can rest, not have nightmares," he told her, wiping away the tear. "Listen, we'll be arriving in Istanbul in no time. We'll find him, my love. We will. I promise you we will. He's fine. You'll see."

As the words left his mouth, though, Steven Galvin knew that he'd been making a lot of promises to his wife these past few days. Promises that he hadn't been able to keep.

13

DESPAIR

New York Presbyterian Hospital

David Collier couldn't stop pacing the emergency-room waiting area. He didn't know what to do, where to go, who to talk to. The attending doctor had asked him to stay outside while they ran a number of tests and scans on Leah. They needed to have full access to her. They would keep him informed as to her condition, but right now David was getting in their way.

So he paced.

When David spotted a young resident come through the doors into the waiting room, he was on him in an instant. This doctor had been shadowing the attending physician who was directing Leah's care.

"Mr. Collier. I'm Dr.—"

"I know who you are," David said shortly. "What's happening to my daughter?"

The resident moved to the side to allow a patient on a wheelchair to be taken through the doors. "Your daughter…Leah…has developed severe electrolyte disturbances. Her blood tests show toxic levels of waste products. She's also suffering from fluid overload. Of course, we have only done a fraction of the tests that need to be performed."

"What's being done for her now as far as medications, dialysis?" David wished Nicole were with him now. She was so much better than he was in this kind of situation.

"We're starting with the blood transfusion. We have to control the anemia. Before we start with dialysis, though, we'd like to admit her."

The young doctor continued to talk, but David didn't have to hear it. He already knew the scenario. They were at worst case. Leah's pediatrician had gone over it with him last week. As a previous recipient of a kidney, Leah would be low on the transplant list. But even if some miracle occurred and they could find another donor, it was very likely that the eight-year-old's body would reject the organ. David was no match to his daughter. Nicole, on the other hand, had been a perfect match. But by the time Leah's illness had been diagnosed, Nicole's cancer had spread through her body.

The young doctor touched him on the shoulder gently and motioned to the window where a receptionist sat. David couldn't see straight. He couldn't hear. His daughter's kidneys were shutting down. David's mind was following suit. He sat down on the closest chair. He leaned over and planted his head in his hands. The pediatrician had told him that in a case such as this, Leah would have to remain in the hospital under continuous dialysis until…until another donor was found. And then they'd start the process all over again.

He was a grown man, but he was crying. Nicole had died and there had been nothing he could do to stop it. And now his daughter…

"I believe you dropped this."

The voice startled him. He lifted his head from his hands and looked at the manila folder the man sitting beside him was holding.

"I don't think so. That's not mine."

"I'm sure it is," he said. "You might want to check inside."

David wasn't in any mood for this. He snatched the folder out of the man's hand and opened it.

His name was hand-written at the top of a cover letter clipped to a thick sheaf of papers. David recognized the letterhead of the research hospital in Germany that he wanted to take Leah to…the one the insurance company had rejected.

"What is this?" he asked in a low voice.

The letter was addressed to him, and he scanned it quickly. It was an acceptance letter, confirming financial arrangements and welcoming Leah to participate in the organ-cloning program.

"What is this?" David asked again. He turned to the man sitting next to him. "And who are you?"

14

FEAR

Istanbul, Turkey

"Your name."

"I'm Nathan Galvin. Age twenty-three. I'm a U.S. citizen. A tourist…and I need water." Nathan had lost count of the number of times he'd repeated the same thing. The man asking the questions today was different from the one who'd questioned him yesterday. That interrogation session had been the only other session that he'd been reasonably conscious for. He was exhausted and very weak, but at least they'd stopped batting his head around.

His interrogator sat across the way, a small metal table separating them. The man's face was visible in the dim light of the bulb, and he didn't try to hide his identity. He was wearing a black print sports shirt, buttoned at the wrists. His hands, when they appeared on the table, struck Nathan as delicate. They were the hands of a musician or a scholar.

They'd untied Nathan's hands and feet yesterday. He knew they no longer saw him as a threat. He'd had no food since they brought him here, and it was taking its toll on him. They'd given him water only sparingly.

"Your name?" the man asked again.

This man spoke English fluently and had a vaguely British accent. Both of these last two interrogators had been unafraid of Nathan seeing their faces. And this scared the hell out of him. He wondered if they were going to kill him, no matter what he told them.

"Your name?" the man asked in the same monotone. No anger, no beatings, just the same question over and over again.

"Please do not require us to use more persuasive means. We only ask that you be honest with us."

"I have been," Nathan murmured. "You're not listening."

"Your name?"

Nathan had to play the same game. He repeated the information that he was authorized to release and nothing more. He didn't know who these people were—Turks, Arabs, Iraqis, Kurds, Iranians? He didn't know which faction of al-Qaida—if they *were* al-Qaida—they were connected with. There were plenty who hated U.S. policy in the Middle East, and Nathan was too green to distinguish between them with any certainty.

The door to the room creaked open, and Nathan saw his backpack being handed in to the man questioning him.

He watched in silence as the backpack was emptied on the table in front of him. Nathan stared at the contents as the standing man pawed through everything. He picked up the small notebook. Nathan remembered that had been in his pocket.

"These are directions. What for?"

The stick drives weren't on the table. Nathan had no doubt his captors had them. "Someone gave me those directions and asked me to exchange a flash drive for him at the Kapali Carsi. That was where I was going…to that shop." He motioned to the notebook.

"Who gave you the directions?"

"I've told you people a hundred times…a kid I met having coffee at the hotel where I'm staying. I don't know him. I just happened to meet him. He was leaving for the U.S. and had forgotten to return the stick drive to a friend."

"Why did you agree to do it?"

"I don't know. He offered me a couple of bucks. I needed the money and it was a good chance to practice the little Turkish I know. I didn't think I was doing anything wrong."

Nathan looked at the other things that were spread on the table. His baseball cap, gloves, a tourist book, cash in liras. Intentionally, he hadn't brought along his wallet. "There was a cell phone in my pocket. It should be among my things. It's not here on the table."

Perhaps if they turned on the cell phone, his location could be traced. Nathan knew his parents would be beside themselves by now. They'd be looking for him themselves.

The man gave no indication that he'd heard Nathan. He continued to paw through the things.

"I know you have it," Nathan insisted. "You want to

know my real name, look at the numbers I've been calling on my cell phone. Call them. Call my parents. I swear, I am telling the truth. I'm a tourist. I don't know what or who you're looking for. But I'm not it."

His captor picked up the notebook but left everything else on the table.

"Touch nothing," he said before walking out of the room and leaving Nathan alone.

15

TERROR

Belfast, Ireland

Finn waited for his wife and two children in the parking lot at Saint Brigid's Church on Sunday morning. Mass would not start for another twenty minutes, but he'd come straight here from the airport.

From where he was parked, near Malone Road, he had a view of the new building's construction next to the old, red-brick church. To Finn, Saint Brigid's was a sign of the times in Belfast. Hardly a hundred years since this church had been built for the area's Catholic servants who worked for the ruling Protestant class. Today, this parish was the fastest growing—and the richest—in the city.

Finn himself had made a sizable donation toward the three million Monsignor Cluny had asked to aid in the construction of the sanctuary next door. Finn had given proudly. This was his family's parish now, since he'd bought a home in this area four years ago. A brilliant move, all things taken together. The bloody house had already more than doubled in value.

These days some of Belfast's most expensive homes were here in the affluent residential district on the south side. They called Malone Road a "mixed" area, where wealthy Catholics and Protestants lived together. A far cry from the neighborhoods where Finn and his brother, Thomas, were raised.

Finn figured this church, this neighborhood, justified the years he was involved with IRA campaigns. But they were done with the killing and bombing now. Most Catholics were considered equal. Or at least, they considered *themselves* equal. He knew he was. And he deserved it. He'd fought for it. He'd lost Thomas to the fight for their bloody rights. He had every right to enjoy what he had, and bollocks to the naysayers still crying about there being problems.

He'd read a flyer last week that said a Catholic male was 2.5 times more likely to be unemployed than a Protestant male, and that Catholics were still under-represented in management levels of companies. No doubt there was some truth to it, but it was someone else's job to fight those battles.

A Mercedes pulled into the lot and honked the horn at him. Finn nodded to the folks in the car. A Volvo followed it in, and there was another wave of recognition by the driver.

When Finn saw his wife's Mercedes SUV come up Malone Road, he got out of the car. For his work, he needed to be away a few times a month, and he missed Kelly when he was gone. He missed the twins bloody awful. He could see the lads already jumping about in the backseat before Kelly had a chance to pull into the parking space beside him.

He opened the backdoor, and Conor and Liam tumbled out. Five years old and an armful, the little devils.

"What did you bring us, Da? What did you get us this time?" they asked at the same time while climbing over each other to get to him.

The pair of them might be two years old, the way they acted. When it came to fighting for his attention, they were little heathens, to be sure.

"I'll tell you after mass," he told the boys, giving them hugs. He tried to straighten their jackets, but they had too much energy to stand still.

"Come on, Da! Now…now!"

"I said *after,* ya puppies. And that's only if you behave yourselves during mass."

"Let me peek in your car," one said.

"Yeah, let us peek," the other agreed.

"What did I say?" Finn said, trying to look stern. "After mass."

"Did you bring us a video game?"

"Yeah, like the last time. Did ya?"

Finn shook his head and hugged the boys against his legs, holding his hand over their mouths playfully. Looking over at his wife, he noticed that Kelly was taking her time getting out of the car. She was looking in the mirror, checking her makeup. Something was not right with her.

"Go in the church, lads, and save a seat for your mother and myself."

The boys raced across the parking lot to the door of the church. Finn walked around and opened the driver's door. Kelly turned and smiled at him.

The makeup and the smile did nothing to hide the tears in his wife's hazel eyes.

"What's wrong, darling?" he asked, crouching in front of her open door. "Were the boys too much again this morning?"

He was around enough Sunday mornings to know you needed eight hands to get the lads in church clothes and keep them reasonably clean until they got here.

"They were no trouble at all." She shook her head and took a pair of sunglasses out of her purse, pulling them on. It was overcast outside. She stepped out and gave him a hug and a quick peck on the lips, before locking the car. "Let's go in. I don't want to be late."

Cars were still arriving. "We're not going to be late. What's bothering you, Kelly?"

"It's Mick."

"What's wrong with him?" he asked quickly. Mick was Thomas's son. Finn had been raising his nephew as his own since before Thomas's death. Mick was now nineteen and smart as a pet fox. He was the first lad in Finn's family to have been accepted at the university.

"He's at the house. A friend of his drove him up this morning and dumped him at the front steps." She lowered her voice. "I tucked him snug in his bed. He's stoned, Finn. Totally."

More parishioners who had parked were coming by the car now, and some began to exchange greetings with them, curtailing the discussion. Finn nodded and smiled, all the while paying no attention to what was said. He took his wife by the hand, and they followed the parishioners.

This was the third time in two months, Finn thought, his stomach churning. Mick didn't touch the stuff when Finn lived at home. He'd been a wholesome kind of kid. No drinking to speak of, no serious girlfriends. A hard-working lad, to be sure. Something was happening to him, though, and not for the better. Finn couldn't let that happen. He had to take better care of Thomas's son.

Monsignor Cluny was greeting the parishioners at the door. "Finn, Kelly, I saw the twins. I thought you'd be coming along behind them."

Kelly made the quick excuse that she'd better see to them. She took her glasses off as she went inside. Finn was ready to follow his wife, but the priest took him by the arm.

"Can you stay on a bit after mass, Finn? I've been wanting to have a word with yourself."

Finn was surprised. Usually the priest liked to get together with his big donors over a cup of tea at the rectory or, for serious money talk, a pint or two down at O'Rourke's after the last mass.

"Sure thing, Monsignor. Something you'd be needing?"

"No, no. Nothing like that. It's…well, we need to be having ourselves a chat about Mick."

16

LOSS

Alanna had to go to work every day this past week. She needed to pretend that nothing had happened. Ray insisted that she keep her routines just as they always were. He didn't want anyone to suspect that he was back in the San Francisco area.

After that first day at her apartment, Alanna didn't know where and when they would meet. She couldn't contact him. He said it was too dangerous. He called her, at least, late every day from a blocked-ID phone number. He told her where to go, what time to be there. She had to be extremely careful that no one followed her.

Every day, they met at a different motel. Wherever they met, however, it was only for a couple of hours. Generally located in San Jose or in Fremont, the motels were the kinds of places that people rarely stayed the entire night in…and only paid cash. One day they'd met at a small motel off the Cabrillo Highway. They didn't even have sex. They just lay on the bed talking, holding each other and listening to the waves of the Pacific pounding against the shore outside the window.

Alanna was seeing herself differently these days. She wasn't offended by any of this. She wasn't even embarrassed. She was happy for every moment they had together. She was being given a second chance at life, and she planned to take whatever it offered.

At the same time, the reality of what she was planning to do—disappear—was pricking her conscience with its details and its consequences. Besides Ray, there were two things that mattered to her in life: her grandmother and her job. With Alanna gone, both of those would suffer.

Immediately after landing the position at NASA, Alanna's first priority had been to situate her grandmother in a place where she'd be comfortable for the rest of her life. She didn't want Lucia to work for anyone again—no cleaning houses and looking after strangers' kids. Of course, Lucia wouldn't have anything to do with that. She liked the family she was working for. The children meant a great deal to her, and until they were grown up and off to college, she was unmovable. So it wasn't until a year ago, at the age of eighty-seven, that she'd finally been persuaded to stop working.

Alanna had arranged for her to move to an assisted-living facility in Mountain View where she had her own room, and all her meals and her needs were taken care of. But that was only the beginning. Now more than ever, Lucia wanted to be closer to Alanna. They spent most Sundays together. And one other day in the week, Alanna had to bring her *abuela* back to her apartment so that Lucia could cook every meal her granddaughter would need for the following week.

Ray's accident had affected Lucia, too. She'd liked him, had doted on him when he'd been around, and had taken his death pretty hard. It was sad that Alanna couldn't share the news of Ray being alive with her *abuela*. And even more tragic for all of them, Alanna couldn't imagine how her grandmother would function if she herself were to disappear forever. Alanna was the only real family her *abuela* had.

Lucia had left Alanna's grandfather years before Alanna was born, but he had passed away five years ago. After the last of Lucia's older brothers and sisters back in Mexico died, her contact with relatives south of the border had gradually and then finally stopped. Neither of them had seen Alanna's mother in almost thirty years. They didn't know where she was or how she lived. Alanna knew that Lucia's loss of her only daughter still gave the old woman great pain. Her grandmother was alone now, except for Alanna.

Guilt was beginning to gnaw holes in Alanna's conscience. But it was even more than guilt, she told herself. It was how *she* felt for Lucia. She didn't know how she could walk away from the woman who'd been there for her all these years. The parent, the foundation of her life, the reason for the strong person that she'd become. She loved Lucia as much as Ray…perhaps more.

Alanna knew it was true. She loved her *abuela* more than she valued her own life.

Sitting at her desk, deep in thought, Alanna struggled as she swam in a deep sea of emotions. She was trying to consider every aspect of their plans…and the consequences of their actions. She didn't know how it could work. It was impossible. Her life was too complicated. She couldn't just walk away.

A knock on her open door startled her. She turned away from the computer screen and the e-mail that she'd been staring at for some time. She hadn't read a single line of it.

"Is this a good time now, Alanna?"

Phil Evans and Jill Goldman were waiting at her door. Phil had mentioned that it was critical that they get together with her today. Alanna motioned for them to come in.

"Are you okay?" Phil asked.

Alanna touched her cheeks. They were hot. She felt flushed. She took a sip of water from her cup, tried to focus on the *now,* on her job and on what was important to the people who depended on her.

"I'm fine…fine. Too much thinking." Alanna tapped her forehead, trying to lighten the mood. "The wiring is smoldering up here."

"Tomorrow is the big day," Jill said nervously.

Since the day Ray appeared, Alanna had found herself beginning to warm up to the young engineer. In fact, she had included Jill in the team that would be making a major presentation to some of the big brass and their guests tomorrow. She knew the quickest way to move up the ranks in this place and earn more money was to put yourself in a position where the top administrators could see you. You had to show them you were capable, comfortable communicating and proud of the work you were doing.

"I'm sure you'll do great," Alanna assured the young woman.

"I e-mailed you my section of the presentation. I hope it was okay," Jill said.

"It's fine. Remember to make eye contact. Don't read it. Talk to it."

"We have three brand-new members of the Congressional House Science Oversight Committee who will be in attendance tomorrow," Phil reminded her. "These guys know almost nothing about what we do, or what the consequences will be if our funding gets cut. And two of them, apparently, are hot on cutting federal spending in space programs."

This happened every year when the new blood in Congress meant the shuffling of committee members. The new members had to be briefed and won over on the importance of what they were doing.

"We're relying on you to dazzle them with your stats and knowledge," Phil told her.

"You mean scare them," Alanna corrected.

"Shock and awe. Impress the hell out of them. It always works. You're great at it."

Alanna knew Phil believed what he said. In fact, everyone who worked on the project seemed to think it. For as many years as Alanna had been involved in managing projects, the grants had been flowing. Other program budgets got cut, but hers grew in size and funding. She was considered a good risk. She delivered what she promised. But it was more than a simple presentation that made everything work. Still, Alanna knew that was a start, so she always made sure she and her team were prepared. She'd be ready tomorrow, too.

Her phone rang. Alanna looked at the display and knew the call was from Ray. Guilt tore at her. She wanted to answer the call. At the same time, she couldn't excuse herself when they were just starting the meeting. She knew Phil's tendency to get extremely nervous when it came time to justify his paycheck. He wouldn't be happy until they'd gone over every point that they were going to tell their audience tomorrow. For Jill's sake, Alanna thought, that was a good approach right now, anyway. The phone stopped ringing.

"With defense spending what it is in the Middle East, we'll be facing the toughest critique of our budget that we've seen in years. We've got to persuade the—"

The phone rang again.

"Give me one second, will you?" she told them, grabbing the handset and turning her back to them.

"I left my coffee on my desk," she heard Phil say as he got up to leave the office.

Alanna pressed the phone to her ear and tried to keep her voice level. "Dr. Mendes."

She was right. It was Ray.

"We can't see each other tonight," Ray said softly.

She should have been disappointed, but relief washed through her. Her own response surprised her. Still, she knew it was the rational, punctual part of her telling her that her team needed time to get ready for the presentation tomorrow.

"I'm sorry," he said.

"It's okay." She remembered Jill was still in her office.

"I'll promise to make it up to you, in a few different—"

"Something unexpected come up?" she interrupted, trying to sound as casual as she could. She could feel her face heating up. She knew exactly how he would try to make it up to her.

"There's someone with you?"

"Yes." Alanna got up and moved to the bookcase behind her desk, putting some distance between herself and the young engineer.

"I'll call you when I can."

"I'll be working late tonight," she told him.

There was a pause. "You give them too much of yourself. Start weaning them. They have to learn to do without you."

She recognized the reprimanding tone. He knew her well enough to know that there were times when her job took priority over everything else. She allowed it to happen. She'd always wanted it this way. And he knew it.

"What's wrong?" she asked, hoping to know the real source of his problem.

He waited a long moment before answering. "I might have to go away."

Her heart sank. "Alone?"

"This time…but don't worry. I'll be back, love. There's someone that I have to see."

"Who?"

"I told you before, Ali. I can't talk about this. But the meeting might give us a way past all this," he said in a confident tone.

She didn't know how anything or anyone could get

them out of this jam. Thinking about the effect of their disappearing on her grandmother had been sobering. This meeting with Phil and Jill was another reminder how indispensable she was when it came to NASA's STEREO-mission project. There was no way she could just walk away from it overnight. Alanna couldn't admit it, but she wasn't sure if she wanted to walk away at all. The logical side of her brain was already slapping her around, forcing her to face reality.

"How can I contact you?" she asked hurriedly, realizing both of them had been silent for a while. They needed to talk. Find a way. If they didn't go away together, maybe they could still see each other somehow. Things would be different now that she knew he was alive.

"I'll text you on your cell phone. You can always text me back if something urgent comes up," he told her. "You can't call me at that number."

"It's important for us to get together before a decision is made," she reminded him.

"We will. I'll let you know," he said softly. "I love you, Ali. Please trust me. Now I have to go."

All logic aside, her throat constricted as Ray hung up. She stood where she was, her back to Jill, pretending that she was still on the phone. She fought the surging emotions. Disappointment, confusion, indecision. She had to put herself back together. Alanna didn't want Ray to meet with this person, thinking that she was free to walk away from her responsibilities.

"Okay, sounds great," she finally said into the phone to no one. "Goodbye."

She turned around, placing the phone back on the

handset. She was relieved to see Phil wasn't back from getting his coffee.

"I'm sorry," Jill said quietly.

Alanna looked at the young engineer curiously. "What for?"

"For eavesdropping. For not leaving your office when you were on the phone."

Alanna doubted the other woman could have heard much—or had made any sense of what the conversation was about.

"It was okay for you to stay. I can be pretty blunt when I need my privacy."

"Oh, I know," Jill said sheepishly. "Do you know the morning that I intruded on you on the bus, a pool started in the department about what time I'd be fired?"

"You mean I could have made some money on you after all?" Alanna asked.

Phil walked back in with his supersize mug filled to the brim with fresh coffee. "Okay, are we ready to focus on tomorrow?"

Alanna was relieved. As upset as she'd been a few minutes ago by Ray's phone call, she now could channel her attention toward only one thing—keeping her twin satellites in space.

17

DESPAIR

New York Presbyterian Hospital

Sometimes, when a life is on the line, the choice between right and wrong, between legal and illegal, is a not a choice at all. David Collier certainly had no choice. There was only one path to take. And wherever this path led, he'd take it with open eyes to the very end if it meant giving his daughter a chance to live.

The man who'd been eager to interview him, Hank Diarte, had been the same man who handed him the letter from the clinic in Germany. After David had failed to show up for the interview, Diarte had called David's house, and the babysitter had told the man about the emergency with Leah. Diarte had then come to the hospital. Little had been said immediately about the job David would be doing, and in a way, it mattered even less to David. Diarte was offering him a way to keep his daughter alive. He would have time to ask questions later.

David met with Leah's pediatrician and nephrologist

once Leah was admitted to the hospital. He was given a brief explanation of what was being done. The blood transfusion had helped, but there were still more tests they were running. When David told them about the arrangement that had been made for his daughter with the clinic in Germany, both men became quite enthused—and obviously relieved. The pediatrician immediately suggested that they conduct a conference call with the doctors who would be taking over Leah's care once she flew to Europe. It was important to discuss the best possible preparation now for the treatment the German doctors would be providing.

As they went off to work out the logistics of the call, David joined Diarte in the hall. This was the first chance he'd had to speak with the man since meeting him downstairs in the waiting area of the emergency room. Now David had time to ask his questions.

"Mr. Diarte, how did you know about my daughter's condition? How is it that you already contacted the clinic in Germany? How did you know that was the best chance of treatment we have?" he asked.

"The same way that we have all of your background information. There's a great deal that we know about you, Mr. Collier."

A lot of David's background was public information from court records. But Leah's medical files were private—and yet these people had accessed them.

"But how was it that your employer made the decision to contact the clinic and make the arrangements? You had not even interviewed me yet. There was so much that you must not have known about me."

"From the first, we understood the critical condition that your daughter is in," Diarte told him. "We sensed the urgency. We wished to waste no time."

"But what if I'm not the best candidate for the position?" he pressed.

"We are very thorough in our research regarding candidates. You *are* the best candidate, Mr. Collier. We knew that before we even contacted you. The job is yours. The interview was only a formality."

David remembered the letter from the clinic was dated before the first call from Diarte. "And what if I'd decided the position wasn't right for me? What if I *still* decide that?"

The other man smiled. "My employer decided that the urgency of your daughter's situation needed to be addressed…no matter what the outcome of our discussions regarding the position."

"That is very generous of your employer."

"Perhaps, Mr. Collier, but not foolish. The risks were weighed. We felt certain that we could come to terms with you about this position."

They stood by a vending machine in an area off the large lounge designated for the pediatric wing. A dozen or so clearly apprehensive parents or relatives were scattered around the lounge. David jingled the quarters he was holding in his hand. He couldn't focus on what to get out of the machine.

"What is it you'd like me to do?" he asked.

"The project begins with a short-term travel assignment. A couple of weeks at the most."

"But what is it you want me to do?" David asked again.

"The position will involve the auditing of some files connected with an international-banking concern."

"Auditing," David repeated, not believing what was being said. No one would pay the kind of expense Leah's treatment would accrue to hire an auditor. "You *are* aware of my qualifications."

"As I said, we know exactly what your qualifications are, Mr. Collier," Diarte said, putting money in the vending machine. "But there is no real need to discuss the project in detail right now. You have something here that needs your attention first. So long as we're agreed on the compensation package we discussed on the phone…"

"You mentioned nothing of the medical benefits that were arranged in Germany."

"At that time, the criticality of it wasn't apparent to us," Diarte told him.

"I assume numbers need to be adjusted to take into effect the expense your employer is assuming," David said. He was willing to work for free—he'd do anything, so long as Leah's health was restored.

"You will find my employer very generous when it comes to monetary arrangements. But as far as the nature of the work itself, we can discuss the full range of your responsibilities once your daughter's health has stabilized."

Whoever these people were, David thought, he appreciated the fact that they understood his priorities. Even so, he'd barely escaped going to prison once before. He wasn't willing to be the fall guy in another scam.

18

FEAR

Istanbul, Turkey

Steven was pleased and surprised to find a Foreign Service Officer from the U.S. consulate in Ankara waiting for them at Istanbul's Atatürk Airport. The FSO introduced himself as Joe Finley, and from the looks of him, he couldn't have been much older than Nathan.

"My superiors are nearly certain that there has been no foul play involved," he told them. "Mr. and Mrs. Galvin, we believe your son will show up any day now. He's probably off on some tourist excursion. This happens all the time."

Denial was one thing that pushed Kei to the edge. Steven took his wife's hand, squeezing gently. He had to take charge before she exploded on him.

"How old are you, Mr. Finley?" Steven asked.

"Twenty-four, sir."

"And how long have you been here in Turkey?"

"Eight months, sir. This is a fascinating country. There is so much to see."

"Are you in the habit of taking off sightseeing without a word to anyone for a week at a time?" Steven asked as they were waved through a special gate at customs.

"Whenever I get a chance," he said brightly. "Turkey is so different from Idaho, let me tell you. Of course, as an FSO, I need to let the consulate know where I'm going."

Finley continued to chat. Steven glanced at Kei. Large sunglasses covered her eyes. She gave no indication that she was being comforted by anything the young man was telling them. At least she hadn't strangled him. Yet.

The Turkish translator and the driver that Steven had arranged for met them by the terminal exit doors. Finley told them that he had been directed to stay with them for as long as they needed or until their son reappeared.

Galvin figured this special attention had something to do with the phone call he'd made to his old friend Paul Hersey before leaving the U.S. The four-term senator from Pennsylvania had held posts in the State Department under two different presidents and had even served as an interim ambassador to the UN. Paul definitely had connections with many top people in the Foreign Service, and he'd told Steven he'd be more than happy to help.

Finley rode in the backseat of the car with them, with the translator—a young woman who introduced herself as Tansu—sitting in front with the driver. Finley's driver would follow them to the hotel where Nathan was staying.

Kei looked very pale to him. So far, she'd shown no inclination to ask even one question of the people who were with them. David didn't know if that was because of his own approach of taking charge or because she wasn't feeling well.

Joe Finley broke in on Steven's thoughts. "To bring you folks up to speed, the consulate has notified the director general of the Turkish National Police and Interpol, as well, of your son's disappearance. I took it upon myself to contact the Istanbul police this morning. They've assigned someone to meet us at the hotel." Finley looked at his watch. "We're looking good, as far as time goes."

The FSO looked ahead at the traffic before turning back to Steven. "I don't want to miss them at the hotel. You should know, folks, that police investigations here don't run with the same...well, sense of urgency...as they do in the U.S."

Kei spoke up for the first time. "Their honesty is more of a concern to us than their speed. How can we be sure that we won't get a bunch of crooks working on the case?"

Steven knew his wife wasn't exaggerating. The trouble regarding Turkey's corrupt police force and judicial system had even made it to American newspapers. The translator turned in her seat and looked intently at Kei.

"We don't care how they get the job done," Steven said to Finley and Tansu. He'd been told that the translator had completed her undergraduate degree at UCLA and was now working on a law degree here in Istanbul. "I don't care if I have to put half the missing persons office, or whatever it is here, on my payroll. I want my son found. That's the bottom line. We need to make that clear. I'll be happy to provide incentives, if that's what it takes."

Both of them nodded. Steven figured he'd made his point. Kei reached over and entwined her fingers with his. Her hand was ice cold. He knew he had to pursue every option, turn every stone. Neither of them did well with waiting.

He turned to their translator. "What are the big newspapers in Istanbul?"

She rattled off a half dozen names of papers.

"We want a full-page ad in every one of them with my son's picture. Every day. I want it to state 'Missing' at the top and that we'll offer a reward." Tansu pulled a pad of paper from her handbag and started taking notes.

"What about television?" Steven asked.

"Yes," Tansu replied. "We can contact the news offices at the—"

"Don't you think we should wait to have the police check into this first?" Finley asked, looking surprised.

"You said just now that the police can't be counted on to move quickly," Steven reminded him.

"Yes, but what happens if he is perfectly fine? He could very well be out on a cruise. It could embarrass him if we jump the gun and put his picture—"

"I'm willing to take that chance. In fact, I'll be happy to weather his unhappiness at what we do, so long as we see him safe and sound," Steven told the other man.

STIGMA

Whatever their strategy was, it was working. They hadn't called or e-mailed him for over a week, and Jay Alexei was getting eaten up with worry.

Jay had lost count of how many nights he'd lain awake in bed. The interview with Mr. Lyons kept playing over and over again in his head. He wished he'd explained things better. He should have shown off more of his technical expertise.

And he wished he hadn't stressed how afraid he was of doing anything illegal—of going back to jail.

Jay had been told upfront that there were more applicants and it would be some time before they got back to him.

All week, he'd gone off to work, increasingly exhausted. His brain, however, wouldn't stop. All week, he'd seen Padma struggling with the pregnancy, as well. She refused to stop working because they needed the money, but every night her feet were like balloons. Her hands had started swelling, too, and she had back pains.

They had a baby on the way. Soon, Jay would have more than the two of them to worry about. Unable to sleep, he'd kept trying to work out in his head how they were going to make it. Hour after hour, he'd kept coming back to the fact that, in reality, he was willing to do anything…absolutely anything that might improve life for Padma and their baby. He'd even go to jail if there were some kind of guarantee that his family would be cared for.

He wished now that there was a way he could say all these things to Lyons. He wanted another interview, another chance to prove himself.

Padma moved uncomfortably and made a noise in her sleep. Her back was pressed to his side. Jay rolled over and gathered her closer to his chest. He'd never realized what love really meant until these past few months. Every day, his affection for her seemed to grow deeper. He knew it was a cliché, but the truth was that, every day, he loved her more than the day before.

Jay felt her tense up in his arms. From deep in her throat came another sighing moan, like she was in pain. He propped himself up on one elbow and looked down at her. The shade on the window next to the bed was up and moonlight poured in. He realized she was only pretending to be asleep.

"What's wrong?" he asked in a whisper.

Her head turned on the pillow. She looked up at him. He saw the tears shimmering in her black, moonlit eyes.

"What's wrong, Padma?" he asked again.

"I think it's time," she whispered.

He was slow to understand.

"I've started labor, Jay."

He sat up as though someone had poked him with a hot iron. He was out of bed and pulling on his pants in one swift motion. He didn't bother with socks, but stuffed his feet into his work boots.

"We have to get you down the stairs…five floors. Maybe I should call an ambulance…your bag…there was something about getting a bag ready." He turned to her. She hadn't moved off the bed. "You can't be in labor. The baby isn't due for another three weeks."

She cried and laughed at the same time. "I wish you could see yourself." She tried to sit up.

Jay came to her side of the bed and knelt down. He turned on the bedside light. He tried to remember some of the reading he'd done on the Internet. "Are you sure you're in labor, honey? First-time pregnancies are kind of tricky."

"No," she said shakily. "No doubt now."

He followed her gaze. Her nightgown was wet.

"My water broke."

"But…this is red! You're bleeding," he shouted in panic.

"It's okay. The doctor told me about it. I'm fine. But the baby could come really fast now." She reached for him. "Help me up."

Jay stood up. In a total daze he followed every direction she gave him. She needed clothing. There was a bag she'd already packed. It was next to the sofa. He had to call her doctor.

"I think this is a big one." She bent over with pain.

Jay held on to her hand and stopped breathing. She looked up at him when the contraction had passed.

"Jay, breathe."

He did as he was told. He wished they'd taken the pregnancy classes they were offering at the hospital.

"I don't know what to do," he said, totally lost.

"I'm doing all the work," she reminded him. "You'll be helping me."

"How?"

"By not passing out." She smiled. "Now call the doctor. Tell her the contractions are four minutes apart."

Jay realized his hand was shaking as he picked up the phone. His mind was blank. He couldn't remember where the phone number for the doctor was. He had to wait until Padma got through another contraction before she told him it was staring him right in the face. The phone number was written on a large piece of paper dead center on the refrigerator door.

Jay considered himself a tough guy. He'd done jail time. But he couldn't remember a single moment in his life when he was more frightened than right now.

They were having a baby.

20

TERROR

Belfast, Ireland

"What in bloody hell do you want from me?" Mick asked angrily, hammering his fist on the breakfast table. The dishes shook and the coffee in Finn's mug spilled over onto the table.

"First of all," Finn said coolly, "I want you to shut up and listen to me."

He blotted up the mess with his napkin and tossed it onto his plate. He'd had to wait until Kelly and the boys were out of the house before he could start this discussion with Mick, but he was damned if he wasn't going to have it now. Finn had set the rules. There were changes that had to be made. The biggest one was where the nineteen-year-old was living. Mick didn't like giving up the apartment near the university. That was too bad. Finn wanted him sleeping every night under this roof. He wanted to know when and where he was going and when he was coming back. He wanted to know the kind of friends he was hanging out with.

"What I want from you, lad, is to stay away from the dope. I want your mind sharp, your habits clean. I want you to study hard and act and do as what's fitting for the name of this family. God's given you a brain, Mick. You need to start using it. Is that too much for you?"

"Fitting for the name of our family." Mick repeated the words in a mocking tone. He shook his head bitterly.

"The monsignor himself had to take me aside after church because he was wanting to tell me tales of two parishioners who'd seen you staggering about down by Donegall Quay this past week…and totally stoned you were," Finn said in a quiet voice. "This might come as a surprise to you, but this isn't what your father and I planned for you when you were grown. This isn't why I work as hard as I do to keep a roof over your head and money in your pocket. We want you to—"

"My da is dead," Mick snapped.

Not to Finn, he wasn't. The nineteen-year-old sitting across from him was a constant and angry reminder of the younger brother he'd lost.

"*I…*" Finn corrected, gathering his thoughts. "I want you to make something respectable out of yourself. I want to look up at you five years, ten years down the road, with pride and say, that's my brother's lad. Made something good of himself. I want to say that Mick did his father proud."

"Don't you think we're a tad too late to be talking of that?"

"You're nineteen years old, lad. Too late for what?"

"To be saving the family name, for one."

"You were given a clean slate the day you were born. You've been given opportunities. You might do some good with it."

"Doesn't matter what I do. There is no focking way I can buy yourself and my da a place in heaven," Mick said in a bitter tone. "I'm not stupid, Finn. Don't you think I know where that money you put in my pocket comes from? Don't you think I figured out long ago what my father was involved with and why it was that he died at the age of twenty-nine?"

Thomas shouldn't have died, Finn thought. It had been his job to protect his younger brother…to get him out of that station on time. He'd failed that day. He'd failed miserably…and lost his own kin.

Mick pushed himself to his feet. "You had a closed casket for his wake, and you don't think I knew why?" He ran a hand through his long brown hair. "My da was blown to pieces. There wasn't much left of him to see, was there, Finn? He was like the others…the ones he'd blown to pieces himself."

"That's enough!" Finn smashed the table with one hand. Mick turned and stood by the counter, his back to him.

There was a lot that Finn took for granted. There were so many things that he'd never explained. And that was not only to Mick. It would be the same when Conor and Liam were of an age as this one. This next generation didn't have to know why he and Thomas lived the way they had—why they had done what they did—why they had taken so many lives. At one time, it might have been easy to explain. Times had changed, though. It wasn't so easy now.

In fact, he thought, explaining only made it worse.

"Whatever you're thinking that Thomas and I did, it has nothing to do with what you owe me as your uncle and guardian," Finn said sharply. "I carry my weight. You'll carry yours. I do my job, and you have yours to do, as well."

"And if it so happens that the weight I carry puts me on a crash course with you?" Mick challenged, turning around and facing him. "I sit through classes, I hear lectures, I read crap every day going on about the value of life. Then, the next moment, I sit back and think about the trip you were on to Budapest or Casablanca or Frankfurt the month before. I think of the lives that you have taken, all in a name of what, Finn?"

Finn didn't know how it was that Mick knew so many specifics. But that was the least of his problems now.

"Don't you be worrying about my sins. You live your life. I'll live mine."

"But you see…this is exactly what I am trying to do. Live my focking life in some way that I can stand it, at all."

Mick stalked out of the kitchen.

"Wait just a moment, you," Finn shouted after him. "We're not done with this, you and me."

No, Finn thought grimly, this argument was far from over.

21

LOSS

Alanna was two distinct souls trapped in one body.

One soul lived for passion, love, happiness, driving Alanna to run away at a moment's notice to join her lover in any corner of the world for all eternity. The other soul fed on reason, responsibility, reminding Alanna constantly of the people who depended on her. The soul of reason placed Alanna's personal needs last.

That wasn't entirely true, either, Alanna thought. She had worked hard all of her life, and she was finally reaping the rewards that reason and responsibility brought. She was an expert in her field. There were many who respected her, counted on her, relied on her knowledge. She was a key figure in a very important chess game. This made her feel valued, proud of the person she had become. Considering her past and her family's lack of education, she was pleased that she had broken the cycle of poverty and powerlessness that had haunted them for generations. She knew she was a positive role model for many women to follow.

The battle of souls could be vicious, though, each demanding its own way. That battle was being waged now, too, and she had felt it from the moment she stepped into the elevator. She didn't see others who were around her. She didn't speak a word, for the noise in her head was deafening.

As the elevator reached its destination, the soul of reason took control. A calm assuredness flowed through Alanna the moment she stepped out into the lobby and saw the large group of suits and military people who were waiting there. They were here to learn about the STEREO mission, the project that she had been instrumental in bringing to life. She was the expert, the one with answers. She knew where they'd been and where they were going with this mission. She knew how much money they needed to keep the project intact and moving forward.

Alanna knew many of the people who were waiting in the lobby. They were NASA people. Others were total strangers.

"Dr. Mendes." One of the NASA directors stopped her and made an introduction to a new congressman.

She didn't follow politics. She had no clue of this man's fiscal philosophy or his political objectives. That kind of information was Phil's specialty. At five feet tall, she barely reached the man's chin, but she knew that by the time she was done with this presentation, he would think she was seven feet tall.

She excused herself after meeting the VIPs. She had to get to her people. There were some whispers in the room and soon many eyes were following her as she crossed the lobby toward the open conference-room doors.

Five people from her group, all engineers, were gathered at the front of the room. They all seemed ready to go. Alanna did a quick check on Phil. He seemed confident. That meant everyone was ready.

The total length of their presentation was going to be about three hours, with satellite footage, taped interviews and a slide presentation to make it more of a show-and-tell. As the current project manager of the mission, Alanna would start the report, with Phil cutting in with some additional details, and she would finish the first segment. She was also responsible for answering questions that would come at the very end. Two of the presenters were new staff, Jill being one of them. The other three were old-timers like Alanna.

She turned to the conference room and realized that the crowd outside had followed her in. Every seat appeared to be full. They had more people here today than at any other time that she could remember. Someone closed the doors and another person adjusted the lights. One of the directors introduced Alanna and her group, spending a great deal of time conveying the particulars of her education and experience.

The decision shifted even more in her mind. The audience already seemed impressed with all of her credentials.

The lights dimmed. The wide screen started with a *Star Wars*–type of Hollywood opening. Alanna smiled at the two young engineers whose visual and audio suggestions to Alanna and Phil had transformed what otherwise would have been just old hat. In front of the podium, the lights also shined on a three-dimensional model of the earth, with the STEREO project's twin satellites in constant motion.

She took center stage.

"The year was 1859. Two hundred thousand kilometers of telegraph wires suddenly shorted out in the United States and Europe. During those long hours, the only means of effective long-distance communication in the world shut down. Widespread fires spontaneously began breaking out in Canada and the western United States. As far south as Rome and Hawaii, the skies turned many shades of red and green. It was like an apocalyptic scene from a science-fiction movie."

Some of the audience murmured in surprise. She could tell the NASA personnel from others. Those familiar with her project had heard this segment of the presentation. Others hadn't.

Alanna continued. "Meanwhile, near London, some of the first ground-based magnetometers were monitoring the behavior of the earth's magnetic field. Surprisingly, quasi-sinusoidal oscillations of the magnetic field lines lasting for periods of a few minutes were recorded continuously for several hours, as if some celestial musician had plucked the strings of the earth's magnetic guitar."

A slide show to the side flashed brilliantly with computer-generated images and actual photographs of the time Alanna was discussing.

"That single event, occurring over one hundred and forty years ago, was three times more powerful than the strongest space storm in modern memory, stronger than one that many in this room might remember, the one that cut power to Quebec in 1989."

She glanced at Phil. Having both of them interact during a presentation kept the audience on their toes. Phil moved next to her.

"Here is a little background for the non-techies in our audience today," he said. "Space storms or solar storms, as they're sometimes called, are linked to twisted magnetic fields in the sun that suddenly snap...and release tremendous amounts of energy. These charged particles race outward. We call this expanding bubble of hot gas 'plasma.'"

Alanna took over. "In 1859, four crucial elements combined to make the strike such a major event. First, the plasma that was ejected from the sun hit the earth. That was relatively routine. The speed of the plasma strike, however, was more unusual. The blob of plasma came at an exceptionally *high* speed. It took only seventeen hours and forty minutes to go from the sun to the earth."

"That is the second element. Solar storms typically take two to four days to travel the ninety-three million miles," Phil explained. "This plasma strike took less than a day."

Alanna continued. "Third, the magnetic fields in the plasma blob—the scientific name, by the way, is coronal mass ejection—anyway, the magnetic fields in the mass were exceptionally intense."

"And the fourth, most important ingredient," Phil said. "The magnetic fields of the coronal mass ejection were opposite in direction from the earth's fields."

"The result of the combination of these four elements of the strike in 1859 was simply this...the planet's defenses were overwhelmed." Alanna paused for effect as the slide show went dark.

"But that was *then,* you might be thinking. And you'd be correct." Phil started again. "In 1859, the technology was practically neolithic compared with today's technology. No satellites, and no GPS systems. No TV feeds, no automatic-teller machines relying on orbiting relay stations, no delicately balanced and overstressed power grids. No cell phones…no *telephones,* for that matter. No, at that time, the telegraph was only fifteen years old."

"Now, could this happen again and what are the potential consequences?" Alanna asked. "First of all, yes, it could definitely happen. In fact, based on a forecast issued by the NOAA Space Environment Center in coordination with an international panel of solar experts, the next solar cycle will be thirty to fifty percent stronger than the last cycle, and it will peak at the end of 2011 to the middle of 2012.

"Scientists at NOAA have issued cycle predictions only three times," Alanna continued. "In 1989, a panel met to predict Cycle 22, which they picked to occur that same year, and the scientists met again in September of 1996 to predict Cycle 23. And in April of 2007, Cycle 24 predictions were made.

"A new field of study has enabled scientists to better predict the severity of the next cycle," Alanna added. "The field of study, called helioseismology, allows researchers to *see* inside the sun by tracking sound waves that are reverberating inside the sun itself, creating a picture of the interior. This is very much the way ultrasound creates a picture of an unborn baby. Using this, scientists can predict for the first time the strength of the eleven-year solar-activity cycle."

"Now," Phil broke in, "some of you have that look on your faces that says, 'The scientists over at NOAA seem to be doing all the work. Why are we pumping more than $560 million into these people's project?'"

"Wait a minute, Phil. If they've given us that much money, how come I'm still taking the bus to work every morning?" Alanna's sharp question elicited a laugh from the crowd.

No one seemed to have fallen sleep. That was always a good thing, she thought.

Suddenly, a close-up visual of the STEREO satellite lit up the screen.

"Just to remind my colleague here, STEREO is an acronym for Solar Terrestrial Relations Observatory. Our project is the third mission in NASA's Solar Terrestrial Probes program. And *that* is quite a tongue twister." Alanna smiled. "We call it STP."

"That's ST*P*," Phil repeated with emphasis on the last letter and getting another laugh. "We're not in the sex-education field."

"Our two-year STEREO mission was launched last year. The twin satellites are already showing us a revolutionary view of the sun-earth system." Another image came up on the screen. Alanna pointed her laser pen at it. "As you can see here, these are the two nearly identical observatories, one ahead of earth in its orbit, the other trailing behind. Between the two of them, we're able to trace the flow of energy and matter from the sun to the earth." She motioned to go to the next view. "Here is a 3-D image of coronal mass ejections blasting through space toward us. As I said, these are eruptions of matter from the sun that can disrupt communication and defense satellites in orbit, as well as power grids on the ground. These eruptions can shut down everything that we depend on in our day-to-day living. And we're not talking about conveniences—we're talking about communicating abilities and power that drive every-thing in our society."

"But you're still thinking, this is one expensive set of cameras," Phil chirped in. "Isn't there an economy model that will do the same thing?"

"Phil's next career is mind reader," Alanna com-mented. "But as you can tell, he's pretty bad at it." With a smile, she turned her attention back to the screen. "Coronal mass ejections, CMEs, can blow up to ten billion tons of the sun's atmosphere into interplanetary space. Traveling away from the sun at speeds of ap-proximately one million miles per hour, they can trigger severe magnetic storms as they collide with the earth's magnetosphere."

The next image showed the earth under attack by magnetic storms. The image was computer generated, but it still had the right effect.

"This is the most important point. What STEREO will do for us is provide an essential and timely warning," Alanna told the group. "With the warning that the STEREO satellites provide, we can activate the technology that we have available to head off potential disaster. Acting either unilaterally or in cooperation with nations across the globe, the United States can take the necessary steps to protect ourselves and the electrical media that we depend on. But all of this has to happen before the CMEs reach us."

They were far from done, but Alanna thought they had whet enough of the audience's appetite that they could now launch into some specifics of design and monitoring, as well as where the money was going now that the mission satellites were safely orbiting in space. Introducing the others in her group and quickly outlining the segments of the presentation that they were going to cover, she then stepped aside, allowing her people to do their jobs.

Her hand moved to her jacket pocket. Standing in the deep shadows at one side of the room, she thanked God that she hadn't felt her cell phone five minutes earlier. She tried to ignore it, but it didn't stop. Her cell phone vibrated back to life again.

She knew who it was. She was certain what it was about. Ray had been determined to find a way for them to go away. He told her he loved her. He wanted her with him.

Alanna looked at the full conference room, at the audience enthralled by the science and the adventure that she'd played a large part in creating. She glanced up at the large pictures of the satellite on the board, at the smaller model in front of their podium. This mattered too much. She'd learned to cope with life without Ray, but, as painful as it would be, Alanna didn't think she could do without this.

She took her cell phone out of her pocket and checked her incoming calls. He hadn't left her a voice mail. She found the message he'd sent her the day before. The one she could use to contact him. She typed in a text message in response.

I am so sorry, Ray, but I can't go. Ever. I love you.

Alanna sent the message and then shut off the phone. This was best for her, for her grandmother and for Ray, too.

It's over, she thought.

22

FEAR

Istanbul, Turkey

The hotel had to be a relic of Turkey's Ottoman days. In its finest moments, it might have had a one-star rating, but that had to be at least fifty years ago.

When the car pulled up out front, Steven suggested to Kei that she stay in the car, but she was having none of that. They went into the small lobby. A glass door to the left led to a tearoom that was apparently closed in the afternoon.

From what Steven could tell, the clerk working the front desk was chief cook and bottle washer in the place. If the presence of the waiting uniformed policemen had flustered the man, the sight of Americans arriving in a car out front seemed to be more than the desk clerk could handle. As they approached the desk, the clerk looked as if he was ready to bolt.

Neither of the two policemen spoke any English, but Steven explained through Tansu to the one in charge why they were here and what they wanted them to do. Joe Finley stood in the background, listening intently to the conversation.

The two policemen were dressed in navy blue pants and nylon jackets, with pale blue shirts and navy ties. Each wore a silver badge on his chest and an ID clipped to his jacket. Steven noted that the more senior officer, perhaps a year or two older than the other, was watching him sympathetically as he listened. The officer ordered his subordinate to write down the information. Steven hoped this was a sign that they were taking the business seriously.

"After we're done here," the translator told them, "they need to have you come to the station to fill out paperwork. This officer is very sorry to have to inconvenience you with details, but he has his procedures that must be followed."

"But we can go up to his room first?" Steven asked.

Tansu repeated the question.

The policeman nodded and said something to Steven before speaking sharply to the desk clerk, who reached behind him for a key.

"What did he say?" Steven asked.

"He says that it is important that you disturb nothing, in case he needs to call for the detectives to come and inspect the room."

Steven nodded.

"Your son…he is good man," the desk clerk told them in broken English as he turned with the key in his hand. "Rent paid up…for next week. He is okay. He won't pay rent if he not come back. Smart. Good with lira."

"I cannot come over," he said to Steven, stumbling

with the words and then speaking rapidly in Turkish to the translator.

"He's saying he's the only one working today. He can't leave the front desk," Tansu translated. "Your son's room is on the second floor. At the top of the stairs, turn left. His is the last door on the left."

Kei reached out to take the key, and the clerk said something else to the policemen.

"The room is very small," Tansu said. "He thinks not everyone will fit in at one time."

They could barely fit in the front lobby, Steven thought.

"I'd like for us to go up first," Kei told Steven. The translator conveyed her request and one of the policemen shrugged and gestured toward the stairs.

As they made their way to the second floor, Galvin asked Tansu to bring up the topic of advertising in the newspaper and on television…and to ask them if he could offer them a "gift" for their efforts and a subsequent reward for positive results. He wanted them motivated. He also wanted her to be making phone calls to the newspapers and getting everything lined up.

At the top of the stairs, Joe excused himself, saying he needed to report in that they had made contact with each other. "The consulate wants to stay informed, in case they can help expedite things from Ankara."

Steven nodded. The policemen and Tansu waited in the narrow hallway by the stairs, and the Galvins walked down toward the room, stepping over trash and bottles stacked outside of rooms.

"We gave him enough money before this trip to stay at the Ritz-Carlton," he grumbled under his breath. "He won't get away with it this time. He's grounded when he gets back."

Steven was relieved to see the hint of a smile on his wife's face at the thought of grounding the twenty-three-year-old. Kei had always been so full of life, until Nathan's disappearance.

The door to a shared bathroom stood open in the hall-way. The strong scent of disinfectant wafted out. There were no numbers, but Steven had no trouble finding Nathan's room.

His hand shook. Doubts about their son's safety were already planted deep in his stomach, but for Kei's sake Steven nodded with assurance before putting the key in the hole.

A musty smell wafted out the moment the door was opened. The room was indeed very small. The bed was made and a polo shirt lay on the shiny pale green coverlet. There was a small window on the far wall. A faded, thread-bare curtain hung across it. The corner of Nathan's suitcase was visible beneath the bed. Some tourist brochures, a Turkish-language book, a map and some change were spread on a table beneath a mirror against a wall. A sport jacket was draped on the back of a chair beside the table, and a shirt lay neatly folded on the seat. By the window a bulky sweater sat on top of a small chest of drawers.

Kei walked in ahead of him.

"Housekeeping must only come in when someone moves out," Steven commented, noticing the coating of dust on the few pieces of furniture. He followed his wife in and closed the door. A towel hung behind the door from a small brass hook.

Kei started across the room, but stopped and picked up the shirt off the bed. She held it up to her face, and Steven thought she was going to cry. She didn't. Still holding the shirt, she went around the bed to the table. Steven looked under the bed. A suitcase and a duffel bag had been stuffed under there. Crouching on the floor, he pulled them out. Inside the bag, he found only a few clothes.

"Steven, look at this."

He looked up. Kei was standing with the folded shirt in her hands. On the seat of the chair, he could see Nathan's passport and wallet and an iPod. In an instant, he was beside her. The wallet had Nathan's driver's license, credit and bank cards, as well as some American dollars and Turkish lira.

"What does this mean?" Kei asked, a note of rising panic in her voice.

He sat down on the bed, unable to think. No matter how hard he tried, he couldn't come up with a logical explanation why Nathan would go away without these essentials.

Suddenly, Kei dropped the clothing in her hand and moved across the room to the chest of drawers. With her back to him, she was looking at something next to the folded sweater. He watched Kei put her hand to her throat.

"What is it? What did you find?" he asked in what he hoped was a steady voice.

"His…" Her voice broke.

"Kei?" He saw her stab at tears.

"His shaving bag. Toothbrush, even his contact-lens case and glasses…they're all here." She held up a chain and a medallion for him to see. "Nathan always wore this."

"Yes, but he told us that pickpockets are a big problem here." He realized he was making excuses. "Maybe—"

"Something has happened to him, Steven." She moved back to him and took the things out of his hand. "What are we going to do? How are we going to find him?"

The tears were streaming down her face now. All he could do was gather her in his arms and hope that his money would be enough to bring their son back.

23

DESPAIR

New York Presbyterian Hospital

"Even though I'm the one who suggested the technique, you should know that therapeutic cloning is very experimental," the pediatrician told David.

"What is it exactly that will happen?" David asked. He knew that both doctors had been on the phone a number of times with their counterparts in Germany.

"First, we obtain DNA from Leah. This step of the procedure can be done right here at New York Presbyterian. We send the DNA to the clinic in Germany where they insert it into an enucleated egg. Once the egg containing the patient's DNA starts to divide, embryonic stem cells will be harvested. From this stem cell, the researchers at that clinic will generate a kidney that is a genetic match to Leah's."

"And that's what they use for the actual transplant?" David asked.

The pediatrician nodded. "The kidney transplanted into Leah should have almost no risk of tissue rejection."

"Has this procedure been done before?"

"Yes. The process is nearly five years old. There's been a fifty percent success rate for those over twenty years of age, and the early statistics are much better, even, for younger patients. But there hasn't been enough data collected to publish any papers on it," the other doctor explained.

"And what are the risks?" David asked.

The two men exchanged a look, and the nephrologist was the one who spoke again. "There are cases where the early steps of culture fails, but these people are absolutely the best at this technique. They have the highest success rate anywhere. The actual risk to Leah isn't what happens in the end, but the wait time. Frankly, Mr. Collier, it will be a challenge to keep her alive for that period of time."

David tried not to let his hopes crumble into dust. "What kind of time frame are we talking about?"

"Generating the transferable kidney could take anywhere from two to six months—*if* everything progresses without a hitch. They'll let you know when they're ready for her."

"And where does she have to be during this time?" David asked.

"Once we stabilize her, she could be in any clinic or hospital where there's access to round-the-clock dialysis," the pediatrician explained. "The doctors at the clinic in Germany will do the actual transplant surgery there, and she'll have to remain with them for a minimum of six weeks, possibly longer, for follow-up tests and studies."

David thought about the job offer and the man behind the scenes who was paying for this procedure. He wondered how long they would be willing to wait before asking him to start in his position. He couldn't leave Leah—not like this.

"When are you taking the culture?" he asked.

"Today…if that's the direction you want to go."

"Absolutely," David said. "We don't have any other choice, do we?"

The two physicians' silence gave David his answer.

24

FEAR

Istanbul, Turkey

There was no reason for them to go to the police department to fill out paperwork. Joe Finley and the U.S. Consulate had arranged for everything to be handled from the Galvins' penthouse suite at the Ritz-Carlton Istanbul.

Steven took an inventory of what was in Nathan's room before they left, and Kei took one of her son's sweaters with her.

For the first time, Steven's fears matched his wife's. There was no logical explanation for Nathan going missing for as many days as he had and leaving all his personal belongings in the hotel room.

It wasn't until they had settled into their hotel that Steven Galvin was told by Tansu that Finley had stopped her from contacting the newspapers. He was angry enough to throw the young man from one of the windows, but—for Kei's sake—he waited until he and the FSO were alone in the suite on the Club Level that he planned to use as base of operations.

Finley began explaining before Steven even had a chance to start laying into him.

"Sir, you have every reason to be angry, but my orders came out of Ankara. The ambassador himself called me. He said to tell you that people who can shed light on the situation are on their way. My instructions were to stop any public reference to the situation until the information officers get here and can meet with you in person."

"Look, I don't give a damn what your orders were," Galvin snapped. "This is not matter of national security. I don't take orders from the U.S. Government. I am looking for my son, and I plan to do everything in my power to find him. So you can get right back on the phone and call the ambassador. You can tell him I am sending you back to Ankara, too, if you plan to interfere rather than help."

"Sir, we have intricate relationships with law enforcement in this region. The ambassador wants you to be assured that we can operate far more efficiently in the face of a delicate situation."

"Don't even try to bullshit me, young man. Yesterday, when I was on the other side of the world, you people were giving me a song and dance about Nathan not registering with the consulate, and about the fact there was not a great deal that you could do," he told him. "I made one phone call, and suddenly you're meeting me at the airport. I tell you that we're going to go public, immediately, and I don't give a damn that the ambassador is sending in the heavy artillery. I don't trust you. I don't trust the consulate. Time is of the essence here. And I plan to do everything in my power to locate my son. So just get out of my way."

Finley's cell phone rang. At the same time, there was a knock at the door and Steven opened it. Tansu was standing in the hallway with two men.

"Mr. Galvin, these gentlemen say they are from the consulate."

Steven cast a dark glance back at Finley. "Thank you, Tansu." He looked at the two men. "Come in."

"Mr. Galvin?" the older of the two men spoke. Badges appeared and introductions were made. The older man was named Siegel, the other Cooper.

Seeing Finley, Siegel motioned for the FSO to wait outside, and the young man quietly slipped out of the room.

"You're the information officers from Ankara," Steven said, confirming what he'd seen on the identification badges.

"Yes and no, sir," Siegel replied.

"Which is it?"

"That is only part of our function here."

"Look, Mr. Siegel," Steven said curtly, "I didn't bring my decoder ring, so why don't you just talk straight to me."

He walked toward the window, then turned back to face them. The two men hadn't moved.

"What's going on, Mr. Siegel? Why are you here?"

The men exchanged a look first. Cooper was the one who spoke this time. "We were sent here, sir, to suggest that you let the U.S. government handle the situation with your son."

"This is the second time in five minutes my son's disappearance has been referred to as a 'situation.' Why?" he snapped, his temper rising. "What do you know? Where is Nathan? If you know something, why can't you people just come out and say it?"

"I'm afraid we have strict guideli—"

"This is bullshit," Galvin interrupted. He'd worked enough years in business to recognize when someone was trying to pull the wool over his eyes. "Do you know where Nathan is? Is he hurt? Is he…is he dead?"

Siegel and Cooper exchanged looks again.

"Mr. Galvin, I can tell you that your son is alive and safe," Siegel told him. "For the moment."

A flicker of hope lit in his chest. "And how do you know that?"

"Because we know."

"That's not enough. Explain," Steven barked.

"What I am about to tell you is classified information. You cannot divulge this information to anyone outside of this room, sir."

"What have you got to tell me?"

"Your son is on assignment."

"Assignment for whom?" Galvin was past controlling his temper. He knew he was snapping and he didn't care. "Nathan doesn't work. He's taking some time off after graduating from college. He's a tourist, for God's sake."

"He's working for the U.S. government, sir."

"That's ridiculous." Steven looked at him sharply. "Doing what?"

"Intelligence," Cooper said in a low voice.

Steven stared at them. "Are you telling me that my son is a spy?"

Siegel nodded. "Because of your status with certain members of our government, I have been given special permission to give you information that is closely guarded…information your son was not at liberty to divulge. Sir, your son is an operative, working with the Central Intelligence Agency. Part of this past year, he trained with us. After finishing his basic training, Nathan was promoted to field operative just three months ago. Turkey is his first overseas assignment."

25

TERROR

Ghana, Africa

Finn loved Irish rugby. He went to the games, checked the scores when he was away. He knew the players. He followed the training news of who was hurt and who was hot. He knew Niall O'Connor had picked up a knock to his left hip in training last week. He'd learned Ferris had been recalled to the squad. Isaac Boss was nursing a calf strain, but that wouldn't stop the captain.

Finn could make predictions with the best as to who was being drafted and who would be ditched. He'd been at the Lansdowne Street Stadium in Dublin on that chilly January night in '99 to watch his Ulster lads whip the Frenchies for the Heineken Cup, and he knew everyone who sat around him for home games at Raven-hill. In so many words, rugger was his sport.

He couldn't say the same thing about football. David Beckham was a silly pop star, so far as Finn was concerned. He never followed the game. Never cared a straw about it. That was why it was easy to get this job done. He was glad Issa Bongben wasn't a rugby player. He was just a bloody football player.

The Africa Cup of Nations was in progress, and the competition provided the perfect screen. He had the name, picture, date, time and place. As much as he made it his business not to learn anything more about his target, it was impossible to miss it in the headlines of every paper. Issa Bongben was the goalie for Cameroon National Football Team, and they were playing Egypt in the finals tomorrow. Bongben had long been suspected of being under the influence of gamblers, but that made no difference to Finn. He was just a bloody job.

The street below him was crawling with people. Finn saw his target leave the hotel restaurant, surrounded by his entourage of bodyguards, handlers and women. As the footballer stepped onto the crowded sidewalk, everyone else disappeared from Finn's focus. He and his mark were the only two people existing in the world at this moment. He stared at the face. He had the right mark.

He fired. The target went down.

Only Finn was left in this world now, and the Cameroon national football team would need a new goalie for Saturday's finals. Finn eased the window shut as the noise of the crowd going wild erupted outside.

"Ninety-eight, Kelly darling," he whispered. "Two to go."

26

LOSS

Common sense told Alanna to end it completely. She loved Ray, but there were too many secrets…too many unanswered questions. Since he'd come back into her life, she found herself wondering whether either of them had truly known the other before. She needed answers. She'd never been the kind of person who let others make decisions for her. She was a leader, not a follower. She wouldn't be led on blindly to wherever. Not by Ray or anyone else.

Emotions tore at her heart, but her head was telling Alanna that the relationship she had with Ray was different now. The blush was off the rose. Too many times she found herself being critical of him. She wondered why he hadn't tried to fight and keep her with him the first time around. She questioned the depth of his love.

She questioned the depth of hers.

Alanna was glad that he wasn't staying with her. She had time to think. Stepping back, she could see the situation with a clearer head. She knew she had to end their relationship. No more secret meetings, no more phone calls, no more uncertainty.

She'd told Ray exactly that when he'd called the day after she sent him the text message. Still, she'd let him talk her into one last meeting. The absolute last time he would bother her, he'd promised.

Ray had asked her to drive up to the Sonoma Valley wine country. For all the years she'd lived in the San Francisco area, she'd never once played tourist and driven up there. That would have been considered a leisure activity. She'd never made time for leisure activities.

She knew about the area, of course, from reading the Sunday paper and hearing about it from others. The Napa Valley wine country had the large wineries and attracted the tourists. Napa became famous in the 1970s when, during a blind taste competition held by the French, a couple of Napa Valley wineries won medals over their French rivals. This event brought with it a great deal of publicity for Napa Valley and then the development of a burgeoning tourist industry. In the wake of that, Sonoma Valley was ignored.

Actually, Alanna thought as she drove, being ignored was exactly what she could use right now. She really just wanted to be left alone. She'd grieved the loss of Ray for so many months. This time, she told herself, it would be easier to let him go because she knew he was alive. She could make it now. She could get through it.

The fifty-five-mile drive to Santa Rosa was a pleasant one on a Sunday morning. She was supposed to meet Ray at the Fountaingrove Inn. She had no trouble finding it. Pulling up to the front door, she told the attendant that she was having brunch in the Equus Restaurant with a friend.

Ray always matched Alanna's sense of punctuality, so she wasn't surprised at all when he came out and greeted her only seconds after she'd arrived. It was one minute to eleven.

He was wearing a wide-brimmed Stetson and sunglasses and, as soon as the attendant drove her car away, he leaned over and kissed her.

She wished he hadn't done that. She didn't want to be tempted. She'd made her decision.

He took her by the hand. "Let's go for a walk."

Alanna very much preferred to say what she had to say in private. She'd made up her mind what had to be, but the pain of doing it, of saying goodbye, was still raw. To have the discussion they needed to have in public only added to her anxiety.

The hotel and conference center had been built on what was once a historic ranch, though only vestiges of the old property remained. The buildings swept out in a low profile, and there was an unobstructed view of a pretty, round barn above. She realized that was where they were heading. The redwood, oak and stone had been carefully blended in the landscaping plans to provide a mix of old and new.

Ray didn't say anything as they walked past two groups of guests strolling back down toward the inn. Alanna looked around, trying to focus on anything and everything but the man walking beside her. She pulled her hand out of his and he let her.

"You changed your mind," he told her when they

were out of earshot of others. There was no accusation in his tone, only hurt. "I don't know why."

"I can't do it," she said passionately. "I can't walk away from my responsibilities…from my grandmother and my work. They matter too much to me."

"But you still love me?" he asked.

"I do…I do, Ray." She looked into his face. "But I know who I am. And I am certain that as happy as I would be with you for the short term, I would suffer in the long term because of my guilt. I would make you suffer. I believe in responsibilities, Ray. And there are just too many things…too many people…who depend on me. It doesn't matter how badly I want happiness, how deeply I love you. I can't choose that life over these other things."

He turned his face and stared straight ahead as they walked.

"You told me that you were a mess when I was gone."

"I was. God knows, I was. But I've thought hard about it. I'll be better this time. I'll know that you're alive and living somewhere…safe."

He reached for her hand again. She let him. "I couldn't stay away before. Do you remember that first day that you saw me in the parking lot?"

She nodded. "I thought I'd lost my mind. You were supposedly dead and here you were walking to the bus stop."

"That was the morning I got back to the San Francisco area. I had to see you. So I just got on one of the shuttles and was dropped off inside the gate. My life was in danger but I was only thinking of seeing you," he told her. "I was lucky that morning that I didn't run into anyone who might recognize me. And the driver didn't pay much attention to my old ID. It wasn't until I was so close to finding you that I realized what I was doing. I had to think this through. I had to do it right this time."

She stared at her feet taking the steps. It hurt to hear his confessions.

"I know I'll do the same thing again if I have to. I can't live without you, Alanna."

"I wish you wouldn't say that, Ray. You had a life before me. You'll have one after, too. You and I are both survivors. We're strong people. You, maybe, even more so than I. But I'm asking you to go. I'm begging you to set me free."

He stopped. She saw him study her small hand nestled in his large one. He removed his sunglasses and looked into her eyes. "There might be another option."

"What do you mean?"

"I told you I was meeting with some people. They have some ideas…that they want to run by us."

Alanna could tell he was nervous. She took his hand in both of hers.

"Run by *you,* you mean," she said. "Whatever decision you make should be right for you. I'm not going to be part of this decision."

He shook his head. "No, this is different. I think you might want to hear what they're saying…that is, if you still love me."

"Ray, don't make this harder for me than it is. I can't go away. I won't," she repeated.

"I think, with what they may be offering, you don't have to. And I won't have to, either."

She looked up at him, confused.

"I want them to explain it to you. To me again, too. I know it sounds too good to be true. But they're saying they can resolve the source of the problem that made me need to disappear. And I think they may really have the power and the resources to do it. That's why you have to be there with me, to hear their offer. Please, Alanna."

"Who are these people?"

"The people I've spoken to only refer to themselves as consultants."

"What kind of consultants?" she asked.

"Technical consultants," he said.

Alanna didn't think there was a more general statement than this. She resented that she had to spell out everything. "Who do they work for?" she asked.

"You can ask them yourself."

"Ray." Her tone was sharp enough to make him focus on her words. "My grandmother has a saying…sometimes we jump over a puddle and fall in the well. Is this what you're doing?"

He didn't answer for a moment.

"Ray, it sounds like they're offering to do something that law enforcement agencies failed to do. This says something about their resources—the way they do business. As far as you know, they could be part of organized crime."

"You don't know that. I won't know it, either, until we speak to them." He took hold of her arms and looked deep into her eyes. "Please, Alanna. They're here at the restaurant. We can talk to them now, hear what they offer…and what they're asking."

They were here. Alanna now understood why Ray wanted her to drive out here. She was annoyed that he hadn't told her this before. "Ray, I think you should go and talk to them yourself."

"No, Alanna. They won't do anything for me. They won't help me unless…unless you are involved, too."

"Why me?"

"Please, just come and ask yourself." He motioned over his shoulder toward the building they'd left behind. "This is a public restaurant serving brunch. They can't hurt us. I know they only want to help us. Let's just go and talk to them."

Alanna didn't want to go. She had decided on the course ahead. She knew how she was going to live through losing Ray again. His actions only made her realize how much easier that would be this time around. But he sounded almost…well, desperate. She reasoned that she had to give him this chance to make his life work.

"If you feel uncomfortable or don't like them, Alanna, we'll just get up and leave. Okay?"

The sky above them was pale blue. They passed through gardens she hadn't even seen as they'd walked out in the direction of the round barn. Nothing was growing yet. It would be another month before the buds of spring began to color the hillside.

Alanna didn't know who these people were or what they wanted. She didn't believe Ray was telling her everything he knew. She was ill-equipped to walk into that restaurant. Still, she did it, thinking of it as doing one final thing for the only man she'd ever loved.

27

FEAR

Istanbul, Turkey

"How do we know what they're telling us is the truth?" Kei asked.

Waiting for Amber Hersey to come back to the phone, Steven put his hand over the mouthpiece. "Why would they lie?"

The agents were cooling their heels in the room two floors below them while Steven and Kei discussed this development in their suite. Steven had told the two operatives that he wanted to talk to his wife before hearing any of their suggestions. He also wanted to call the one friend back in the U.S. who might be able to get him some answers. Because of the time difference, Steven figured his only chance to get the senator was to call him at home.

Paul wasn't home, but his daughter, Amber, was trying to find her father and get Steven a forwarding number. Amber was the same age as Nathan and the only child, with a bit of a history of wildness. She'd been very close to Nathan when the two of them were growing up. College and friends had separated their paths. But anytime they got together or whenever Steven and Kei saw Amber, it was like seeing their own child.

"Can they send a message to Nathan and have him call us?"

"No, they say he is undercover, and it would be dangerous for anyone to contact him."

Kei seemed to have much more energy again. She was pacing the room, the entire time holding Nathan's sweater. "Did you know about this?"

"Of course not, love."

"Did you know he was looking for a job with them?" she asked.

He shook his head. "Like you, I believed him when he said he wanted to take some time off and travel. I mean why…why the CIA? Why do something so dangerous?"

"He must get that from your side of the family," she told him. "I'm nothing more than a couch potato."

"Come over here, potato." He held out his hand. Kei sat next to him. She shivered.

"Cold?"

"I keep having chills run through me. I can't believe this. He's fine. I have to make myself believe it. Nathan is fine."

"Believe it," Steven told her.

"Why didn't he tell us?" she asked.

"He can't. He isn't supposed to. If I hadn't threatened to put Nathan's picture in every newspaper in Istanbul, we probably still wouldn't know."

She rubbed her cheek against the sweater. "When is his assignment finished?" Kei asked.

"They couldn't give me an answer. We can ask them again."

"Please ask them," she encouraged. "By the way, I'll kill him when we see him."

"You may. You're his mother," Galvin said. He knew how she felt. Steven himself had already learned a lesson from all this. He needed to do a better job of communicating with their son when he returned. Just because Nathan was twenty-three and on his own, that didn't mean there weren't ties that still connected them.

Amber came back on the phone. "I just spoke to my dad on his cell phone. He'll call you back in a few minutes. He said he has to get to a secure telephone."

"Thanks, sweetheart," he told her.

"By the way, how's Nathan doing?" she asked. "Are you having a good visit?"

When Amber had picked up the phone, Steven had fabricated a lie regarding why he and Kei had been in Istanbul. It was obvious that Paul hadn't mentioned anything to his daughter about their earlier telephone conversation. They all knew what good friends Amber and Nathan were. There was no reason to worry the young woman.

"He's fine...doing great." Steven hoped it wasn't a lie.

"Tell him he was supposed to call me," she said in a mock-complaining tone. "I'm still hoping to make a trip over while he's there."

"I'll tell him," Steven promised.

"Say hi to Kei. I miss her."

Steven thanked the young woman and hung up. He relayed the gist of the conversation with Amber to his wife.

"You think Paul can help us?" Kei asked.

"As Co-Chair of the Senate Intelligence Committee, he has his connections. I'm sure he can at least verify that these two men are who they say they are. Also, he might be able to confirm if Nathan is really employed by the CIA."

Kei hugged the sweater tight to her chest. "I want to be on the phone, too, when he calls back."

"Absolutely." The two families had known each other for nearly twenty years. Paul and his wife had divorced seven or eight years ago, but everyone stayed in contact.

They didn't have to wait long. The senator called them back in under five minutes. Kei picked up the second phone in the room. "Hello, Paul," she said.

"Hello, Kei. I'm glad I have both of you on the line with me."

Steven took a couple of minutes and told his friend about the CIA operatives from Ankara and what they'd told him.

"I know all of this already," Paul told them. "After your phone call yesterday, I did some digging here. My committee works hand in hand with the directors over in Langley. It was not difficult to find out what's going on with Nathan."

Galvin felt relieved. It was so much easier to imagine Nathan in this job, now that he knew his friend was involved.

"Paul, why would he do this?" Kei asked. "Why would he get involved in something so dangerous?"

"I don't know, Kei," the senator replied. "Duty, perhaps. Or adventure, I suppose. Those are questions that you can ask him when you see him. I did find out that he applied before he even finished college. After the standard training program, they had him taking a number of specialized classes. He's a career operative now."

"Where is he, Paul?" Steven asked. "What is he doing?"

"I can only tell you that he's in Turkey and that he's on assignment. That's all my questions would get me. But I was assured that he's fine. I was also told that it's not a good idea for you and Kei to be over there right now. I don't think there is any way you'd want to jeopardize his cover any more than you have already. It could put him in danger, you know."

Steven looked across the room at his wife, wondering if she was satisfied with what she was hearing.

"If he was going to be gone for a while, why didn't he take his personal belongings?" Kei asked.

"Because we've given him everything he needs," Paul told them. "We don't want any proof out there that he's someone other than who he says he is."

Steven took a list out of his pocket that he'd made when they were in Nathan's bedroom.

"And who exactly does he say he is?" Kei asked.

"I can't answer that. Tell the truth, I don't know. But you have to understand that these operations require… well, discretion."

"Nathan does have a couple of personal items with him," Steven told the senator on the phone. "When we checked out what was left in his room, I found his watch and cell phone missing."

There was a pause on the line. "The watch shouldn't be a big deal," Paul commented. "I don't like the idea of him taking his cell phone."

"He used it to call us every few days or so," Kei admitted. "It was when we couldn't contact him on that phone that we became concerned."

"I was told that he had been instructed not to have any personal belongings in his possession," Paul told them. "It could be that he lost the phone, or ditched it. Really, there's nothing to be concerned about regarding those two things. Listen to me, you two, as a friend speaking. My suggestion is for you both to go back to Connecticut and wait where he knows how to get in touch with you."

Steven and Kei's gaze met across the room. He gave a small nod to his wife. She frowned but didn't fight him.

"It's very possible that Nathan might be able to break away and try to call you, just to let you know he's okay."

Steven didn't want to remind his friend that Nathan would know to call them on their cell phones if they weren't home. The phone call aside, though, he did think that it would be better for his wife to be back home.

"I want to hear his voice," Kei whispered into the phone.

"Don't worry, Kei. You will," Paul assured her. "And in the meantime, I'll keep an eye on his situation over there. You two just get back home."

28

STIGMA

Jay Alexei pressed his fingers to the cold glass. He wanted to reach inside, pick up his son. The baby was crying.

Couldn't the two nurses working inside the fishbowl see he was upset? From ten feet away, he could see the baby's tonsils. He was getting purple in the face. The blue cap on his head looked ridiculous. He wanted to hold him again, run his fingers through the fuzz of dark hair, touch his little nose.

Jay tapped on the window. Neither nurse paid any attention to him. He tapped again, harder. One of them turned and glanced at him. He motioned to his baby. The nurse smiled at him and went back to talking.

"Looks like he's got a good set of lungs on him," some guy beside him said. "The next Pavarotti, maybe?"

Jay didn't have to look to recognize the man. The accent gave it away. It was Hank Diarte. Surprise, and then a wild sense of relief rushed through him. He tried to keep it cool. Not ask him what he was doing here.

"He's trying out his vocal range, but the nurses

seem to have already gotten used to him. They don't even hear him."

"How much did he weigh?" Diarte asked.

"Six pounds, four ounces. Twenty inches long. I think he's twenty-one inches long, but the nurse in the delivery room couldn't hold his feet long enough to get an accurate measure." Jay knew he sounded like a proud father. He loved the feeling.

"And how's your wife doing?" Diarte asked.

"She's amazing," Jay said, smiling. He'd found himself smiling a lot over the past twelve hours. What he'd witnessed in that delivery room, what Padma had gone through, was truly a miracle. He couldn't stop thinking about it. It had been a natural birth. Four hours total. The nurses kept saying that was really good for a first-time delivery. Jay didn't think he would have survived it if it had been any longer. "She's exhausted, but amazing."

"It is an amazing thing. No doubt about it."

He nodded. "So how you are doing, Mr. Diarte? I didn't expect to see you here." Jay couldn't wait any longer. He had to ask.

"Well, we like to keep track of our prospects," he said. "Have you chosen a name for him yet?"

Jay shook his head. "We haven't even talked about it. The baby was early. They're sending us home this afternoon, though. So I guess we'll have to come up with a name this morning."

Jay remembered that they still didn't have a crib. The only baby clothes they'd bought were a couple of one-piece sets they'd found on clearance racks a couple of months ago. Padma had bought a few packages of diapers at the store where she worked. There was so much that they were missing. One hand sank into his pocket. He had forty-six dollars in cash left until his next payday, which was three days away. He had to get a taxi to take them back home. He remembered that the nurse had mentioned something about baby car seats. They had to have one. But he didn't even have a car.

He turned to Diarte. "Are you still doing the interviews?"

"No, we're finished."

"And?" Jay was too afraid to hope.

"That's why I'm here."

"Yes…you're here," Jay repeated, feeling almost giddy.

He watched Diarte bend down and reach into a briefcase on the floor between them. When the headhunter straightened up, he had a large manila envelope in his hand. He handed it to Jay.

"All the details regarding how to get there and when, your tickets, and the contacts that you'll need to have are in here. Oh, yes…" He reached into the briefcase again and took out a much smaller envelope. "This is a congratulations gift from your new employer to you and your wife and…the baby to be named later."

Jay opened the second envelope. Inside, there was a congratulations card…and an American Express gift card for a thousand dollars. "I…I…this is…this is very generous."

Diarte handed him a business card. "Call this car service when you and your wife are ready to go home.

The service has been paid for. The driver will come and pick you up."

This was already much more than he'd expected. Jay was feeling a little light-headed.

"Please…please thank Mr. Lyons for me," he said, overwhelmed. No one had ever treated Jay with this kind of generosity. "Please tell him that he won't regret his decision. I'll give him everything I have."

Diarte leaned down and closed the top of the brief-case and picked it up.

"There's one more thing that your new employer wanted me to suggest…but this is only a suggestion, and you don't have to feel obligated to accept it."

Jay didn't think any suggestion or offer could top what he'd already been given.

"He wants you to know that you're more than welcome to bring Mrs. Alexei and your son with you to the islands for the period of time that you need to be there. It might be a very good thing for all of you. But again, that's only a suggestion."

Jay smiled and looked at the baby, now sound asleep in the nursery. Mr. Lyons wouldn't have to ask him twice.

29

FEAR

Istanbul, Turkey

Nathan had lost count of the days.

There were no windows, no clocks. The single light-bulb dangling from the ceiling was on all the time. Nathan had no clue at any time if it was day or night.

He didn't know what his captors wanted…or more importantly, what they were waiting for.

Perhaps two or three days after talking to the man in the black shirt, he'd been awakened, handcuffed, gagged, blindfolded and half dragged outside. He was quickly shoved into the back of a truck or a van. He knew it must have been nighttime when he was moved; there was no sense of light through the blindfold when he stumbled from the building to the vehicle. And during the ride to the new location, there also seemed to be very little traffic.

Where they took him, Nathan had no idea. He didn't know if he still was in Istanbul or if he'd been taken out of the city. His new prison seemed like an actual jail cell, of sorts, though it had the feel of something held over from the Middle Ages. There was no lightbulb dangling from the ceiling in this tiny room; the only light filtered in from around the single metal door. In the corner of the room, there was a hole about three feet deep that had already seen service as a latrine. A rusted iron pipe stuck out of one stone wall, and someone had placed a rusted metal bucket beneath. A constant drip from the pipe was Nathan's only source of water. At some point, happily, they'd decided against starving him to death. A dish of unrecognizable food was brought in once a day.

Nathan always knew when one of them was coming into the cell. The locks on the metal door had to be rusty. There was always a lot of noise before anyone came in.

Three different men seemed to have been tasked with guarding him. One was the person who'd set up the trap at Kapali Carsi. Nathan had no difficulty remembering his scarred face. The men rotated the duty, so that two were always there when it came time to give him dinner. It bothered him that none of them tried to hide their faces, though it was almost impossible to see them anyway. They all spoke some English, though one spoke better than the other two. When they delivered the food, one of them always came in holding a flashlight and a metal dish, while the other waited in the hallway, right outside the door. The one in the hall always carried an AK-47.

With the exception of the living conditions and the fact that they kept him half-starved, Nathan hadn't been badly treated. There'd been no beatings since he'd been moved. They said a few words to him here and there, but the questioning had stopped. A couple of times, in the early days, Nathan considered fighting his way out of here. But there was no opportunity. The armed man in the hallway was a definite deterrent.

Still, try as he might, Nathan couldn't come up with any reasonable explanation why these people had taken him…or what they wanted. He kept wondering if they'd made a mistake of some sort. It just didn't make sense.

Lying in the near darkness, Nathan thought about his parents a lot. He remembered the opportunities he'd had—the paths he could have taken. So many choices, and he'd taken none that they'd recommended. Adamant about finding his own way, he'd made the decision to accept this job almost on impulse. He wanted to be a success, though not so much financially. His father had made enough for the family to be set for ten generations to come. Nathan wanted to find a life and a career that was his and be good at it.

He couldn't remember now why on earth this had been the path he'd decided to take.

When he wasn't exercising, trying to keep his muscles from atrophying, he lay on an old mattress in the corner. He'd put it in the farthest corner from the reeking hole in the floor. But now, he heard one of them coming in. He stood on his feet. He always did. It didn't matter which one of them came in, they always told him "Sit!" as soon as they saw him.

The door creaked opened. The same one who'd brought him a dish of food last time came in, carrying a lit floor lamp that was attached to an extension cord that ran out into the hall. Another of his guards stood outside, watching intently.

Nathan was surprised that the guard did not tell him to sit. He also carried no food. In his other hand, he held a digital camera.

"Wall," the man told him, motioning to the wall. "There…stand."

They were going to take his picture. Nathan actually felt a jolt of happiness at this little change in routine. Perhaps this meant that they were going to tell someone out there that they had him. He remembered the images of kidnapped westerners that showed up on Al Jazeera broadcasts. Some died in the hands of their captors, but many of them would live. He hoped to be one of the latter.

"Wall," his captor repeated.

"Don't you want to be in the picture with me?" he asked, feeling his spirit lift for the first time.

"Stand…wall," he repeated.

The armed guard from the hall stepped into the room. He stared at Nathan menacingly, his finger on the trigger of the AK-47 in his hands.

"You've kept me alive this long. You know, you should get some reward for that," Nathan told them.

He'd been thinking about this for a while. He stepped toward the wall.

"If you're going to send my picture to the U.S. government, then send a copy of my photograph to my parents. They'll pay you a lot of money…many U.S. dollars…to know I am okay."

The camera flashed.

The guard looked at the image. "Look…" he said,

pointed toward the door. Nathan turned his profile to the guard. The camera flashed again.

"A million dollars. Even more," Nathan said hurriedly as they started to leave the room. "They'll pay you anything you ask. I am their only child. Google my father. Steven Galvin. You'll see. He's worth a billion dollars, and I am his only child. Contact him. He'll pay you."

The door closed with a loud bang, and the only answer to Nathan's suggestion was the sound of locks being snapped shut.

30

LOSS

Whatever Alanna's imagination had conjured up regarding what branch of organized crime these "consultants" were part of, the mental image didn't match their looks and manners. Both men, clearly close to retirement age, were definitely desk types, and both were extremely polite and professional.

They introduced themselves, with Mr. Diarte deferring to his employer Mr. Lyons. Rather than sitting in the Equus Restaurant, which appeared to be crowded, they were directed to the Pegasus Lounge, where they could have the place practically to themselves.

An elegant baby grand piano sat silent in one corner, and Alanna glanced at the large antique sepia-colored photograph of the round barn from the days when the area was ranch land. Moving to the far end of the wood-paneled room, Diarte led them to a table in a private corner, a good place for them to talk.

Alanna had been in business long enough to recognize immediately that both men were eager to please.

The realization came as a surprise, considering that Ray was the one who needed their assistance.

"What is it that you two gentlemen do?" She got to the point as soon as they were left by the hostess, who'd offered to bring them mimosas or Bloody Marys, if they preferred. Only Ray took the young woman up on her offer.

"Hank Diarte works for me, at present," Lyons explained. "I'm a principal in a consulting company. We manage projects."

"What kinds of projects?" she asked.

"Mostly projects of a technical nature."

Alanna waited for the man to say more but he said nothing. "That's pretty wide open, Mr. Lyons," she persisted. "Can't you be more specific?"

"I'm afraid not. At least, not until we have some indication from you that you are willing to consider working with us."

"Me?" She glanced at Ray in surprise. His gaze seemed to be everywhere but on her. Her earlier suspicion that there was a lot more that he hadn't told her about this meeting was coming true. "I'm afraid you're mistaken. I'm not looking for a position."

"Oh, we know that, Dr. Mendes," Lyons replied quietly.

"Then I don't understand."

"Let me explain. The projects we manage are generally of short duration—anywhere from a couple of days to a month, rarely ever more. The way we run them is to assemble the absolute top experts in the field for the required tasks, and just for that short length of time. Now, most of the people who work with us, people like yourself, have no interest in permanently leaving their present situation. That works out just fine. Many use personal time or vacation time. The compensation alone makes it more than worthwhile."

Alanna leaned back in the chair and studied the three men who were sitting at the same table with her. Ray could as well have been a stranger.

"I'm getting more confused by the second."

She turned to Ray. His gaze was now fixed on a wine list.

"Ray, how did you find these people?" she asked him directly.

"They found me."

She turned back to Lyons. Diarte was scribbling notes on a small notepad. "And how did you do that, considering the fact that he was in a witness protection program?"

"We have connections in many areas, including the government," Lyons said. "And our connections are not necessarily illegal. A lot of the information that we receive, as well as the projects that we manage, come to us from some of the most respectable people and organizations in America."

"Don't insult my intelligence, Mr. Lyons," Alanna told him shortly. "This is just so much double-talk. Why would you think I would take what you say at face value? I don't know you. And, to tell you honestly, this all sounds very suspicious to me. I've been asking direct questions. I expect straightforward answers."

Ray opened his mouth to say something, but Alanna placed a hand on his knee. He stopped.

"Mr. Lyons. We really don't have all day," she continued. "So unless you are willing to get to the point of who you really are and what you can do for my fiancé—as well as, what, exactly, you want in return—then this meeting is over."

Diarte was watching his superior, but Lyons never took his eyes off of Alanna's face. Finally, he nodded and opened a briefcase that he'd placed on the floor when they sat down. He took out a folder.

"I respect your directness, Dr. Mendes," he said politely. "I should have expected nothing less, having—as I do—a pretty thorough knowledge of how you conduct your own projects. I apologize for not getting to the point sooner."

As Lyons continued, he laid his hand flat on the folder as if he were swearing on a Bible.

"We are exactly what we said we are." He opened the cover of the folder, took out a sheet of paper and slid it in front of her. "This list contains the names and phone numbers of some of our references. The individuals listed here are experts who have worked with us on projects in the past."

She scanned the list of ten names, with positions, names of companies, and phone numbers. She was surprised to see that she knew a couple of the people through her work.

"As far as what we can do for Mr. Savoy, we know all the specifics of the investigation he was involved with," Lyons explained. "As you are probably aware, he was the only witness willing to cooperate with the prosecution of the case, which of course exposed your fiancé to the very real threat of retribution and certain death."

Alanna didn't know any of these details, but she didn't think this was the right time to admit it.

"Fortunately, we have access to three other witnesses in the same case who never stepped forward. With proper financial compensation, they have all now agreed to testify. In fact, two of those witnesses have agreed to provide evidence in support of far more serious charges."

Ray's attention was, for the first time, totally focused on Lyons.

"I don't want to bore you with every little detail, but once before we were able to resolve a similar situation." He slid another piece of paper in front of her. "You may be familiar with that name. It is all a matter of public record now, and the witness involved is living without fear. In this case—similar to the situation with your fiancé—the witness came out of the federal protection program." Lyons paused to let his words sink in. "It's fairly easy to eliminate one witness, but three or four…"

"And you were the one who made the arrangements in this other case?" she asked.

He gave a small nod. "You won't find our names in the public records, but my company was instrumental in making it happen. That phone number will allow you to talk to the gentleman directly."

Alanna gazed at the paper. She remembered the case. It was a high profile court case involving two major corporations.

"Who are the other witnesses?" Ray asked.

Lyons gave a small laugh and shook his head. "I'm sorry, but I can't tell you that. Let's just say that we are not prepared to go forward until Dr. Mendes decides her course of action."

There was so much that Alanna didn't know about the situation that Ray had been involved with. She needed to speak to an attorney before she could know for sure whether or not what these people were saying was the truth. Or even legal. She saw Ray looking at her hopefully. He was allowing himself to be convinced far too easily. Of course, he had a lot at stake.

But so did she.

"What is it that you want from me?" she finally asked Lyons.

"We'd like you and Mr. Savoy to join the rest of our team for two weeks—three at the most—at a resort on Grand Bahama Island."

Alanna stared at Lyons incredulously. She motioned to him with her hand to say more. She knew her expression spoke of her impatience.

"The individual who hired us for this recruitment—"

"What individual?" she interrupted.

Despite her interruption, Lyons kept his composure. "Our task here is to recruit a highly qualified group of individuals with specific talents for a predetermined period for this project. All of you will join us in the islands at the same time."

"You're serving as headhunters?"

He nodded. "In this case, you're correct."

"You could have said that to begin with," she reminded him. "So this is not your project. You are simply interviewing people for whatever this project is?"

He nodded again.

"And the fact that I am a United States government employee makes no difference."

"You are not being recruited to work for any foreign government, Dr. Mendes, I promise you."

"But there are still confidentiality issues with my job that can't be compromised in any situation."

"We understand that."

"Okay, then, why me specifically?" she asked. "There are many others in my field with very similar qualifications. People who don't have the trouble my fiancé and I are dealing with. People who would be far less costly for you to employ."

"Dr. Mendes, I know that what I am about to say does not make our bargaining position any easier, but we believe you will be very happy with what we are prepared to offer…above and beyond what we will do for your fiancé which as you know is very substantial. The bottom line, Dr. Mendes, is that there is no one else who has what you have to offer. The individual who hired us to assemble this team specified that you must be part of it. There can be no substitution for you."

Alanna looked from Lyons and Diarte to Ray. She wanted to shake him at this moment. There were things that he knew but hadn't revealed to her. She was unprepared for this meeting.

She loved him…that was why she was here. But he wasn't reciprocating. She looked back at Lyons. "Well, that brings us back to who that individual is who wants to hire me, doesn't it?"

Lyons nodded. "Yes, I believe it does."

31

TERROR

Belfast, Ireland

Tea was for leisure time, coffee for work hours. It was nine-thirty at night, but Kelly knew Finn was working.

She poured her husband a mugful of ink-black coffee. No sugar, no milk. Strong enough to have a spoon stand in it straight.

At the top of the stairs, she heard the twins giggling. "You'd best be in bed," she warned from outside their door.

Immediate silence followed, but a few seconds later the door opened a crack.

"Da hasn't come in to tell us good-night yet," Conor whispered, peeking out.

"No, he hasn't," Liam repeated, edging in front of his brother into the doorway.

"You both get into your beds, and I'll go get him."

They stood where they were, looking up at her with their bright green eyes—testing to see if she meant it.

"Now." She took a step toward the door, drawing a screech from them as they ran to jump into their beds.

Kelly smiled and shook her head. Going by Mick's bedroom, she paused again. The door was closed. She could hear the sound of American rap music. She liked to think things were improving. Mick was coming home every night just as Finn had ordered him to do. As far as she knew, he was going to his classes every day at the university. She hadn't seen him stoned since that Sunday a couple of weeks ago. Still, she didn't like the fact that Finn and Mick didn't talk much. They behaved like two strangers. Polite, obligatory in responses to questions, but that was it. Kelly didn't like it at all. There was trouble brewing. She felt the crawl of it on her skin.

At the end of the hall, she tapped once on the door to Finn's office and walked in. Her husband was engrossed in a file spread on his desk. The safe to the side of the desk was open.

"I brewed you a new mug of black-mud pie," she told him.

"That's my sweet."

Kelly noticed that he pushed some photographs under the other pages as she approached. She knew everything about Finn—where he'd come from, all that he'd done and what he was doing now. She'd been working with him years ago when she'd been a student, falling totally in love with the IRA group leader. It had taken him a while to notice her, even longer to fall in love. But here they were, married and raising their own family. She couldn't wait until Finn gave up the job he was doing now. They didn't need it. With the money he'd

made and invested in Belfast property, they were all set
financially.

"Only two more," she told him as a reminder, putting
the mug on his desk.

"Yeah, about that," Finn said, reaching up and taking
her hand. "I have some good news and some bad news."

Kelly gave him a narrow glare. "I don't care for the
sound of that. You're not going back on your promise,
now?"

Finn shook his head, then nodded.

"Finn," she said through clenched teeth.

"I know…I know. I'm not doing it intentionally." He
tugged on her hand until she was standing next to his
chair. He wrapped an arm around her waist. "This is absolutely the final job. This job and I never will accept
another one. That's my promise."

"Ninety-nine. I'm happy with that. So what's the
problem?" she asked.

"Look at this."

She looked down at the number he'd underlined a
couple of times on the cover letter. Her head spun a
second. "That's…that's a lot of money, Finn."

"'Tis," he said. "But that's not for one, but three."

"Three?" she repeated.

"Still, it's double the normal rate per."

Kelly didn't say anything. She had to trust him to
make the decision here.

"It's all or nothing. I take on the three jobs or get none
of them." He reached for the mug of coffee and sat back
in his chair. "This would be a grand style to finish,
though, wouldn't you say?"

He looked up at her. "What do you think, darling?"

"I won't kick if this is the end. But it must mean, Finn, that you need to be finished after this. Forever."

"Finished I *will* be," he said with a smile. "This will be it."

Both of them looked up at the sound of the door creaking. The twins peeked in. "Da…"

"Didn't I tell you two to stay in bed and your da will come and hug you good-night?" Kelly headed for the door and so did Finn. The parents took the boys back to their bedroom.

A moment later, as Kelly and Finn disappeared into the boys' room, Mick emerged from his own bedroom and moved quickly toward Finn's office. Mick looked back down the hallway and slipped in.

He knew where Finn kept his money. The safe was open. He hurried to it and took out what he needed. Not too much. Finn wouldn't even notice it. He wasn't robbing his family. He just took enough to pay his man what he owed. The price of blow was on the rise lately, what with the crackdown on importers.

As he turned back toward the door, the folder on the desk caught his eye. He saw the number underlined on the paper. Quickly, he thumbed through it, saw the names. He stared for a moment at the pictures.

Sliding the pictures back beneath the rest of the papers, Mick went quickly out and back to his room.

Finn wouldn't even know that he was there.

32

FEAR

Washington, D.C.

Steven Galvin could see the surprise still on the face of the senator as he entered the politician's office.

"Come in, come in," he boomed, walking over to shake Galvin's hand warmly.

Paul Hersey was a large man, built like the ex–football player he was. He had a solid presence and square-jawed, all-American good looks. None of those qualities ever hurt him around election time.

"I didn't think I heard my secretary right when she told me you were here. In all the years I've known you, I think this is the first time I've seen you on Capitol Hill."

He was correct. Steven had always made it a point to keep his distance from Washington.

"Luckily, we in the industry always had Bill Gates to act as the lightning rod for us."

"True," Paul said. "For all his complaining, I don't

think he ever *really* minded speaking before one committee or another."

Steven nodded. Bill was an interesting guy, that way. As for himself, Steven just preferred to stay in the background. Run things in a way that didn't draw attention to himself. Part of that meant keeping clear of House and Senate subpoenas.

Not that he wasn't interested in politics. It just wasn't his forte. That was what lobbyists were for…along with his substantial financial contributions to one or the other's campaign funds. Paul Hersey, in addition to being a longtime friend, had been a primary recipient of Steven's generosity over the years.

The senator motioned for Steven to sit down, and he sat in the leather chair next to him.

"So, is Kei with you?" He didn't wait for an answer. "You know Amber has moved back in with me. Graduate-student housing or Dad's house. She took the latter. And I have to say, it's very nice having her around. We are getting so much closer now than we were when she was a teenager. A whole new relationship."

"I'm glad, Paul."

"I am, too. When June and I got divorced, I gave in too easily when I let Amber stay with her mother. Now I realize how much of my child's life I've missed. She's so mature. And wicked smart. Too much of an idealist, but living in Washington will fix that soon enough. All and all, she's a great kid. Beautiful, too. How many years has it been since you saw her?"

Steven searched his memory. "I don't know…maybe a couple of years. Nathan brought her to Connecticut for a weekend. I think it was the summer of their junior year in college. I did speak to her when we were in Istanbul and looking for you. She sounded happy."

"Yes…yes. You did talk to her," he said. "I can't wait for you to see her again. She told me she misses you and Kei. We have to get together for dinner while you're in town."

Steven wondered if he sounded like Paul. When Nathan was young, it was the wallet foldouts of a dozen pictures. Now it was their child's accomplishments.

"Kei isn't with me. I flew in just for the day. I need your help, Paul." He decided to get right to the point.

"Anything," the senator said sincerely. "You know me. I'll do anything I can for you."

"It's about Nathan," Steven said. "It's been two weeks now and the line we're getting about him being undercover, that he'll get back to us when he can, isn't cutting it anymore, especially for Kei. She's a mess. *I'm* a mess. We need something more substantial. Some news that says someone has seen him out there. That someone has been in contact with him. We're afraid that he's disappeared off your radar. Paul, you're a father. I know you understand this."

"I do understand."

The senator's face grew very grave. He paused, as he was trying to gather his thoughts, to find the right words. It was not a look Steven recollected ever seeing on Paul's face.

"Nathan's situation hasn't dropped off my radar, Steven. Not for a single day. I have been following it very closely. I have been staying in contact with the people at Langley. We're…we're in the process of getting his situation under control."

A one-ton weight dropped in Steven's stomach. For a few seconds he couldn't breathe. His heart was beating so fast that he thought it could burst out of his chest at any second.

"What's happened to him?" he finally forced out.

Paul leaned forward, his elbows on his knees, his face reflecting a great deal of stress. "Nathan was intercepted by someone before connecting at his rendezvous point. He has been kidnapped."

This was the knockout punch. He stared at Paul, trying to make sense of the words. "It can't be. When did this happen?"

"I'm sorry, Steven."

"Who kidnapped him? How do you know all this?"

"They sent us a photograph of him. It's definitely Nathan. It's obvious from the photo that he hasn't shaved for a few days, but otherwise he looks fine. He's definitely alive."

"When were you going to tell me this?" Steven asked angrily.

"Hopefully, never. I was planning on returning your son to you instead."

"He's my son. You should have told me." His voice shook.

"Steven, I couldn't. National security req—"

"You can't just hide something like this under a rug," Steven barked at his friend, interrupting whatever excuse the other man was going to use. "He's my child,

Paul. Flesh and blood. I have a right to know what's happening to him."

"Nathan works for the United States government. To be specific, he is an operative for the CIA. Because of the Kurdish problem, we're caught in the middle of a very sensitive situation with Turkey right now. We can't allow news of his abduction to come out."

Paul droned on. It was all gibberish as far as Steven was concerned. He pushed himself to his feet. For an instant, he didn't think his legs would support his weight. "Being in the public eye is the only chance he has of living."

"Not so," Paul disagreed. "You know that publicly we don't negotiate with terrorists. Right now, though, we *are* negotiating with them. That's the only reason the incident has been kept quiet. We have to keep it at this level or the whole thing will blow up in our faces. Of course, if they decide to go public via Al Jazeera, everything changes."

Frustrated, Steven ran a hand down his face, through his hair. He started pacing the office, and the senator was silent while he thought. He didn't know how he could tell any of this to Kei. They'd been down, then up, and now way, way down. He honestly didn't know how she'd take it.

"He's only been working for the CIA six months," Steven said finally. "Why would they kidnap a kid like him?"

"Some erroneous information led to this, I've been told. It apparently misled our people as well as the contacts. These people, whoever they are, have been operating over the past two weeks under the assumption that they'd abducted a different agent. One with a lot of experience."

"Exactly who are these people?" Steven asked. "Are they al Qaida?"

"It really doesn't matter," Paul said.

"It does to me," Steven snapped. "Who are they?"

The senator looked at his friend for a long moment and then shrugged. "They're what is left of a resistance group that operated in southern Iraq. That group was broken up…either killed, absorbed into other insurgent groups or run out of the country. My understanding is Langley believes that this kidnapping was intended as retribution for an incident that involved this other agent when he was working in the field in Iraq. Payback. A quick assassination. Luckily, the kidnappers had immediate doubts that Nathan was the person they were after. Since they sent us this photo, we're almost certain now that they know they've got the wrong man."

Steven let out a long, shaky breath. Assassination. His boy. God. This would destroy Kei. The information was destroying him.

"So now that they know…now that we've told them they have the wrong person…are they going to release Nathan?" he asked in a pleading tone.

"As I said, we're negotiating that right now."

"Who's negotiating?" Steven asked.

"Our people," Paul said calmly.

"Don't give me that bullshit…our people!" Steven shouted. His temper was now boiling over. "I want to know who is negotiating. I want to know what they're doing for Nathan right now. I want to know what these people will take in exchange for my son."

Before Paul even began to speak, the gravity of his look gave it away. "So far, they want what we can't give them."

"They want the other agent," Steven said it aloud. "And that's not going to happen. Someone with that kind of experience is not expendable, but my son is."

"No, we're not looking at it that way. We will get Nathan out," Paul told him. "There are other things that we can use to negotiate. Political-prisoner release, money. We will get Nathan out, Steven. I give you my word on it."

"How much money are you offering them?"

"We haven't come up with an amount yet."

"That's where I help, Paul," Steven told him. "Make the offer so large that they can't refuse it. Start at the top."

"We will, and I appreciate your offer—"

"This is not an offer. I'm telling you."

"Look…Steven…" Paul pounded one fist onto a meaty palm. "There is a standard procedure that needs to be followed here. Those who are negotiating for us are professionals who do this kind of thing every day. They know what they're doing. They also know that whatever amount they settle on this time will have to be duplicated the next time one of our agents falls into the hands of a terrorist group."

"I don't care about other agents. I don't give a damn about the future or about procedures or any of that. There's only one thing I care about right now, and that is getting Nathan back. Do you understand me, Paul?"

The senator let out a frustrated breath. He looked up

at Steven. "I'm on your side. I'm trying to help you. But this isn't the first time this has happened."

"If you don't help me, Paul, I'll get someone else who will," Steven said harshly. "I don't care about this professional mumbo jumbo. We're talking about the life of my only son. I have got to be involved, every step of the way, until he's back."

Paul stood up, ready to argue the government's position.

Steven held up his hand. "If this were you in my place, if someone kidnapped Amber, how far would you go to get her back? Be honest, Paul. How far would you go?"

There was no pause before the senator answered. "To the end of the world."

"That is how far I'm planning to go," Steven told him. "Now, are you going to help me or do I find someone else?"

The senator stared into his face for a long moment and then nodded.

"I'll do everything in my power to help you," Paul said. "But I'm going to need you to trust me."

33

DESPAIR

New York Presbyterian Hospital

David was allowed to visit Leah in the pediatric intensive care unit for only five minutes at a time.

He'd been told that she'd be here for a few days at the most. After that, she'd be moved to a wing where end-stage renal-disease children waited. David had already had a walking tour of the wing. Well lit, colorful and open by design, the cheery space had lots of distractions and play spaces to keep kids occupied. But nothing they did about the physical surroundings could hide the truth that, for many children in Leah's condition, this was nothing more than hospice care.

For too many, it was the end of the line.

The pediatric intensive care unit, curiously nicknamed "Pink U," was a different story, though. There was no fooling around with surface appearances here. This unit was all business.

David shook off the gloom-and-doom sensation and

walked into Pink U. Hospital beds surrounded by electronic equipment and monitors formed a circle around the center of the room, and every bed was filled with a child dealing with various life-threatening ailments. As he crossed to Leah's bed, he glanced around at them. At almost every bed, a parent or caregiver—looking as troubled and helpless as he was feeling—stood by their child. Looking at them, David felt almost a sense of kinship. They all were suffering, and he knew that every one of them would sacrifice his or her own life to give their child a chance at a fresh, healthy start.

Leah was drifting in and out of sleep when David reached her bedside. A partially closed curtain separated the eight-year-old from the little boy in the adjoining bed. He touched her hair. It was so soft. Wires and tubes ran to monitors and a dialysis machine. At the sight of the equipment hooked to his daughter, David tried to ignore that familiar knot in his throat, that same crushing sadness in his chest.

"Don't let the negative forces overpower the positive," he muttered to himself.

He forced himself to think of the door of opportunity that had just swung open for both of them. He took hold of her small hand. She opened her eyes.

"Daddy," she whispered, a weak smile breaking across her pale face. Her fingers grasped his. "You're back."

"I told you I wasn't going far."

"I know," she whispered.

"Hey, I hear they're moving you out of here in a couple of days," he told her.

"Can you take me home?"

He squeezed her fingers. "Not yet, honey, but pretty soon."

"Then, will you stay with me?" she asked. "I don't like all these strangers."

"They won't let me hang around too long here. None of the parents are allowed to stay long. But once they move you, I'll be right there beside you, love."

"I'm scared, Daddy," she whispered, clutching harder at his hand.

"I'm right here, sweetheart," David said, fighting to keep the tears from welling in his eyes. "Everything will be okay, honey. You'll see. Everything will be fine."

Diarte had come back today to talk over the start date for the project. The job was about to begin in a couple of weeks. When David asked him to be more specific about the project, Diarte had shown some fancy footwork. He clearly didn't want to talk about that with David yet. Somehow, the topic kept coming back to Leah and her care.

The only thing that was firm so far with regard to the project was that David had to be ready to go to an island in the Bahamas for a couple of weeks to a month.

David wasn't stupid. He knew it had to be something illegal. A project requiring him to work at an offshore site for a few weeks? A job that they were willing to compensate him for more than handsomely but wouldn't be specific about? And it wasn't just money they were offering. They had gone to enormous trouble and expense with regard to Leah.

David had spoken to the clinic administrators in Germany. All anticipated expenses for Leah's care had been prepaid, *including* the transportation costs from New York to Germany. And all the costs that David's insurance wasn't covering while Leah was here in New York.

He wasn't worth that much…at least not for a legitimate project. He just couldn't imagine what he'd be useful for in an illegal operation.

David had already spoken to his half sister who lived in Philadelphia. She was willing to come to New York and check on Leah daily at the hospital while he was away. But despite this arrangement, he didn't know how he could leave Leah. He didn't have any idea how he could explain it to her. He didn't really think either of them would be able to handle it. Not when his daughter's life was hanging by a very thin thread. The doctors would give no assurances about Leah's ability to stay alive for any length of time. No estimate whatsoever. Her condition was evaluated day to day.

David knew his daughter well enough to know that her spirit would be a factor in how her body reacted. Nicole's death had caused a major reduction in Leah's kidney function. David didn't want to think how she would react if she knew he was deserting her, for weeks and possibly up to a month.

Efficient to the second, one of the ICU nurses came around to kick the visitors out. David was relieved that Leah had fallen back to sleep. In the hallway, an idea came to him.

After tracking down Leah's pediatrician and asking a few questions, David dialed the number Diarte had given him.

"Mr. Diarte, I have a proposal I'd like to make… something to move the project forward."

"Excellent, Mr. Collier. What are you thinking?"

"Money appears not to be an issue with regard to my joining your client's team."

"Are you requesting a higher salary, Mr. Collier?" Diarte asked cautiously.

"No," David told him. "But I would like arrangements to be made so that my daughter can accompany me to the Bahamas."

"But she's in the intensive care unit now," he replied.

"That's true," David acknowledged. "But she's scheduled to move out of ICU and into regular care at the hospital in a couple of days."

There was silence at the other end.

"I can't leave her," he said, working hard to keep his emotions from affecting his tone of voice. "I'm all she has. If you can arrange it so that Leah comes with me, I won't ask another question."

"Let me call you right back, Mr. Collier," Diarte said, hanging up.

David found himself standing at a window at the end of the hallway. Below him, the black waters of the East River reflected the lights and the traffic of the Queensboro Bridge. Beyond Roosevelt Island and the Triboro Bridge, Queens stretched out like a carnival. Jets landed and took off at La Guardia with rhythmic precision. He could see, in the distance, the Whitestone Bridge. Bridges to everywhere, it seemed.

It was only a few minutes before Diarte called him back, but it felt like an eternity to David. He assumed that

Diarte would need to discuss this proposal with his superiors. He knew that Leah would require medical staff close by, as well a facility where she could receive dialysis.

Diarte had mentioned that they were heading to the Bahamas. That was only a half-hour flight from Miami. People lived there. It was a civilized place. There had to be hospitals. And he'd already checked the dangers of moving Leah with her pediatrician. They could do it. Eventually, they'd have to move her to Germany.

David's phone vibrated in his hand. Diarte was on the other end.

"I'm happy to say that this is absolutely a go, Mr. Collier. We'll start making the arrangements on our end."

34

LOSS

Alanna called five of the people on the list Lyons had given her.

Each person she talked to spoke highly of the experience. Interestingly enough, they all had engineering backgrounds. Two of them were involved in the start-up of a new inventory system. They had taken three weeks off from their regular job and the compensation had been amazing. Another person she'd spoken to was involved with product testing. All the projects had been handled the same way. All spoke of Lyons's straightforwardness in negotiations, followed by secrecy about the project until the work actually began. Each job had required going away to a remote location for a short length of time.

The five people she'd spoken with all told her the same thing. If they were offered the opportunity, they'd do it again.

She'd asked each of them if they knew the reason for all the secrecy. The answers had been diverse. The best one was from one of the engineers she personally knew and who worked for NASA. He'd told her that what Lyons had him doing was like policing the police. The engineer had the sense that Lyons regularly hired on specialists to serve as short-term watchdogs—often testing something that had been already tested. So it was important to not allow the word to get out. He also had a sense that Lyons was somehow taking orders from someone in the government. Someone big.

Alanna had other questions, too. Questions about things like confidentiality and possible violations of security. When it came to the work they were doing for NASA, the agency required all employees to sign document after document swearing to keep the work they did confidential. Again, the answer had been positive. Not one individual working in the private sector had encountered any conflict with their "day" jobs. Alanna knew her responsibilities fell into a far more sensitive area, but even the other NASA engineer had affirmed the reports the others had given.

Ray called her on Wednesday night, as soon as Alanna arrived home from work. She'd spoken with him, but she hadn't seen him since the day they'd met at the Fountaingrove Inn. He sounded ecstatic.

"I talked to my contact at the U.S. Marshals Service. I also called my attorney. They both agree that this could work."

One huge difference between Alanna and all the people she'd spoken to was the fact that Ray had put her into a corner. He was in a jam and that conceivably put her in one, too. What Lyons was offering Ray seemed shady, at best. Nothing was cut-and-dried in this case, but she was surprised that leaning on witnesses…or paying them to come forward…was not frowned upon by prosecutors.

"I wish you'd give me some of the names of your contacts," Alanna told him. "At least someone at the Justice Department that I could speak to. I'm not comfortable with this, Ray."

"You don't trust me to look after my own life?"

She heard the hurt tone. She was used to taking charge and handling things herself.

"I do trust you," she said gently, wishing that she believed her own words. They were talking about his life, his future. She was being dragged into it.

"So, does that mean that you're going to give it a try?" he asked hopefully.

"I still don't have any of the details of what they want me to do."

"I spoke to Lyons on the phone," Ray said. "He told me that you'd be given everything when we arrive at Grand Bahama Island. At that time, if you have any doubts about whether you want to do the job or not, you can back out. They'll arrange for us to take the next flight home."

Alanna had never realized until now how untrusting her nature was. Everything that she'd been told seemed more or less reasonable, the background checks had held up, but there was still a huge question mark at the end that kept her stomach jittery.

Ray, on the other hand, had no problem with any of it. When she thought about it, she supposed this was another reason why she'd been attracted to Ray to start with. He was the kind of person who jumped in first and learned to swim later. She, on the other hand, felt she had to be an Olympic-level swimmer before she put her foot in the water. They were different people. They had different approaches to life. She wondered if those differences had already opened an ocean between them that would be too wide to cross.

"Two weeks on a Caribbean island, Ali," he said quietly into the phone. "No crummy motels. No looking over our shoulders. The two of us, together for a few sunny weeks. A lot like before. Please tell me you want this as much as I do."

Alanna sat down on the edge of the chair in her living room. She closed her eyes and took a deep breath. She couldn't fool him or fool herself. She had to speak what was on her mind. "Ray…things are not the same as they were before you left. I think, when I was in mourning for you, I crossed a line back to the life I had before we met. And though it was far from perfect, I…I…"

"Ali, please. I've been under a lot of stress and that's why things don't seem the same. Give us a chance."

She rubbed the back of her neck, trying to ease the headache that was beginning to pound.

"Ali," he said softly. "I'm asking for a chance to live again. You still say you love me. What they're offering is the first opportunity I've really had to get my life back."

She let out a frustrated breath and then nodded to herself. Her job, her grandmother, nothing would be knocked off its orbit if she were to go on some "vacation" for two weeks.

"Okay. Okay," she said finally. "I'll put in for the time."

35

FEAR

Nathan was so tired.

This had been an excruciatingly long and difficult journey. At times lately, he realized he couldn't remember how it had all started. He had no idea how long he'd been here. He also had no idea if it would ever end.

But these past few days, since having his picture taken, Nathan felt a new sense of hope emerge like a bud in spring. One moment, it seemed that all he would ever face would be this interminable murk of winter. Then, he would remember the flash of the camera, and he would think that there *might* just be an end in sight, after all.

When his spirits buoyed at the thought, the possibilities for release were endless. Nathan imagined his photo being sent to U.S. officials at home. In his mind's eye, he saw a daring rescue by U.S. Marines. In another version, he imagined his captors believing what Nathan had been saying about Steven Galvin. He could see them receiving cash from his father in a black case at one of the nightclubs under the Bosporus Bridge. They'd release him then.

Sometimes, Nathan's mind wandered to thoughts of gathering enough strength and courage to fight his captors and escape by himself. That was the most exciting, the most pleasing thing to dream about. He should have attempted that when he was first captured. He couldn't remember now if he'd ever had an opportunity. He didn't think so.

The familiar noises in the corridor told him that someone was coming. Nathan felt a stir of excitement in his stomach as he pushed himself to his feet. The sound of latches. The door opened.

Nathan watched as two men entered. He was getting to know them pretty well, but he suddenly wished he knew them better, at least knew their names. Their faces gave away nothing. He was surprised, though, that neither told him sit, as they always did. As always, however, the one closest to the door held the AK-47.

"Your name?" one asked, shining the flashlight at him.

This triggered memories of the early days of his imprisonment. He shrugged it off.

"You know, I don't even know your names."

Nathan stretched his arms out. Soon, it would be spring. He wondered if he could be back in Washington in time to see the cherry blossoms. He was starting graduate school. He'd made up his mind. This career was over. He'd invite his mother to come and see Georgetown. They'd go out for lunch.

"You took my picture," he continued. "I assume you sent it to the U.S. consulate. I just hope you sent a copy to my parents. I'm Nathan Galvin."

"They told…you lie to us."

Nathan stared at the man holding the flashlight.

"No, I didn't. Who told you I lied?"

"All lies," the man said as the other with the AK-47 took a step closer.

"I don't understand," he said. "My father—"

But Nathan never got the chance to finish, for the other guard lifted the rifle to his shoulder and fired.

BOOK 2

Come, "the croaking raven doth bellow for revenge."

—Hamlet

36

Amber Hersey sat in the very last row of the large auditorium. The lecture today was mandatory for all graduate students taking the Freedom and Self course. The event had also been recommended to law students at Georgetown.

She wouldn't have missed it, anyway.

The guest lecturer, Senator Paul Hersey, had delivered his speech on "The Future of Human Rights" to a maximum-capacity crowd. The question-and-answer period following the forty-five-minute speech was going very well, with her father weaving together the perfect balance of humor and fact to win over the audience.

A lifetime of involvement in politics, and Amber realized that this was the first time in her life that she had sat through one of her father's complete speeches. Paul Hersey was confident, believable, charming. He looked so comfortable, so commanding, standing on the platform, the center of attention. Amber wished she had inherited some of those qualities. But at twenty-four, she had developed into more of an introvert. In terms of personality, she was definitely becoming more like her mother. Quiet and shy, with an occasional burst of wildness, and then back into her shell again.

A comment of the senator's made the audience burst into laughter. Amber smiled, realizing she'd totally missed whatever it was he'd said.

"He's totally amazing," the young woman sitting next to Amber said under her breath.

"And handsome, too. How old is he?" another grad student two seats over asked.

Amber bit her tongue to keep from saying, *too old for you.* She didn't know any of the students sitting near her. None of them had any idea that she was actually Senator Hersey's daughter.

The audience's thunderous applause signaled the end of the lecture. Amber had made no plans to meet with her father this morning. She had a meeting with her adviser in an hour about taking time off for the upcoming book tour. The children's book about the adventures of a ten-year-old girl getting lost in the White House and encountering the ghosts of past presidents had been a surprise hit. She figured the senator had tons of things on his schedule for what was left of the morning, too. She guessed he'd leave through the same door as he'd come in—closest to the stage.

She pushed up to her feet and turned to the exit door.

"He's coming out this way," the woman sitting next to her announced excitedly.

Amber turned and was surprised to find her father weaving his way through the students and up the steps toward her.

"Excuse me… Thanks very much… Thanks… Excuse

me," he was saying as he passed students who were trying to talk to him. "Excuse me…I have to catch up to my daughter."

A warm feeling rushed through her. Heads were turning, and people were noticing her. Amber could feel herself blushing under the scrutiny. It was awkward, but it also felt good.

The senator finally reached her.

"Well?" he asked, putting his arms around her. "How did I do?"

Amber hugged him back. "You were brilliant."

37

Age had made her wise but not cynical.

Well, Alanna thought, healthy skepticism wasn't exactly cynicism.

She'd thought she could leave her doubts behind and come on this trip with an open mind, but she was wrong. The arrangements alone only served to fuel her anxiety.

For their flight from Oakland to Miami, their seats had been up in first-class. Alanna made an excellent salary, but this was the first time she'd ever flown that way. In all the times she'd traveled for business, she'd never been able to justify spending that kind of money on herself. She looked for the cheapest fare from point A to point B. She didn't need pampering.

When they arrived at Miami airport, there'd been an attendant waiting inside the terminal with one of those golf carts. Their luggage would be taken care of, they were told. She and Ray climbed in and were whisked off to a turboprop plane sitting fueled and ready outside a private hangar.

They met the pilot and copilot standing in the shade of the plane's wing. They were the only passengers on the King Air C90B, a six-seater. The 125-mile flight would take about half an hour. Inside, the accommodations were even nicer than the first-class seating they'd enjoyed earlier on their flight cross-country.

"Now, this is the way to live," Ray said as they boarded the plane.

"You would think someone is trying to impress us," she replied, moving to one of the cream-colored leather seats. She immediately buckled her seat belt.

"I can't see why not. You deserve it," he responded.

Four of the seats came together around a maple tabletop that the copilot clicked into place once Alanna and Ray were seated. Before going back outside, he pointed out the door to the restroom and the refreshments stocked in the handy built-in coolers. The plane couldn't have been more than a couple of years old. Everything still looked and smelled brand new. Ray reached into the cooler and took out a Heineken.

This was the first time in days that they had been able to be together like this with no one else around. A door separated the cockpit from the rest of the cabin. Outside the small window of the plane, Alanna could see the pilot and copilot inspecting the craft. As she watched them, she saw a cart drive up to the plane, bringing their luggage. She wondered how much a private arrangement like this cost. It had to be a lot.

She looked at Ray. "Why?"

"Why what?" he asked.

"Why do I deserve it?" she asked. "What is it that they want me to do?"

Ray shook his head, taking a sip of his beer and

putting it in a cup holder on the table. "I guess we'll find out when we get there."

She looked around the cabin again. She played with some of the buttons on the armrest. A personal screen slid down from the ceiling, and entertainment options rolled onto it. She glanced at Ray and saw him put his feet on the table. He looked ready to doze off again. That's what he'd done the entire length of their flight from California to Miami. She'd wanted to talk, but he'd slept. She heard a compartment door close somewhere beneath them. She figured their luggage was in.

"Ray, please tell me everything you know about these people."

"I only know what you know." There was a hint of dismissal in his voice, as if she was bothering him with her question.

She didn't believe him…which was extremely sad. She was here because of how she felt about him— because she loved him—and yet she didn't trust what he was telling her.

The pilot and copilot boarded the plane. Vaguely, she was aware that they were saying something to her and Ray, but Alanna was too consumed by her thoughts to be listening. Ray spoke to them and the two men went through the door into the cockpit, shutting it behind them.

Ray reached over and touched her hand. "Would you like some juice or a water bottle?"

She shook her head as the engines fired up. "There has to be more that you know about this Mr. Lyons…or Diarte. You took me to meet them."

He shrugged. "Sorry, you know everything that there is to know."

"Come on, Ray. You spoke to them," she said in a determined tone. "Did they call you? How were they able to reach you? You weren't staying in one place. I wasn't even able to get hold of you. Please think back. You have to remember that first conversation with them."

"Sure," he whispered, getting out of his seat and crouching beside her. "But we only talked about you."

He brushed his lips across hers. His fingers traced her cheek. He started to deepen the kiss…and then stopped.

"It's been a long time since we had this kind of time together. What do you say we put this flight time to good use."

Alanna pulled back as if stung. The plane started to move. She looked out the window, feeling as if her face was on fire. They were heading toward the runway.

"Ali?" Ray asked, taking her hand.

She pulled her hand away and tucked her fingers under her leg, out of his reach. Confusion was tearing her apart. When she was with him, she had no time to think. Lately, they'd spent a lot of time apart. They'd only talked on the phone. The last time that she'd seen him, before today, was when they'd met with the men who'd arranged this trip.

He touched her cheek. "What's wrong, Ali?"

She should have felt embarrassed, guilty for the way she was acting. At the same time, she was starting to feel as if invisible threads were attached to her hands and feet. He was controlling her. He tugged whenever she got out of line. She hated that feeling, but…this was Ray. She looked into his eyes.

"You're my weakness, Ray," she whispered. "You know it…and they know it."

"Let them. You're my weakness too. My everything. That's what happens when people are in love."

The pilot's voice came through a speaker in her headrest. They were about to take off. Ray moved back to his seat and fastened his seat belt.

"You're exhausted, my love. Why don't you close your eyes and try to catch some sleep. I—"

"No, Ray. I don't want to sleep," she blurted out. "I don't want to stop asking questions. I don't like being distracted when I'm *asking* questions. We're like the blind leading the blind. We don't even know *really* where these people are taking us. But it bothers me most that we don't know what they want from us."

"But we do." He lowered his voice, motioning with his head to the cockpit. "You checked the references yourself. Neither Lyons nor Diarte look or act like some criminals. There's no one holding us at gunpoint. You're panicking for nothing."

"Ray, *you* have nothing to lose," she reminded him.

"But *we* have everything to gain."

Alanna wished she could convince herself of that. The plane took off. She leaned back in the seat, looking out the window. They were immediately over water.

"There's a good reason why I'm feeling like this." She decided to say everything that was on her mind. "I went through hell the months that you were gone. Guilt… mourning…regret…loneliness…depression. I would have done anything in the world—absolutely anything— to get you back."

He leaned forward and touched her arm gently.

She stared at him. "And then my wish came true. One day, you were back. And now I know I'm expected to keep my end of the bargain."

"We were given a second chance at happiness. That's what this trip is about. Why should we think of anything but our future together? That's all that matters."

She continued to look at him. There was something bothering him. It was in that…something…in his voice. It was in the way he looked at her…or rather, in the way he couldn't hold her gaze. She was forcing herself to keep her mind open, refusing to let her heart distract her.

And then she felt it and everything changed in an instant. She could see through him.

"Ray, don't you think I deserve the truth?"

He shook his head, as if perplexed. "What do you mean? Of course you deserve the truth. What is it that you think I'm not telling you?"

"You have to tell *me* that." She leaned toward him, forcing him to face her.

"I don't understand you, Ali."

"Maybe that's true. But I've had time to think on this trip, and it's just come to me."

"What are you talking about?"

"You were supposed to keep me swept off my feet until we got there," she told him.

Ray laughed, scoffing. He put a hand up. "You are scaring me now. You're letting your imagination get the best of you."

Alanna let silence be the inquisitor for a few long moments. He visibly shifted in discomfort in his seat.

"Who are you, really?"

"I don't find any of this funny." He sat back in his chair, putting his feet up on the table. He reached for a magazine from a compartment in between them.

"Handsome, smart, tall, young playboy suddenly falls head over heels in love with older, short, plain, Mexican-American scientist who's never had a steady boyfriend in her entire life. You know, I never stopped to question what could be the attraction. I never wanted to know."

"Ali, stop talking about yourself that way. You're beautiful…and six years is nothing. You know that." Ray tried to lighten his tone and pasted on a weak smile. "Okay, you might be considered petite, but I think you're perfect."

Alanna's heart tightened in her chest. She could see it more clearly by the second. The embarrassment was there, the guilt he no longer could hide.

"How far back does this scheming go, Ray?" she asked.

"I'm not talking to you anymore. Not when you're being like this." He opened the magazine.

"It was no accident that we met the same day that you started working at Moffett," she told him. "Whoever these people are who hired you have some serious connections with NASA security, don't they?"

She tried to keep her voice level, her eyes dry, but inside, her heart wept. She'd been the biggest fool.

"Did you ask for extra money when you saw me in person?"

"Stop!" he shouted at her. "Do you hear me? Stop it!"

He undid his seat belt and got to his feet. She wondered where he was going to go.

"This hurts me!" he snapped. "I don't know what I've done to deserve this."

She watched him in silence.

"You don't trust me?" He put one hand against the small screen still hanging in front of her. "You don't love me? Okay. Fine. If that's what you think, Alanna, no problem. As soon as this plane lands, you just get back on the next plane home."

"I will, Ray."

He raked his fingers through his hair. "You just can't be happy, can you, Alanna? You just don't know how."

38

Grand Bahama Island

"Mom would have liked this place a lot."

At Leah's words, David tightened his fingers on the handles of the wheelchair. His daughter's first view of the island made her think of Nicole.

Funny how their minds worked so similarly.

Finances had been very tight during the last couple of years of his wife's life. They had taken no vacations at all. He wondered if Leah remembered the last time they'd gone away as a family. Just the three of them. Probably not. She'd been barely four years old.

"You're right," he replied. "She *would* have liked this island."

Leah's nurse and an assistant moved around them to strap the wheelchair to a lift that would lower it to the airport tarmac. Leah's condition had been stable for two weeks now, and as long as she went through dialysis every day, her doctors felt there was no reason to keep her in the hospital.

David's new employer had made every arrangement

possible to smooth the way for this trip and their subsequent stay. David had been told that there was one hospital on Grand Bahama Island, in the heart of downtown Freeport. There were also three private clinics with dialysis equipment. With Florida less than a half hour away by plane, David felt it was much better for Leah to be with him than to have her a thousand miles away in some state-of-the-art hospital in New York City. He hoped he was right.

Two nurses had been hired to work in shifts watching Leah while on the island. The dialysis equipment and medication were supposedly waiting for them where they were staying.

"Do they have any TVs where we're going?" Leah asked.

"I'm sure they do," he told her. The main source of entertainment for the eight-year-old this past couple of weeks had been watching movies or TV at the hospital. "But there's also the beach and books and maybe we'll get a chance to play some games."

"It's not fun to play with only two people," she told him. "You always win."

"That's not true. I let you win every now and then." He adjusted the baseball hat Leah was wearing. She was extremely pale. The trip had taken a lot out of her. The late-afternoon sun wasn't much of a threat as far as getting burned. Still, David had been told to watch out for a number of things. Leah's resistance was very low.

"See. I knew it. You *let* me win."

"I'm just kidding. When you win, you win on your own."

"Daddy, you're fibbing," Leah reprimanded him.

"Seriously. I'm just trash-talking."

The lift settled onto the runway, and the nurses undid the straps.

"I'll take her," he told the two women.

He took his sweater off and draped it on the back of Leah's chair. The air was balmy, quite a change to the freezing rain they'd left in New York City.

A young Bahamian who was pulling their luggage out of a compartment in the side of the small plane stopped and turned to him. "There's a van coming to get you, sir, if you'd care to wait over by that hangar. They just called. They should be along in a few minutes."

David thanked him and looked around. Another small plane was sitting next to theirs. That one, too, appeared to be a newly arrived flight. A worker was taking luggage out of it, as well. The airport was very small and clearly private. David knew that Freeport had an airport that handled the tourist traffic flying in aboard commercial jets, but this airport was not it. A number of smaller planes that looked to be privately owned were parked in a row along a fence. One unmarked jet was parked near a small building that he figured must be the airport office. There wasn't any sign of life there, but that wasn't the direction he'd been told to go, anyway.

"He told us to go that way," Leah said, pointing toward a small hangar fifty yards from their plane.

He started pushing Leah's chair in that direction. The hangar, with its doors open at both ends, offered shade, at least. Two people, who seemed to be waiting, stood there. From their body language, David decided they were in the middle of an argument. He slowed down a little, but continued toward them.

He knew there would be a team of people working on the same project here on this island. Beyond that, he didn't know where they would be coming from or what their specialties were.

"I want to learn how to play chess," Leah announced as David pushed the wheelchair toward the hangar.

"I haven't played chess in years. I don't know if I remember how to play anymore," he told her. He stopped in the shade, just inside the hangar door. The hangar was empty, except for a few workbenches along the walls, some hoses and parts, and a partially dismantled World War II vintage fighter in a far corner.

"Good. We can learn together." She smiled up at him. "That way, if I win, I know it's fair and square."

He reached down and pulled her ear and smiled back. These days, David did a lot of smiling. He was taking control of his own chessboard, square by square and piece by piece. Leah's DNA samples had been sent to the clinic in Germany, and the cloning was apparently progressing as it should. In addition, his daughter was with him. He was already receiving a salary and benefits, even though he still didn't know what his job was. But that part didn't matter. If they asked him to embezzle funds from the Dalai Lama, he would clean him out and send a thank-you note later. Whoever his employer was, David was indebted to him for what he was doing for Leah. He was keeping her alive, and David owed him.

"Do you know how to play chess?"

David realized Leah was speaking to the couple standing in the hangar.

"Yes, I do," the woman told her.

"Sweet," Leah said. "Are you staying on the island?"

David noticed the uncomfortable look that passed between the two people. The guy walked off and stood outside the open doors, hands in his pockets, his back to them, looking out at the small airport runway.

"More than likely, I'll be leaving on the next flight out," she told Leah.

"That's too bad," Leah said. She then tried to push her own wheelchair forward. David helped her. "I'm Leah. He's my dad."

The woman's face softened into a smile. David figured she was about the same age as him. Not much more than five feet tall, dark hair, dark eyes, delicate features. Most likely Hispanic. She wore no makeup and was dressed in black business dress pants, a white collared shirt and a black cardigan sweater that she had to be warm in.

"I'm Alanna." She shook Leah's hand. "Alanna Mendes."

"Dr. Mendes?" someone called from the set of doors.

She turned that way. A young man in a royal-blue polo shirt approached, clipboard in hand.

"We checked on your request. The earliest flight we can get you on leaving the island is tomorrow morning," he told her. "Is it okay if we move your belongings to the resort for the night and drive you to Freeport for the flight tomorrow?"

"So nothing is leaving from this airport?"

"No, ma'am."

"What about the plane I flew in on?"

"Both of those planes are taking off in about an hour, but one's going to Bermuda and the other is going to…" He glanced at his clipboard. "Oh, yeah. Curaçao."

She had a very expressive face. David could see the struggle reflected in her features. She looked over her shoulder at the man who was standing by the other set of open doors to the hangar. He hadn't moved.

"I guess it's okay," she said quietly.

"Thank you." The man pulled out his cell phone as he left the hangar.

"Does this mean you'll have time to teach me how to play chess tonight?" Leah asked.

"Leah," David scolded his daughter gently. He turned to the woman. "I'm sorry. My daughter and I didn't mean to eavesdrop. I'm David Collier."

Her handshake was firm when she shook his hand. The touch of a smile was back. She looked at Leah.

"Do you know if we're staying at the same place?" she asked.

The eight-year-old shrugged and looked up at David.

"I really couldn't say," he replied.

"What's the name of the resort you're staying at?" she asked.

He and Leah exchanged a look. "I believe it's a private resort. I don't remember hearing a name to it."

"I'm glad I'm not the only one who seems to be short on answers," she told them.

"So that's good, isn't it?" Leah asked. "We must be staying at the same nameless place."

The smile reached her dark eyes. She seemed totally entertained by Leah.

"If nothing, my daughter is persistent," David told Dr. Mendes. He noticed that she glanced again in the direction of her friend. He no longer was there.

"So what kind of doctor are you?" Leah asked her.

"You don't have to answer that," David cut in immediately. "A lot of times my daughter forgets that not everyone is interested in being interrogated by her."

"I don't mind," she said to Leah. "I'm a scientist. I have a Ph.D. not an M.D."

"That's good. I'm not crazy about doctors," Leah told her. "Medical doctors, I mean."

David noticed that Dr. Mendes's gaze involuntarily flickered toward the wheelchair and Leah's legs.

"Why don't you like medical doctors?" she asked.

"Plenty of reasons," the little girl said. "They didn't save my mom, for one. She had cancer. She's dead now."

"I'm so sorry," Alanna said quietly, looking up at David.

He was surprised and alarmed to hear his daughter express her opinions like this to a stranger. In many ways, Leah was an eight-year-old beyond her years. Still, he'd never known her to open up to someone that she didn't know. He also didn't know how much of Leah's opinion was reflective of what she might have heard David say about doctors.

"And I don't like what they're doing for me, either," Leah announced.

David reached for Leah's hand and took it gently in his. "I'm not sure Dr. Mendes wants to hear about our disappointments with the medical profession, honey."

"Oh, no. I'm really very interested. But please call me Alanna."

Leah squeezed his hand. He had a sudden sense that she was telling him that this woman was okay.

"I have kidney disease. I've already had one transplant. But it didn't work."

"I'm sorry," Alanna whispered. She crouched down until she was at eye level with Leah. "You're very young to have gone through so much disappointment."

"It's okay. I have the best dad in the world. A lot of kids don't have that."

David stared down at Leah. He was suddenly speechless. Emotions welled up in him. There was so much of her childhood she'd missed because of health problems and Nicole's death and David's loss of job and legal difficulties. He realized now that he never thought there was anything Leah could feel positive about. Least of all, him.

"He gives me five bucks to say that," Leah said next.

There was a moment of silence then a burst of laughter escaped the scientist.

The sound of a plane landing drew their attention. Dr. Mendes was frowning as it taxied toward the hangar.

"For a place that has so many planes coming in, I don't understand why I can't get one going back to Miami."

"Maybe they just don't want you to leave right away," David suggested.

"That's okay with me," Leah chirped in.

Alanna smiled at the little girl and then peered out at the incoming plane. It was slightly larger than the one David flew in on.

"Dad, I wonder if these are more people who'll be

staying where we are," she said. "We should go and check on them."

She motioned to David to take her toward the open doors.

"Sorry, more victims," he said to Alanna.

The scientist smiled, and David had a feeling she was in a far better mood than she'd been when they first came into the hangar.

39

A van and an ancient Suburban pulled up to the hangar just as the passengers on the last flight began to disembark.

Alanna was not happy about being unable to fly out until morning, but there appeared to be nothing she could do about it. If she made enough noise, she could probably get them to take her to a hotel in Freeport. Still, in spite of Ray, there was something curiously unthreatening about this situation. The latest arrivals confirmed her opinion.

A very young couple with an infant came across the concrete to the hangar. They were apparently the only passengers on this flight.

Alanna knew her argument with Ray had wounded him deeply. He was the last one in the van and took the front seat next to the driver. He didn't say a thing or even glance in her direction. The van had three benches behind the driver, and Alanna took a seat on the back row. The young couple and the baby sat in front of her. Leah and her father were behind the driver, with the little girl's wheelchair folded and placed inside the door once everyone was in and seated.

The old Suburban, loaded with their luggage and the

employees who'd greeted them at the airport, followed behind the van.

There was a difference in the way Alanna was seeing things now. She knew it had to do with the way a sick but feisty little girl looked at life and the people she met. Alanna looked out the window, admired the landscape flashing by. Amid the green growth, the trunks of count-less fallen trees lay on the ground, all lined up side by side, as if they'd been placed that way on purpose. When she asked, the driver told the visitors that the fallen trees had been knocked down by a couple of hurricanes a few years back. The storms had leveled much of the vegeta-tion on the island, but everything was coming back now.

Both rows of seats in front of her carried people who appeared to be risking a lot more than Alanna in coming here. Clearly, they all were here for the same project, but David Collier was here with a daughter who was so weak that she needed a wheelchair to get around. The couple in front had introduced themselves to her as Jay and Padma Alexei, and they were here with their newborn son. The infant couldn't have been even a month old. The couple looked young enough to be in high school. In a way, she thought, life is a matter of perspective. Alanna felt much more confident now, looking at what was going on. She seemed to have the least at stake.

Even so, she would be out of here in the morning.

She looked at the back of Ray's head. He appeared to be lost in his thoughts. There was so much that she didn't understand about what had happened between them—what was happening now. They'd never fought before, and Alanna wondered if her admission of not trusting him had pushed their relationship to the point of no return. She cared for him. She loved him. She hurt inside about what she'd said. At the same time, she knew she had spoken what was in her heart and what she thought was the truth. She was certain there were things he wasn't telling her. It was the extent of what he wasn't telling that bothered her.

The small caravan turned left onto a main road that ran along the water. As they turned, Alanna looked at a run-down boatyard on the right filled with weathered hulks of sea vessels. The sea was a magical blend of aquas and darker blues.

"How long before we get there?" Leah's question forced Alanna out of her gloom. She found herself smiling at the eight-year-old, who didn't even wait for an answer. Instead, Leah was already turned in her seat and making soft noises to the baby.

"Almost there, miss," the driver replied. "We just had to drive the long way around the airport. Some of the roads in West End were washed out by the storms and haven't been fixed as yet."

Alanna knew from looking out the windows of the plane that they were at the western end of Grand Bahama Island. From the air, the white ribbon of concrete that constituted the airport appeared to be a stone's throw from what looked like a resort with a marina on a spit of land surrounded by the sea.

"Is it a boy or a girl?" Leah was asking.

"He's a boy," the young woman answered.

"What's his name?"

"William Harsha Alexei."

"That's cool," Leah responded. "What does Harsha mean?"

"It means joy or delight," the young mother told her. "It's an Indian name."

"I never had an Indian friend before," Leah told her. "Can I call him Harsha instead of William? I like that name a lot."

The young woman nodded. "We like the name, too. But when he gets to be your age, his friends probably call him William or Will."

"Or Bill," Leah added. "But we'll call him Harsha, okay?"

Alanna was amazed by Leah's ability to draw people out of their shells. Everyone in the van seemed much more relaxed because of her. Everyone but Ray, Alanna corrected herself. He was paying no attention. She looked out the window, trying to focus on the beauty that surrounded them.

Living and working in California, Alanna's only trips east had been for professional conferences set in major cities like New York, Boston and Atlanta. She had never in her life been to any islands like the Bahamas. In fact, she'd never been to Florida before today.

The road they were traveling on was in great condition, but from where she was sitting, Alanna had a good view of a variety of different lifestyles. Half-painted, concrete-block houses with ancient fishing boats and rusted trucks and cars in front sat side by side with new vacation homes, built away from the road but high enough to have an unspoiled view of the ocean. Women wearing thin cotton dresses and headscarves sat on porches of shacks with shutters for windows as they watched children playing with dogs in overgrown yards. The van passed a couple of middle-aged tourists in bathing suits and visors, straddling bikes and talking to two local fishermen by a narrow strand of beach. The fishermen were tossing fish from their boat into a couple of battered coolers as they chatted.

At least at West End, Grand Bahama Island appeared to be a comfortable mix of new and old, wealth and poverty, stranger and local.

The van slowed down as the driver drove through a gate where the main road ended. Palm trees lined both sides of the divided driveway and flowers flamed color-fully in the center median. As they drove along, Alanna saw on the left a handful of houses with fishing boats and sailboats that appeared to be docked at their back-doors. More high-end houses were being built there as well. On the right side, she looked out at a beach and the open Atlantic.

Everything seemed so civilized here. It was far from what Alanna had imagined. There was no compound behind high, chain-link fences. No armed guards with Dobermans to thwart any chance of escape.

The driver slowed down and stopped at a bend in the road. Just beyond was a gated entrance, though there still was no fence anywhere. A guard came out of a small house. Alanna decided he had to be about ninety years old. Dressed in a short-sleeve tan polo shirt, black shorts and a baseball cap, he smiled and waved at them as he lifted a wooden bar.

The place was absolutely beautiful. The view of

manicured grounds, small cottages and white beaches beyond was breathtaking.

"Are you sure this is work?" the young man sitting in front of her asked his wife.

Alanna wondered if her request to fly out of here the next morning had been premature. The van pulled to a stop in front of a sprawling, one-story building that was situated beside a protected marina. Two huge cabin cruisers and half a dozen sailboats were parked alongside a number of smaller boats at the docks. Three men dressed in the same colors as the gatekeeper came out to help them.

Doors were opened and luggage pulled out. Leah had a hundred and one questions for everyone helping them. Alanna sat patiently in the van until the others had gotten out. She watched Ray ask something of one of the men outside before disappearing into the building.

No matter how she looked at it, Alanna felt uncomfortable about her situation. She and Ray were in the middle of a disagreement. She didn't know if he would want to stay with her now, even if she changed her mind. If she didn't fulfill her part in this project, she honestly didn't know if Ray's life would be at risk. At the same time, how could she feel comfortable, not knowing who her employer was and what she was expected to do here? It was more than a notion; she just didn't believe Ray was speaking the truth.

"Dr. Mendes?"

She realized that one of their greeters was talking to her. She was the only one left in the vehicle.

"I can show you to your cottage, if you'd like to follow me," the man told her.

She worked her way out of the van. The breeze was stronger at this part of the island, but it was warm, and the salt air smelled so nice.

"Actually…" She turned around 360 degrees. She could see guides leading the others across the manicured grounds to their cottages, which spread out like fingers around the main building. "Actually, I'd like to meet with our host first."

The man nodded as if her response was totally expected. "Absolutely, please follow me."

She'd seen no sign, as yet, of the two men she and Ray had met with out in the Sonoma wine country. Rather than talk to Lyons and Diarte, though, Alanna hoped this time to speak with the actual person who had requested her services. She left her luggage in the care of the attendants who were loading the bags onto carts.

Alanna followed the young man in through the same door that Ray had used. Inside, she entered an open reception area decorated with a couple of comfortable sofas and alcoves with chairs. Although the place was obviously privately owned, it had been designed to handle groups of guests. Alanna recalled that none of the references she'd spoken with had talked about being brought to Grand Bahama Island to work. She wondered why they had been brought here, specifically.

"This way, please." The man motioned her through another set of doors and into an enclosed walkway that separated the reception area from another section of the building. As she walked along, Alanna looked out the large plate-glass windows at the sun beginning to descend in the afternoon sky. Once again, she felt a sense of awe at the beauty of the place.

At the end of the walkway, she entered what had to be a man's residence. Even in the entrance hall, masculine tastes had dictated the choice of colors and furnishings. She was led into a wood-paneled library and asked to wait.

She couldn't force herself to sit down and relax while she was waiting. She had no name, no face, no information whatsoever about this person. To her left, there was a long table that looked as if it had been taken out of a university library somewhere. A carved mahogany desk sat at one end of the room. Floor-to-ceiling shelves of books covered two walls. On the desk, a couple of picture frames faced away from where she stood. Alanna thought it would be intrusive to check them.

She moved to the bookcases instead. The collection of books was diverse and not organized in any particular order. There was a mishmash of fiction and nonfiction. Self-help books sat next to classics. Old leather-bound volumes next to paperbacks. Mystery and romance, English and Russian literature, volumes of poetry. She touched the frayed spine of a paperback copy of *One Hundred Years of Solitude* and an equally worn copy of something called *The Thistle and the Rose.*

In a way, the collection was endearing. It wasn't a set of volumes professionally selected and arranged by a decorator with aesthetic appeal in mind. Rather, it showed an individual with diverse interests.

"My wife was an avid reader," someone said behind her.

Alanna hadn't heard anyone come in. She turned

around, then stopped abruptly. She wasn't much into following the "People" section of the news. This face, though, she had no trouble recognizing.

"Dr. Mendes," he said pleasantly, taking a step toward her. "Welcome to West Bay. I'm Steven Galvin."

40

Gocek, Turkey

Finn always tried to keep business separate from pleasure. He made a point of never taking his family to the location of a job he'd done. Of course, there were exceptions to the rule. Some major cities couldn't be avoided. Ireland was home. Still, the last thing he'd imagined was to come to this small town of three thousand and immediately start planning a trip with his family for next year.

Set on the southwest coast of Turkey and at the deepest point of the Gulf of Fethiye, Gocek was a gorgeous Mediterranean village. Nestled at the foot of pine-covered mountains, the town overlooked a number of small islands, scattered about the bay like jewels in a blue satin box. In short, the place was brilliant.

Finn could already see himself fishing with Mick and the twins while Kelly wandered in and out of the shops in the center. The place had plenty of good places to eat, and fine places to stay. This was exactly the vacation they needed as a family, some time away from the everyday drudgery.

This was truly what Mick needed, Finn thought. The lad needed time away from the bloody lowlifes he called his mates.

And after this contract, he was done with it all. Then, he and Kelly could use a little bit of celebrating.

The sight of the slick powerboat cruising along the sparkling waters from the marina jarred Finn out of his retirement-planning mode. He glanced at his watch and opened the folder in his laptop case. His target's picture was right on top.

As quaint as the village of Gocek could be for vacationing tourists, it wasn't the ideal location for a hit. No hustle and bustle of the city. No crowds that would make one go unnoticed. No skyscrapers. Finn had to change some of the details. He had to shadow the target for days before picking the time and place.

Utku Ahmet was vacationing in the affluent waterfront town with his wife and infant daughter. They were staying in a private property on a hill overlooking the marina. The villa offered no clear range area where Finn could make his shot.

After a few days in Gocek, though, Finn was familiar enough with Ahmet's routine. There was one thing that the young Turk enjoyed every evening. Making the most of the unseasonably warm January weather, each night Ahmet would take his wife and daughter out into the harbor to watch the sunset.

Finn knew it was his best opportunity, but the shot itself presented a few difficulties. First, he had to set up on a hill above the harbor. At almost twelve hundred meters, the distance was greater than he preferred. The wind variable would be a factor, as well, but luckily the strong breeze was coming directly at him over the water tonight.

The problem was really how to get clear after the shot. To get out without a problem, Finn knew he had to make it a clean shot, in spite of the distance, while the Turk was offshore. With any luck, Ahmet's wife would be so unsettled that she would take some time getting the boat to shore…long enough for Finn to dispose of his weapon and get down to his car.

It was not an ideal situation, considering all the variables. Despite the negatives, though, Finn was glad he'd taken the job. This would be one hell of a place to come on holiday with the lads and Kelly.

The sun was dropping quickly now. As Finn watched, Ahmet throttled down the boat in almost exactly the same spot he'd stopped the previous two evenings. Finn moved two paces to the right and placed the rifle's bipod stand on the soft, needle-covered earth. Lying on his stomach, he set himself up, looking through his scope past branches of pine trees below him on the hillside.

Finn could see Ahmet holding the daughter in one arm. The baby was patting the father on the face. Little fists moved in the way. Finn lowered the crosshairs to the man's heart. The baby's arse would take the bullet.

"Give the lass to your wife," Finn directed under his breath.

No one was listening to him. He rechecked his distance: 1,187 meters. Wind, ten kilometers per hour straight in. He could do this. The sun was sinking deeper, dipping into the western sea. In a minute, it would be too dark to do the job.

"Come on, woman," Finn ordered Ahmet's wife. "Take your baby from him."

The young woman was as much a nuisance as the baby. She'd moved into the path of the bullet.

The sun was nearly gone. The golden colors on the water were growing darker by the second. Finn knew that this was the time if he was to finish the job. The boat was steady. He did a quick recalculation.

"Give up the bloody baby, man."

As Finn said the words, Ahmet stood up and handed the child to his wife. Taking a camera from her, he raised it to his eye to take a picture of the horizon. The wife moved beside him and pointed the baby's hand at the sun.

That was all the Irishman needed. He squeezed the trigger.

A second later, the Turk's body jerked forward toward the sunset before dropping over the side out of sight.

41

"I have your ex-wife on the phone," Susan told him through the old-fashioned intercom on his desk.

Paul Hersey paused only long enough to press the speaker button on his phone before going back to signing the documents that were piled up on his desk.

"June, thank you so much for taking my call," he said in his charming tone. "How are things?"

"They're fine, Paul," she said shortly. "What do you want?"

Despite the passage of more than a decade, to say things were not smooth between them was an understatement. They remained civil for the sake of Amber and the media, but Paul knew very well how she felt about him. Their occasional personal contact was brief and to the point.

"I heard your VCA bill is going on the ballot in Pennsylvania this fall again. I'm so glad," Paul commented, retaining his friendliest tone.

June had always been one to pick a cause and spend the following umpteen months dedicating her every waking hour to it. This one was particularly annoying. Voters Choice Act bills made it much easier for independents and renegade politicians outside of the two parties to run at election time. He was, of course, dead set against the idea. But June didn't have to know that.

"What's the forecast for getting it passed this time?" he asked.

She started rattling off their latest polls and stats. Luckily for Paul, when it came to politics, June still trusted him for some reason. She had no clue that he'd been working behind the scenes to undermine efforts to have the VCA on the ballot this coming November.

His secretary, Susan, tapped lightly on his door and poked her head in. She had another armful of files for him to go over. He motioned for her to come in.

"Remember, I'm here for you." He pushed the letters that he'd already signed toward Susan. "In case you need some arm-twisting in Washington."

"Thanks." Pause. "So what's this call about?"

Paul figured it was time to get to the point. "Pretty awesome about Amber and all the publicity her publisher has decided to do on her book, don't you think?"

"Definitely. I think it's absolutely wonderful."

"She tells me you're thinking about going on her European signing tour together," he said. "That's great."

"She *asked* me to go."

"So you *are* going."

"Is there a problem?"

He paused a couple of seconds and held up his hand for his secretary to wait. There was a problem with the letter he was about to sign.

"Well, that explains the call I received," he said soberly.

"What call?"

"She's trying to find a way around the suggestions the Secret Service has made regarding her security." He leaned back in his chair. "The bottom line is that Amber is ignoring her safety."

"What's going on, Paul?" she asked, her voice taking on a note of urgency. "Has there been a threat made on Amber's life?"

Her response was quicker than he'd expected. She'd already taken the hook. "She's the daughter of a front-runner in the run for the White House, June. That puts her in a different kind of spotlight. Anytime you're in a situation like this, you have to become…well, cautious."

"The Secret Service is against her going on this book tour. Is that it?"

"Well, no…and yes." He paused again for effect. "You see, when it comes to providing security for Amber, we're in limbo because it's still early in the campaign. If we were closer to the convention or already nominated or elected, there would be no question—she'd be escorted everywhere she went. But we're not quite there, yet."

"But the Secret Service is concerned," she said, clearly worried.

"Not exactly. It's just that their hands are tied right now."

"Then untie them, Paul," she replied. "Use your connections. There must be a way to get that protection for her."

"I've already contacted some people. And called in a few favors." He tapped his pen on the paper a couple of times. "But let me tell you the way it was put to me. If Amber were going on this tour alone, then they'd have no trouble assigning a couple of agents to accompany her. But with you on the trip with her…"

"I won't go," she offered immediately.

"I've already spoken to Amber about this. She'll be pretty angry with me for suggesting it to you," he said.

"She won't know. I'll find another excuse. I can take care of it," she said quickly. "Paul, you and I have had our differences over the years. But we both know that Amber's safety is the one thing at the top of both of our priority lists."

"Of course."

"Well, I'm not going. I've already thought of an excuse. Get the Secret Service to send a team."

He could have pushed the issue further, but he decided there was no point in belaboring it.

"Okay, if that's the way you want to go with it," he said. "I'll go to work on that here. I'll make sure she'll be safe."

He ended the call and found his secretary staring at him.

"Senator, I didn't want to interrupt," she told him. "But I'm certain arrangements have been made for the Secret Service to send a team of agents with Amber, regardless of whom she travels with."

"That's true, but my ex doesn't have to know it. June had Amber for years and couldn't keep her. Now my daughter is with me." He looked down at the document in front of him. "And I plan to keep her."

42

All along, Steven had known she would be his most reluctant recruit. He was right. He'd received the phone call that she wished to leave the island the moment she arrived.

The good news was that her handshake was firm and confident. She didn't look like a woman that frightened easily. There was still hope.

"Mr. Galvin. I have to tell you I'm surprised."

Almost half a decade out of the business, Steven was never really sure if people would still recognize him. She obviously did.

"Why surprised, Dr. Mendes?"

"Would it be wrong to assume Mr. Diarte and Lyons interviewed me for a project of yours?"

"That would be the correct assumption. And please, call me Steven."

"Do they work for you?" she asked.

"Only on a consulting basis," he told her. "They're excellent at putting together teams of people for specific projects. I have used their services before."

"Why the secrecy?" she asked.

"Dr. Mendes, that's a difficult question to answer in ten words or less."

"I'll give you twenty," she said. "And you can call me Alanna."

"Thank you. In Seattle, we always operated on a first-name basis." He motioned to a set of chairs near the window. She followed him and they both took a seat. The sun was a golden red ball dropping brilliantly toward the horizon. He smiled. "I'm afraid twenty words still won't let me get my point across."

"How many words do you need?" the scientist asked, looking out at the sea.

"I do think that a day or two would be enough time."

She wasn't afraid to make eye contact. She studied him for a few moments. "Enough time for what? You should know up front that I don't care for the way I was lured here."

"Yes." Steven nodded. "I'm sorry about that. You're such a key part of this project that we…I…needed to be sure you came."

"You could have just asked me and told me what the project entails," she told him.

"You're right. We could have," he conceded. "But I couldn't risk you saying no."

"That kind of talk doesn't really fill me with confidence."

"I can understand that, but I promise you that everything I tell you from here on will be the truth."

The scientist looked at him intently, measuring him up.

"I need your involvement in this project, Alanna," he said. "I'm asking you now to hear me out, to listen to what I need from you, and then to make the decision whether you'll work on this project with us or not."

"What's the project?" she asked again.

"If you won't mind, I'm planning to explain it to everyone who arrived today at the same time. I was planning to discuss it after dinner."

She looked at him and then nodded. He was relieved when she didn't object. She was thinking of something else right now, and Steven knew what it was. Her former fiancé. He waited. She started to ask him, but then stopped. He saw her look around at the library again.

"You have a beautiful place here," she said finally, gesturing to the scene outside the window.

"Thank you."

"Is the entire resort yours…the grounds and cottages?"

He understood her need to have some answers. He understood how her mind worked. It was very much like his.

"Yes, it's mine."

"It's pretty spacious for a private residence," she said.

"It was originally a business investment, actually. I bought the place in 1989, I think it was. It was my wife's idea. She always thought I worked my managers too hard. So she found this place. For years, there had been a hotel here, dating back to the thirties. Pretty famous with the yachting crowd. Movie stars, too. They'd all come out to fish and drink and gamble, I guess." Steven paused. She actually seemed interested. "We have a bunch of photos from the glory days, in the dining room and the bar. A couple of the pictures show Ernest Hemingway and Errol Flynn partying it up here, in fact."

"What happened to the hotel?" she asked.

"It started to go downhill from lack of business during the Second World War. The airport was built in the fifties to make the hotel more accessible, but it didn't make any difference. The place went out of business in the late sixties after a hurricane did a ton of damage. It was a total wreck when we bought the property."

"The one constant in life is change."

"That's true," he replied. "And my wife loved making changes that improved life. This property, as run-down as it was, suited her perfectly. It was just what she wanted. She had a vision for the place and supervised the project. We tore down the old hotel and built this. After that, she'd force me to hold staff meetings here a few times a year. Everyone would bring their families…" He found himself looking at the picture of Kei on his desk. Her dark eyes, the smile reminded him of happier days. "Everyone had a great time."

"American business, for most part, hasn't discovered the importance of finding a balance. I'm guilty of that, myself. We tend to work so hard until we burn out." Her voice softened. "Your wife is wise."

He'd tried to keep as much of it out of the news as he could. That's the way Kei would have wanted it.

"A very wise woman," he agreed. "But that too has changed."

"What do you mean?"

"My wife is dead, Dr. Mendes."

43

The television screen showed two political pundits, but only one was holding forth as Jay came out of the bathroom.

"...promising start for his campaign, but we're still nine months from the first presidential primary. A lot can happen. One big thing the senator has going for him is the solid campaign financing he's starting out with. Hersey's campaign has raised an estimated fifteen million dollars in the first three months of this year. Add that to the sixty million in the war chest from last year, and the early frontrunner is in terrific shape. Even more important, though, Hersey's campaign manager has made a point of getting the word out the senator has put up a hundred and thirty million dollars of his own money to set the stage. Major donors like to see that, Chris. Nothing like seeing a presidential candidate put his money where his mouth is. Even at this point in the race, they're clearly in great shape for the long h—"

"What are you watching?" Jay asked, padding across the marble tile into the sitting area.

"I don't know," Padma said with a smile. Cuddled

with the baby in the corner of the sofa, she was feeding him. "I turned it on just for the background noise."

"Why don't you sit on the patio outside, so you can enjoy the view?" he asked.

"I'm breast-feeding him," she said in shock. "I can't go out in public."

Jay laughed. He picked up the remote and turned off the television, then moved next to her on the sofa.

"And you shouldn't walk around in a towel. What happens if someone comes in?"

"The door is locked," he whispered, kissing her over the baby's head. "And nobody's coming in."

"This is an amazing place, Jay."

"And that's one amazing shower in there. Enough room for both of us, you know."

"We still have to wait two more weeks," she whispered to him. "But I guess *only* a shower wouldn't hurt."

He laughed and kissed her again. Trailing the back of his fingers across the soft skin of her neck and shoulder, he thought for the thousandth time how mad awesome it was having Padma and their baby here with him. The place was like something you'd see on a TV show. Tile floors throughout, with some kind of natural-fiber woven rugs here and there, a little kitchenette and a sitting area with a monster flat-screen. On top of that, they had two bedrooms with a crib already set up in one of them when they got here. And from their bedroom and the sitting area, French doors opened out onto a covered patio. From there, you could walk right across a cut grass lawn to the beach.

Already, Jay thought he'd died and gone to heaven.

Harsha made a noise as he ate. Jay placed a soft kiss on his head.

"Greedy little bugger he is, isn't he?"

Padma's laugh sounded like music in his ear. "Listen, you jealous beast, you'd better dress. You are supposed to meet the rest of them in that dining room at the main house for dinner."

"I hate to leave you alone here," he said.

"This is part of your work," she reminded him. "That fridge and freezer are packed with all kinds of good stuff to eat. Besides, the person who brought our luggage in said I can call in and order anything I want for dinner. There's a menu there on the counter. They run this place like a resort."

"Good, if you call for something, I won't feel too guilty."

"I'll think about it. You just go meet your coworkers," she told him.

This was the big night, Jay thought. He was dying to know what they wanted him to do.

"The other people in the van looked a lot older than us," he admitted.

"And so serious," she replied. "That guy in the front never said a word till we got here."

"Yeah, they all were…except for the sick girl." Jay sat forward and gazed at the empty TV screen. "I hope Mr. Big doesn't change his mind when he sees me."

"Why would he change his mind?" Padma told him. "Jay, baby, you're smart. Don't you forget that. You'll do great. I know they're lucky to have you."

"I'm the lucky one…because of you."

Jay stood up and started toward the bedroom. Before coming out to the island, she'd forced him to use the gift card and buy himself a pair of khakis and a few polo shirts.

"I think I'm going to check on Leah after you're gone," Padma called in to him. "I think they're in the place right next to ours."

Jay had been relieved to see someone else arrive with their family. At the same time, he'd felt bad about the wheelchair. "Do you know what's wrong with her?"

"She can walk. I saw that, but she's really weak. Her father probably will be with you, and I heard a nurse was going to be staying with her all the time. But maybe she could use more company."

"That will be really nice," he encouraged her.

Jay really liked the setup here. There were other people that Padma could talk to. She could take walks. The weather was great. If it worked out, he'd make more money at this gig than he would be working his entire life at the warehouse.

It was all right. He just hoped that they hadn't made a mistake and that he was qualified to do whatever it was they wanted him to do.

44

Wherever Ray was staying, it was clear to Alanna that he wasn't staying with her.

When she realized that his things hadn't been delivered to her cottage, Alanna couldn't decide if she was relieved or disappointed. She missed him—and they had so many things to talk out—but at the same time she knew she had to make her decision about staying or going in a rational fashion and without the distractions that their relationship entailed.

She tied her hair back quickly and frowned at her reflection in the mirror in the sitting area.

"Now you're thinking of your relationship as a distraction," she murmured to herself. "That's not a very good sign, Alanna Maria."

Going to the glass doors leading to the patio, she closed the blinds and went into the bedroom. Alanna hadn't bothered to unpack anything but her bathroom things and a change of clothes for dinner. She picked up her red cardigan sweater off the bed and went to close the blinds in that room, as well.

She paused, looking out at the moon, already ten degrees off the horizon. It was nearly full, an amber disk casting a thousand flecks of light on the water. If things were a little different, it would have been a very romantic image. She drew the blinds shut.

As Alanna headed for the door, she turned and looked around at the accommodations. Steven Galvin's people called this a cottage, but the square footage was greater than her apartment in California. She glanced at her laptop and frowned. She would have liked a chance to do some research on Steven Galvin, but she wasn't going to be late for dinner.

Outside, she draped the sweater over her shoulders. Alanna was glad she'd brought it along. The breeze off the ocean was cool. The pathway leading to the main house was well lit and took her to the edge of the marina. The water was lapping at the docks and the boats, but there didn't appear to be anyone staying in the boats themselves. From her outings with Ray, she knew that back home the marinas were a hub of social activity during the summers, at least. She glanced back at the other cottages and wondered which one Ray was staying in.

As she walked toward the main building, Alanna had to admit that she'd felt a huge sense of relief when she discovered Steven Galvin was the man behind the curtain. A decade ago, he was almost as well known as Bill Gates in American business. An absolute poster boy for success. What she knew about him was only headline material, of course, but all of that had been complimentary.

He was the quintessential self-made man. Instrumental in elevating a number of companies to Fortune 500 status, by the time he was fifty he was solidly entrenched in the who's who of the rich and powerful. And then, he'd simply retired early to spend time with his family and pursue his numerous philanthropic projects. While she hoped this project was one of those, she couldn't imagine why he'd need her for it.

Alanna couldn't recall much about Galvin's family except having a vague image of his wife in some business-publication photos. She was of Asian descent and extremely beautiful. Alanna thought how sad it was that she was dead.

As she thought about it more, she had a vague recollection of something about him in the newspapers in this past year or so. She had been—and still was—too consumed with the STEREO project to pay much attention to the real world, but there was something gnawing at her memory. Alanna wondered if it was his wife's death that she was thinking of.

From a pathway to her left, Alanna saw Leah's father coming toward the building. She considered going in, but then decided to wait for him. She was good at putting on the appearance of confidence and intelligence, but deep down her insecurities never went away. As a woman engineer operating in a man's profession, she'd learned early that it was always good to walk into a situation like this with another person. It was easier to deflect attention that way.

David Collier, realizing she was waiting, smiled as he approached her.

"Thanks for waiting," he said, coming up to her. "I hate going into these things alone."

"I was just thinking the same thing," she admitted.

"Quite a place, isn't it, Dr. Mendes?"

"It's beautiful. Please call me Alanna."

"Okay." He gestured toward the main building. "Shall we?"

She nodded. "So how does Leah like it?"

"The little imp has explored every inch of our unit. She likes it a lot. My only hope is that it rains outside every day that we're here."

She looked up at him, surprised.

"She has dialysis tubes protruding from her body," he explained. "Infection is a huge concern. She hasn't asked yet, but going swimming in the ocean is an absolute no-go. Even playing in the sand outside can have serious complications." His eyes met hers. "How do you tell a kid not to be a kid?"

Once again, Alanna was reminded how minute her problems in life were compared to what Leah and her father were facing.

"I'm sorry," she said, realizing as she said it that everyone probably said that to him. "If we get out of here early enough tonight, perhaps I could visit with your daughter and give her a crash course in how to play chess?"

She might as well have told him it was Christmas come early.

"That would be just great," he replied happily. "To be honest with you, she asked me if I would see if you wanted to come over. But I didn't want to impose."

David Collier had the signature marks of an executive—expensive sport jacket and designer tie, good looks, impeccable manners. He'd be the kind of person that Alanna assumed could get anything just by asking.

But one look in his face and you could see that life's strains were leaving their mark. Alanna recalled Leah saying that her mom had died of cancer.

They reached the door, and a young man in a white shirt and black pants opened the door for them as they approached.

Alanna realized that she might know more about who their employer was than David Collier did. They hadn't had a chance to discuss any of that, though, and it was too late now.

A young woman serving as the hostess greeted them inside. "Good evening, Dr. Mendes. Mr. Collier. Cocktails are being served in the library this evening," she told them in her lilting Bahamian accent. "Right this way, if you please."

Before they reached doors leading to the walkway to the library, the front door opened again and Jay Alexei came in. Immediately, he cast a nervous glance at David's sport jacket and tie.

Their hostess extended the same invitation to the young man.

Alanna was not very good at guessing ages, but she thought Jay looked very young and extremely nervous. He looked younger than the kids they hired right out of college. She remembered his wife and child.

"Hello, Jay," David greeted him warmly. "That is so nice of your wife to have dinner with Leah."

"Oh, sure…sure," he said, joining them.

Alanna saw the young man pull uneasily at the collar of his shirt.

"You look great," she told him quietly.

He looked at her, surprised, and then gave her a small nod of appreciation. The three of them followed the hostess to the library. This time, however, Steven Galvin wasn't going to make a grand entrance the way he'd done with Alanna. He was waiting for them.

She was glad to see the same bowled-over expression on David Collier's face when he recognized their host. Even Jay, as young as he looked, appeared to know the man who had arranged for them to come here. He was a little stunned, too.

Alanna looked around the library. She was disappointed to find no sign of Ray. Steven immediately introduced himself to the two men accompanying her and, after a cordial exchange, pointed them toward the bar.

"Please help yourselves at the bar over there, and to the hors d' oeuvres that we've laid out on the table over here. That fish spread on the right is a particular favorite of mine. It's made with fresh yellowfin tuna that we catch right here."

From their faces, she could see that David and Jay were both surprised that she'd already met Galvin. She looked at the others in the room. From the way everyone was conversing, it appeared that they were either employees of Steven's or people who'd worked for him before. There were men and women of varying ages.

"Alanna," Steven said, touching her arm as the other two moved off. "Are your living arrangements satisfactory?"

"Yes, absolutely. Everything is lovely," she told him, looking around the room again. "Was my friend, Ray Savoy, invited to this gathering, as well?"

She had to know, and if there was one person who knew the answer, it had to be Galvin.

"Yes, of course," he said, looking past her. "But he's not here."

She nodded. The hostess came up from behind her.

"Pardon me, Steven. May I have a word, sir."

"Sure." He looked back at Alanna. "Excuse me for a moment."

As he walked away, she turned around to find David Collier, two glasses of wine in hand, standing next to her.

"White wine okay?"

"Sure, thanks," she said, taking the glass.

David nodded toward their host's back. "You knew about him?"

"I only found out this afternoon," she told him. "When we got back from the airport. I was really surprised."

"Did you have a guy named Hank Diarte interview you for the position?" he asked.

"I had two people interview me," she told him. It was nice to talk to someone who admitted being as confused as she was. "One of them was Diarte. The other was Lyons."

"I don't see any sign of Diarte."

"I didn't see Lyons, either," she told him. "I guess since we're here, their job is done."

Galvin was speaking to Jay Alexei. If Alanna thought the young man was nervous before, he showed no sign of it now. She figured, like herself, adrenaline rush took over in the situations that really mattered.

"You wanted to leave here today," Collier continued. "Would you mind my asking why?"

Alanna looked toward the door again. No sign of Ray. She didn't think she was ready to confess to someone she'd only met today about her doubts with her fiancé.

"It was something personal," she said quietly, taking a sip of her wine.

"I saw your friend leave this afternoon," David said casually. "About an hour after we arrived."

Alanna looked up at him in surprise. "My friend?"

"I thought he was your friend. I might be wrong. I thought you two were arguing at the airport. He sat in front in the van on the ride over here. His name was… Roy…Ray…"

"Ray Savoy," she told him. "We…we came here together. You said you saw him leave?"

"On one of the powerboats."

"Oh." She thought about that a moment. "Maybe he was going on a sightseeing tour. He likes boats… fishing."

"Maybe," David said quietly. "But I saw them load his luggage onto the boat."

45

Dundalk, Ireland

The people working at the Hughes & Hughes Bookstore were definitely going out of their way to be accommodating, but Amber Hersey knew that nothing short of going on the street with a lasso would bring people in. Other than selling a book to the store manager and one of the employees, they hadn't had a single customer. Of course, the teeming rain might not be helping.

The whole tour was ridiculous, though, and she knew it.

She was a twenty-four-year-old American graduate student. True, she'd written a reasonably successful children's book. Still, without stressing her brain too much, Amber could list ten reasons why she shouldn't be here. But it was even easier to list ten reasons why she *was* here, after all.

First, she was the daughter of a longtime senator from Pennsylvania and the current presidential front-runner. That was why her book had been published by a major New York publisher in the first place.

Second, she was the daughter of a longtime senator from Pennsylvania and the current presidential front-runner. That was the reason for this international book tour.

Third, she was the daughter of a longtime senator from Pennsylvania and the current presidential front-runner. That was why everywhere she went, her picture showed up in the local papers.

Real authors couldn't buy this kind of publicity with any amount of money, but the truth was that the press coverage of an American girl with one book out just wasn't going to help sell books in a rainy, gray Irish town…unless she was Lindsay Lohan or Paris Hilton.

But that wasn't the point.

Amber knew that the campaign publicity machinery was getting great, positive images to use as a sidebar for her father's press releases.

When Amber's cell phone rang, she decided not to bother remembering any other reasons that she was sitting here talking to herself.

Her father was on the phone. Impeccable timing.

"Well, how's the grand tour going?" he asked.

"This was a mistake, Dad," Amber said in a tone hushed enough not to hurt the store manager's feelings.

"No customers?" he asked.

"Zip," she replied. "Once again, another country, another city, another beautiful and charming bookstore, and zip, zip, zip in book sales. Has the publisher called looking for the advance back?"

"No. That money is yours to keep."

"I know, Dad. I'm kidding…sort of."

"Listen, honey. You aren't really there to sell books,"

her father said in an upbeat tone. "You're there to travel, to have a good time."

"Oh, yeah! How could I forget?" Amber said quietly, looking toward the front of the store, where one of her escorts was sitting and reading an Irish-names book. "It's *such* a good time traveling with two Secret Service agents who have the combined personality of a dried lentil. I don't think I could stand having any more fun."

"Why don't you call one of your friends and have them meet you in Ireland for the weekend. I'll even spring for it," he offered.

"I have no friends, Dad. None that like me enough to hop on a plane and come to Ireland for a weekend and sit in a bookstore with me."

She didn't want to complain about her mother backing out on the trip. These two found enough faults with each other without any extra help from her. Amber knew things would have been a lot different if her mother had come. They'd have had their arguments and fights, but she'd also have had someone to talk to and go sightseeing and shopping with.

"Well, after this, you've just got London and then home, right?"

"And then, next summer, all those children's book-stores in the U.S.," she reminded him.

"Hey, if you don't want to do that tour, I'm sure you could get out of it."

She sat back in the chair, realizing what she was doing. She was bored out of her mind, but that wasn't her father's fault. Nobody had forced her to try her hand at writing a children's book. She'd enjoyed it. And going on a book tour had sounded great to her, at least in theory. But Paul Hersey was too classy a father to remind her of any of that.

"I'm sorry, Dad," she told him.

"Sorry for what?"

"For whining like a three-year-old," she admitted. "Actually, that'll be my next book. A whiny three-year-old who moves into the White House when no one is looking. I'll name the character after myself, Amber. How does that sound?"

His laughter coming through the phone made her smile. "Honey, you can always cut the trip short and come home."

Amber had thought about that herself. It was nice to get this kind of encouragement, too.

The chimes above the front door tinkled as a customer entered. The tall man stepped inside and with him came the smell of rain and wet wool.

"I think the real Ireland just came in."

As she talked, the man peeled a wool hat off his head and curly brown hair tumbled down to his shoulders. He nodded to the Secret Service agent sitting by the door, and then turned and smiled in her direction.

The reaction was immediate. Amber felt a swell of heat wash right down into her belly. Ireland just got a lot more interesting.

"Sorry, Dad. I have to go."

"What is it?"

"I might have a customer," she said, hoping.

46

There was nothing to keep her here, but she'd stayed.

Around eight-fifteen, Alanna stopped looking for him. Ray never showed up during the cocktail hour, nor was he here for dinner. Alanna noticed the extra setting at the dining-room table that was removed after everyone sat down.

She did find it curious that Steven Galvin didn't know that her fiancé had left. Maybe he did, she thought, but didn't want to be the one bearing bad news.

In any event, she was determined to enjoy the night in a civilized manner. No matter what was going on with Ray, Alanna had decided that she was leaving tomorrow morning on the first available flight.

Overhearing the conversation at dinner, she learned that Galvin had other employees, aside from the three arriving today, who had been moved down here for the short duration of this project. Some talked about their families being here with them. Everyone appeared to be staying on the property.

After dinner, she and David and Jay were led back to the library. The long table had been cleared of the hors d'oeuvres and the room was spotless. Four chairs had been carefully spaced around the table, she noticed, with enough distance between one person and the next. Galvin clearly didn't want anyone feeling crowded. He took his seat on one side of the table where his open laptop sat, and gestured for everyone to sit down.

"I know each one of you is anxious to learn why you're here, what this mysterious job is that requires your particular talents or knowledge." He made eye contact with everyone at the table. "And I'm sure you have dozens of other questions that you have been waiting to ask."

Alanna was relieved that Galvin started right away. She didn't need any more cocktails or dinners or general schmoozing. He paused and played around a couple of seconds with whatever file he'd brought up on his laptop. She guessed he'd be making a presentation.

"I know that at least one of you is still not committed to staying," he continued without looking up. "That's fine. I appreciate the time you're all giving me to present my offer. There."

He pulled a remote from his pocket and pressed a button on it, causing a projector screen to descend from the ceiling by the bookcase at the end of the table. At the same time a small overhead panel opened and a projector appeared.

"I'll go through the background of this project and my proposal and how the expertise each of you possesses fits into my plans. You are welcome to ask any questions that you wish at anytime throughout or at the end of my presentation. I mean that—please feel free to interrupt me at any time."

He looked around the room, made eye contact with every one.

"The only thing that I ask of you is that if you choose not to participate in this project, you will honor my request of confidentiality. This is extremely important to me."

Alanna wasn't imagining it. Galvin was looking only at her now.

She nodded. She was almost certain that she wouldn't be given the opportunity to walk away if the project involved some major security violation. She couldn't imagine someone with Galvin's money and influence and reputation being involved with something illegal anyway.

Using the remote, he dimmed the lights in the room and sat back in his chair.

If she was looking for some 3-D, high-tech, attention-grabbing opener, what came up on the screen wasn't it.

A baby picture. A bald-headed, chubby little baby lying on his stomach and wearing only a diaper.

"My son," he started, his voice husky. "Nathan Robert Galvin, born September 7, 1985."

It was a timed slide-show presentation. The next picture showed Nathan as a toddler sitting on Steven's shoulders. Next to them stood a stunning young Asian-featured woman.

"Nathan, age two and half," Steven continued, his voice clear now. "And this is my late wife, Kei. This picture was taken at the Grand Canyon, during the good old days when I used to actually take time away from work and go on vacation with my family."

The slide show continued, showing Nathan on his fourth birthday, blowing out candles on a cake, but Steven wasn't looking at the screen anymore.

"I haven't lost my mind and forgotten why you're here. I promise to get to the point very shortly," he told them. "The only reason I've started with Nathan's pictures is to have you understand the trigger behind what I am going to ask you later to do."

He looked at Jay. "You are a new father, Mr. Alexei."

Jay nodded.

"And you, Mr. Collier. I know you'll go to the ends of the earth to be there for your daughter."

"That's true," David said cautiously.

"You both know how far a parent will go to protect their child."

Both men nodded.

Alanna felt suddenly defensive that Galvin thought she might not have that understanding. Her defensiveness quickly gave way to sadness; the truth was, she did lack such love from a parent in her life. Her grandmother had been her only support. She'd had no mother or father to go to the "ends of the earth," as Steven put it. At the same time, she knew deep inside that she *was* capable of having such strong emotions toward another human being—especially one who depended on her.

She'd come here.

The photos now showed Nathan graduating from high school. The proud parents were in some of the photos. He'd become a very handsome young man, a combination of both of them in looks. The pictures following it were of the young man working on a roof, hammer in hand, doing some kind of community-service project. Nathan was getting older before their eyes.

"There comes a time in every parent's life when you have to let go. As painful as it is, you have to cut the ties and let your son or daughter float free and start that adult chapter of his or her own life. That time came for me and Kei when Nathan graduated from Georgetown."

The next few slides showed the young man's college graduation. Again, the proud, smiling parents.

"He had no interest in engineering or going into the line of business that I was in. Nathan's one love was travel, seeing the world. So when he told us that he planned to spend some time traveling, we did the only thing we could. We let our only child go."

A picture of Nathan came up that was obviously taken at an airport. Baseball cap, a backpack on one shoulder, wearing a T-shirt and jeans. Unlike the others, the photo didn't advance. It remained on the screen.

"This was the last time Kei and I saw our son," he said in a low voice.

Alanna looked at Galvin. He was staring at the picture. This might have been what she couldn't remember from the headlines before. He'd lost his son and then his wife. No one said anything. The air in the room had become scarce.

"Nathan Robert Galvin, age twenty-three, was kidnapped from Kapali Carsi, the Grand Bazaar in Istanbul, thirteen months ago," Steven announced.

Shivering involuntarily, Alanna sat straighter in her chair. She'd never expected to hear that.

"Five weeks later, we were told that we needed to

make the arrangements to bring Nathan's dead body home," Steven said unsteadily. "Twenty days after Nathan's funeral, my wife Kei took her own life, deliberately overdosing on prescription antidepressants and sleeping pills. She couldn't stand the pain anymore."

They were all frozen at the table. Alanna didn't know how to respond. She didn't think any of them knew. They were here because of what had happened to Nathan.

The picture of Nathan remained on the screen. Steven raised the lights and turned to them. "I'm sorry. I guess I caught all of you by surprise."

"The ones…" Jay started hesitantly. "The ones who kidnapped your son…were they caught?"

"No," Steven answered. "Unfortunately, the Istanbul police didn't pursue the criminals as vigorously as they could have. Even Interpol failed to act as we…as I believe they should have. There were no arrests, not even fake arrests for our sake. In fact, as to the cause of Nathan's death, the final reports that were made public were so vague that no individual or groups could be held responsible for it."

"Why your son?" David asked. "Why kidnap a tourist?"

Steven Galvin looked away from them, focusing on the faded image of his son.

"Nathan was in the wrong place at the wrong time," Galvin explained. "I was later told by the U.S. government that they believe the kidnappers thought him to be a CIA operative."

To have the kind of wealth these people possess and to be so helpless. She couldn't imagine it.

"I hope you don't mind me asking, Steven," Alanna said gently. "But did you try to offer money for his return?"

He nodded. "We tried. I used every contact I had in Washington, overseas, in Turkey. I was willing to pay any amount, but it was too late. The communications were botched. We were never able to establish a clear dialogue with the kidnappers."

Silence settled again in the room. Nothing could take away the pain that this man was living with. He'd lost two people that he loved. Alanna remembered how she felt last fall when she thought Ray had died in the boating accident. She'd shut down, mentally and physically. She couldn't remember a blacker period in her life. But Ray's accident had been a setup. That nightmare had been staged.

Alanna's gaze wandered, coming to rest on David. She thought he must understand better than anyone else in this room what Galvin had gone through. His own wife was dead. His daughter had a potentially terminal illness.

"Well…there you are," Steven told them. He still didn't seem to have his emotions completely under control. He shut off the photo of his son. Alanna watched the screen and the projector disappear into the ceiling.

"I don't need to describe to you the anguish I went through over Nathan's and Kei's deaths," he said, clearing his throat. "But I'm the one who is left. And it hasn't taken me too long to figure out what I have to do."

"If I were you," Jay said quietly, "I'd be looking for revenge."

The statement rang true. She could easily see herself angry enough to want an eye for an eye in a situation like that. But how?

"I wanted revenge more than anything else," Steven agreed. "But I didn't have the names or faces of the animals that kidnapped and killed my son. So I hired detectives. I worked with agents and former agents of the U.S. government. I went to Istanbul myself, repeatedly. I retained the services of an international security outfit that looks after private contractors working in the Middle East. I wanted information. Anything they could give me."

"And did you have any success?" Alanna asked.

He nodded. "Yes. I was able to discover the terrorists who kidnapped Nathan were operating under an umbrella organization that funded them. They were definitely not just run-of-the-mill kidnappers, grabbing a tourist. That much was true."

Alanna was familiar enough through the news of the constant battle that western governments had been waging with such organizations. They funded terror. And they seem impossible to shut down.

"Al Qaida?" Jay asked.

"Not exactly."

"How large is this umbrella organization?" David asked.

"I can't tell you. They are an amorphous, shadowy group. But they seem to have a steady stream of money, and as long as the funds are there to support them, the terrorist activities they fund continue." Steven looked at each one of them in turn. "And that's why I invited a scientist, a banker and a computer security specialist to join me in this battle. I don't intend for you to help me go after individuals. I want to dry up the well. My plan is to wipe them out the only way I know. I want to ruin them all financially."

Alanna didn't think it was exactly the right moment to mention that something like that was impossible. Western governments had been freezing assets and following money trails for years. They'd even tried isolating entire nations, like Cuba and Iran, just for that purpose.

She noticed Jay shifting uncomfortably in his seat. Finally, he sat forward.

"Look, Mr. Galvin. I honestly feel for you," the young man said. "But you are well aware of my background. I doubt Dr. Mendes or Mr. Collier know it, but I spent two and half years in prison for hacking into a system that I shouldn't have. I have a family now. I'd prefer…I'll do anything to help you, but at the same time, I won't go back to prison if I can help it. I don't want to break any laws."

So their computer security specialist was a hacker, Alanna thought. She couldn't help but wonder if he'd been twelve years old when he'd gone to prison.

"I perfectly understand your concern, Jay," Galvin said calmly. "And Mr. Collier and Dr. Mendes haven't said it yet, but I think it's safe to assume that neither of them would feel comfortable participating in anything that they would consider illegal."

She was glad Steven said what was on her mind.

"My proposal *bends* but doesn't break U.S. laws, though to make you all more comfortable about it, I've based the operation here, offshore." Steven paused before continuing. "But I'm not playing softball, either. We're going after these killers in ways that governments can't. We aren't going to simply freeze assets. My plan is to drain the liquid assets of this organization altogether. I want to cut them off without a rial."

"You could be talking about hundreds of millions, maybe even billions of dollars. Transfers of amounts that large won't go unnoticed, by the people losing it or the banks charged with protecting it," David said, not trying to keep his skepticism out of his voice. "And there have to be recipient accounts that the money gets transferred to."

"Exactly. My suggestion is that the recipient accounts be a few thousand charity organizations that we've been covertly lining up. The transfer will be direct…no middleman, no fingerprints. On the books, it must only look as if they made the donations themselves."

"Won't we be getting these smaller charity groups in trouble by having them receive money from a terrorist organization?" Alanna asked.

"No," Steven answered her. "These people have hidden their money in thirty-seven Dubai accounts that we have identified. The accounts have been created with smoke screen on top of smoke screen. Finding them has been no small feat, and it's already cost me a well-spent fortune. But these have been set up in a way that no government out there has been able to touch them…first of all, because the banking concerns we're focusing on are based in Dubai; and second of all, because they cannot be linked directly to the terrorist activity we know they're funding. In the end, though, this money will go where it can do a lot of good."

"I don't mean to sound like some gutless geek, Mr.

Galvin, but…but I'm thinking there could be some pretty powerful people behind this," Jay put in. "Like maybe a dictator or two—or at least some members of royal families. I have to be straight with you. Those guys scare me more than any prison term. They'll come after our…I mean, I would be worried about my family."

Galvin looked up at the bookcase where the images of his son and his wife had been projected. He looked back at Jay and nodded grimly.

"I understand your concerns. There's nothing gutless in that," Galvin told him. "But you all know who I am and what I've done in my life. I am not a person to leave the planning of a project half done. I've always been a details guy. Once I explain the plan to you all, you'll see that there will be no fingerprints. Nothing will tie us to those accounts or to what we do. In fact, that is exactly where you and Mr. Collier fit in."

"So, I won't exactly be auditing accounts, as Mr. Lyons told me," David said in a low voice.

"No, Mr. Collier. I couldn't—"

"It doesn't matter where we are, offshore or on Mars, Mr. Galvin," David interrupted. "In my mind, we are still breaking the law. And operating outside of the law is a huge concern to me. I've spent more years than I care to count fighting legal battles to clear my name of false accusations. Something like this could destroy the little ground I've gained. Never mind that it could put me behind bars, where I would be no good to my daughter."

"The same thing I told Mr. Alexei applies to you." Galvin was looking hard at David. "I believe the ethical…rightness…of the project speaks for itself.

Once you hear the specifics, you'll see that there's absolutely no danger of your being tied to this project. Think of the arrangements that were made directly by my people in Germany. I wouldn't go through all of that if I thought you'd be locked away and unable to enjoy the results of it."

Alanna had no idea what the arrangements were that Galvin had made for David. Whatever it was, though, it didn't need further explanation, for David became silent. She could see that Galvin held both of these men on a string; a gentle tug was all it took to put David in a more amenable position.

"Will you explain some of the specifics of your project to us tonight?" Jay asked, breaking the silence that had fallen on the room.

"That's certainly a possibility." Galvin nodded. "But before we get to any of those specifics, you should know that nothing will go ahead unless we can convince Dr. Mendes here to join us."

He turned to Alanna.

"So what can we do to convince you to come along?"

47

Dundalk, Ireland

"We barely made it here," she said breathlessly, her head dropping back against her hotel-room door.

Just as the book signing ended, the rain had stopped. Amber hardly noticed the weather, however, as she and Mick walked along the wet streets. And she had definitely no longer been thinking of book sales.

The invitation was to go together to a quaint pub a few streets over called the Beerkeeper. She'd heard they served a hundred different kinds of beers. Instead, as they walked, he'd whispered a few words in Gaelic into her ear, and Amber had physically steered him in another direction. With the Secret Service trailing in the car furnished by the Irish government, the two had nearly run to the tired little hotel where she was staying.

They'd never bothered to take their clothes off. They'd never made it to the bedroom. He'd barely had time to slip on the condom. And then he'd taken her right there against the door of the suite. Their lovemaking had been explosive.

Now, he carefully lifted her, disengaging his body from hers and setting her feet on the floor. She laid her head against his chest.

"I can't believe we did this," she said with a laugh. "I'm not usually so easy. I've always made it a rule never to have sex with someone on the first date. But this wasn't even a date, was it? I think we may have shocked my escorts."

"Hush, woman," he whispered against her mouth. He kissed her tenderly on the lips. "Is that the bathroom?"

"Ask it in Gaelic," she said, hoping to get lost in his accent again and forget the foolishness of her actions.

He smiled. *"Cá bhfuil an seomra folctha?"*

She let out a heavy sigh. He was absolutely gorgeous. "That's the door to the bedroom. The bathroom is in on the right."

Amber watched him pull up his jeans. He didn't bother to zip them. He picked up his hat and jacket from the floor and threw them onto a nearby sofa and disappeared into the bedroom.

She looked down at herself. Her winter jacket was half off her shoulders. Her black wool dress was twisted around her waist. Her thong was still dangling around the ankle of her boots.

"This would be a great story for the newspapers," she whispered to herself, shaking her head and putting her underwear—for want of a better place—in her jacket pocket. Slipping the jacket off, she straightened her dress. "He is gorgeous, though."

He was in the bathroom, so she hurried to the sink in the little kitchenette off the living room to clean up.

She didn't even know his last name. His first name was Mick, and he was a college student in Belfast. He'd approached her table, given her that heart-melting smile and asked her in that accent, "Didn't I see your picture in the paper?" That was all it took. Amber had been ready to jump him right there.

Standing at the counter, she pulled off her boots. She still couldn't believe what she'd done. Her problem was that it had been too long since she'd gone out with anyone. She'd had her wild days, of course, during high school and college, but she just wasn't into hooking up so much anymore. Of course, you couldn't tell by the way she'd acted tonight. She was glad he'd had the sense to use a condom. God knows, *she* wasn't thinking about it.

The breath caught in her chest when she saw him come out of her bedroom.

"You seem to have lost your clothes," she announced in case he didn't know.

He came around the counter into the kitchen. She backed into the corner.

"What did you have in mind?" Her eyes moved down his body, and she almost laughed at the ridiculousness of the question.

"Well, lass. I just thought maybe we'd fock some more." He pulled her dress up and over her head, and dropped it on the counter.

She reached around to undo her bra. He wasn't much into taking his time—not that she minded. He lifted her up and sat her on the counter.

"That sounds a bit rough, Mick. Can you say it in Gaelic?"

He laughed, pulling her to him.

"Woman, fock is fock...*mo mhúirnín bán.*"

48

There was nothing like being put on the spot.

As she'd listened to Steven Galvin talk, Alanna had realized she was putting her earlier decision of leaving on the first flight on hold, but only for the time being. And now, every eye in the room was on her.

"I just can't commit to staying until I know more about the project," she said. "What do I have to offer?"

"The STEREO satellites," Galvin told her.

Alanna could already tell she wasn't going to like this. The others might be able to hide their activity, but she was the owner of the STEREO mission. She'd be the first person suspected if anything malfunctioned.

"Those satellites provide an important service to the world. I won't do anything that compromises the success of that mission."

He nodded. "I wouldn't expect you to."

"Then how can I help?" she asked.

"There are test cycles that you personally schedule," Galvin told her. He glanced at David and Jay. "To bring these gentlemen up to speed, the test cycles are a kind of emergency-response system. Isn't that right? They assure that everything functions as it should."

This was confidential information, but Alanna wasn't going to bother to ask how he knew so much. Government clearances didn't appear to apply to this man.

David broke in. "Actually, I don't know anything about this STEREO mission."

Jay answered for Galvin. "Two satellites were launched into orbit around the earth. They monitor solar storms and warn us when we're going to be hit by the energy. Keeps us from having unexpected power disruptions."

"That's a very accurate description," Steven said. Alanna was impressed by the young man, as well.

"So, what about the tests?" she asked Galvin.

"At the onset of any of these tests, you have a highly secure list of recipients that get communications from you, indicating that this is only a test and that no emergency backup needs to be activated."

Once again, this was true. Alanna didn't think he needed confirmation that he was right.

"What I am asking you to do is to schedule a test cycle to fall within our desired work window. Then, I want you to activate that communication that this is only a test. What Jay will do is to make sure that some of the key contacts on your communication list have, well, a delay in receiving your message."

"You want them to activate their backup system," Alanna asked.

"Exactly," Steven replied. "I already know that this portion of the switch over is automatic in the institutions we'll be targeting. Because of their international nature, the banks we are interested in can't afford to lose time looking for an administrator to make a decision. They have taken the human delay out of the procedure. Also, they don't like the risk of power-grid structures going down in waves, so they have configured their response to shut down ahead of the blackout. They power up in their own security mode."

Jay spoke up again. "So, if they don't receive word that the signal is actually a test signal, their computers automatically reconfigure the security coverage as they activate the switch over to the secondary power source."

"That's right."

Alanna shook her head. "But there should be no difference between the security coverage when the backup power source is activated. I don't understand what you hope to gain."

"One minute and twenty-three seconds. Eighty-three seconds total. With the banks that we are interested in, that is the dead time between the power down and power up in the switch-over. We have the eighty-three seconds to empty the accounts."

Alanna looked at him. She still didn't understand how, during those eighty-three seconds, they could gain access to those accounts. But that wasn't her area of expertise. That was why David and Jay were here.

"When this is over, you will have done nothing wrong," Galvin told her. "You will have followed every step of the procedure as it's done month after month."

"Except that some people won't get the communication," Alanna reminded him.

"They will get it, but late. And the reason for that won't be because of any error you make. The problem will be a hiccup in their mainframe. The timing of your signal will coincide with a barrage of attacks on their sites, flooding them with traffic from botnets."

It was David's turn to ask. "What are botnets?"

"Thousands of PCs unwittingly hijacked with hidden software," Jay told him.

"But I will know I've done something wrong," she said.

"In what we are trying to do, how does the word *wrong* apply?" Galvin asked philosophically. "We will be taking money out of the accounts of those who fund terrorist activities around the world. That isn't wrong. We are giving that money to a large number of organizations whose sole goal is to help people in need. That isn't wrong, either. We're not robbing anyone of their lifesavings. We're taking money away from those who use it without consequence to themselves to hurt others. There is no legal authority that can act against these people, Alanna. They have successfully insulated themselves within a cocoon of evil and international finance. But we're not going to let them continue. This is a Robin Hood project…but with an edge."

Put that way, Alanna felt like an unfeeling robot. An inflexible idiot who followed orders and never stepped out of line.

"I have to think this through," she said. "I can't commit to anything like this until I can consider everything that is involved from my end."

"I would have expected nothing less from you," he said politely. "Is it safe for me to assume that you will stay on the island until you've made your decision?"

She nodded. "I shouldn't take too long. And I'm sure I'll have questions for you as soon as I walk out of here."

"I'm available twenty-four hours a day to you. Just pick up your phone or come over here or tell me where to meet you. Whatever. I'm available."

She felt funny sitting here. It appeared that the explanation portion was over, at least until she'd given them her decision.

"Then I think I'll go back to my room."

The three men stood up. She was surprised and touched, especially by Jay. She didn't believe his age group knew anything of old-fashioned courtesy. Alanna stopped at the door and turned to Galvin.

"Oh, I already have a question."

He nodded encouragingly.

"What happens to the job offers you've made Jay and David if I decide not to participate in the project?"

"I'd prefer not to discuss their situations with you, if you don't mind."

"But you said yourself that my input is key," she reminded him.

Steven looked steadily into her eyes. "A decision on your part not to participate would seriously jeopardize moving ahead with the project."

"Right," she said. "That's what I thought."

Alanna didn't have to look at the two men to know how devastating that decision could be in their lives. Just as Ray's situation mattered to her, she had a feeling Steven Galvin had chosen his candidates based on their degree of desperation.

"I'll let you know," she told him, walking out.

49

Dundalk, Ireland

Amber heard the door in the other room close. She sat up in bed, still groggy. The bedside clock read 3:23 a.m. She looked over her shoulder at the other side of the bed. He was gone.

"Mick?" she called, getting out of bed. There was no answer.

The hotel room was cold. She pulled the blanket off the bed and wrapped it around her naked body. From the light spilling in the window, she could see that the bathroom door was open.

She turned on the bedside light. His clothes were gone.

"Mick," she called out, still hoping. She went into the empty bathroom and turned on the light. Her reflection surprised her. She looked happy and relaxed. She wasn't a novice at sex. She'd had half a dozen boyfriends over the years. Not one of those relationships, though—even at their best—had approached what she'd felt with him. Tonight had been amazing.

She walked into the living room and turned on the light there, too. His jacket and hat were gone, too.

"I sure hope you left me a note." Amber looked around on the counters and in the living room. It was as if he'd never been here. Nothing had been left of him but the empty wrappers from the fish and chips they'd ordered from room service.

She sank onto the sofa and slapped her hand on the cushion. She didn't even know his last name. She had no phone number. And how many university students in Belfast were named Mick? She could have cried just thinking about it. They hadn't run into anyone after leaving the bookstore. There was no one she could ask who might know him. She'd waved off the Secret Service agents when they reached her hotel. She hadn't even given them a chance to learn anything about him.

Amber heard her cell phone ring. She looked around, remembering that her phone was still in her bag. She padded across the room to the counter where she'd left it.

She turned on the light over the counter and looked inside her bag. Her cell phone stopped ringing. She froze, realizing that her wallet was open. She took it out and saw the cash that had been in there yesterday was gone.

There hadn't been much in there. Ten or twelve Euros, maybe…if that. She checked her credit cards. They were all there. Her passport was still in the pocket. He'd just taken a few paltry euros. What a fool she was.

The cell phone began to ring again.

"Are you okay?" he asked when she answered. It was her father.

"Why wouldn't I be?" she asked.

"I just talked to one of the agents…and—"

"What are you doing, spying on me?" She cut him short. Her sadness about Mick's silent departure turned immediately to anger. She figured Mick's exit would have been noticed by the Secret Service, but having the news reach her father so quickly was ridiculous.

"Amber, there's a reason why those men travel with you," he said reasonably.

"Yes, so you can call them in the middle of night and find out who I hang out with and—"

"Listen to me. A security bulletin came through tonight. You could be in danger there. I want you to cut your trip short and come home. If you've got a pencil, I'll give you the flight arrangements we've made."

Amber said nothing. From her father's committee work, she knew that the State Department and Homeland Security put out security bulletins every day. No, it wasn't that. Her father was telling her this because he knew about her spending the night with an Irish stud who had left her in the middle of the night. He was trying to give her an out.

"Okay," she said, stabbing at a tear on her cheek as she fished a pen out of her bag. "Okay, shoot."

50

The last thing David Collier expected when he returned to his cottage was to find Leah and Alanna sitting on the patio playing chess.

When Alanna had left the conference room, he'd wanted more than anything else to follow her and explain how this job meant the difference between life and death for Leah. But he couldn't do it. As much as he wanted to, he couldn't put pressure like that on another person.

He had his own reservations about doing this job. Through thick and thin, no matter how far down his luck had taken them, he'd stayed on the right side of the law. But he had no choice here. The little that Galvin had said in response to David's concern had spelled it out clearly to him. Whether they were operating in a gray area of the law or not, David would go along or the arrangements in Germany would disappear.

Each one of them had his or her own problems. Those problems—or their solution—seemed to be the driving force that had brought them to this island. He didn't know what Alanna's crises were, but she had to decide on her own.

"She's been very busy tonight," the nurse explained

as he came in. The woman told him about Leah's dialysis and the dinner she'd had afterward with Padma Alexei and her baby. "Considering the hours of travel on top of it, she's probably asleep outside and only propped up with pillows."

"Her mouth is moving, so she must be awake," David told the nurse.

He thanked her and sent her off for the night. He'd already told them that, aside from setting up and administering the dialysis, they would only need to be on call to look after Leah when he was working. Or unless there was some emergency.

He went out through the glass door into the patio and both of them looked up, surprised to see him.

"Daddy, you're back," Leah said excitedly.

There were pillows around her, a blanket draped over her shoulders.

"Aren't you two cold out here?" he asked.

"No, it feels good," Leah replied. "The ocean smells so salty."

From the way Alanna had her arms crossed, she definitely looked cold. She looked up at him and smiled. "Actually, it feels very good."

He shook his head in disbelief and went back inside, got another blanket and came out. He draped this one around Alanna's shoulders.

"I thought you had a lot of work to do tonight," he asked her directly.

"I'm working right now."

"Is teaching me how to play chess hard work?" Leah asked.

"Teaching you was no trouble," Alanna answered. "But beating you is very hard work."

The giggle from the eight-year-old made David smile. She knocked down one of Alanna's pawns. "Check."

There was only a handful of pieces left on the board.

"This is interesting, Dr. Mendes. I didn't take you as the kind of player who would allow an opponent to go past five or six moves."

Alanna made a move. She looked up at him. "I tried to teach her finesse chess. That way, I could have checkmated her just as you say. But your daughter, curiously, enjoys playing a more bloody game. So we have a killing field here, as you can see."

David pulled a seat close to the table and sat down, watching them.

"This is a really fun game, Daddy," Leah told him. "Do you remember how to play?"

"I think I do," he said. David realized that Alanna had set her level of playing to that of his daughter. Leah made a move that put her queen in jeopardy. Rather than taking the queen, she told her about it and had Leah replay the move.

"Softie," he said to her.

"No, nice person," Leah corrected. "She is teaching me, Daddy. *Teaching me.*"

"Softie," he repeated when the next move put Alanna in a checkmate position.

"A smart player always lets them win the first time, so they want to play again," Alanna told him. "Now, tomorrow we'll play for money."

"Cool," Leah said excitedly. "Daddy, how about if you and I play now?"

"Leah, how about it's two hours after your bedtime now?"

The eight-year-old let out a frustrated sigh. "Rules, rules, rules."

"You got that right, young woman."

He got up to get the wheelchair. Leah stopped him.

"I don't need it. I want to walk." She slowly pushed herself to her feet.

David watched her every move, staying close enough to give her a hand if she needed it. He was surprised when his daughter opened her arms to get a hug from her playmate. Alanna hesitated for a second, but then she had the young girl in an affectionate embrace.

"Can we play again tomorrow night?" Leah asked.

"You can count on it." She folded the blanket that he'd put around her shoulders.

David thought that sounded too good to be true. He didn't want to ask in front of Leah, though.

"I should head out."

"Would you mind sticking around for just a couple of minutes?" he asked. "I have something work-related to ask you."

She nodded, understanding. David walked with Leah to the bathroom.

"I can brush my own teeth, Daddy," she reminded him when he hovered in the doorway. "I can change and get into bed by myself, too."

"I'm worried you did too much today. With all the travel and…"

"I feel great." She smiled. "I haven't felt this good in a long time."

He kissed her forehead, believing what she said. Emotionally, this was the happiest he'd seen her in a very long time.

"Go," she ordered. "I can get to bed all by myself."

"But you can't tuck yourself in and kiss yourself good-night," he reminded her. "I'll be back in five minutes."

"Daddy…?"

"Yup?" He turned around.

"Thanks for bringing me with you," Leah said. "Today was very cool."

He smiled. "You're welcome."

Alanna was waiting for him on the patio. She had straightened the pillows where Leah sat and moved the wheelchair inside the door. He didn't want Leah to hear their conversation, so he closed the door behind him.

"Have you made a decision?"

She nodded. "I'm staying."

"You didn't spend much time thinking about it," he told her.

"Leah told me they're growing her a new kidney in Germany," she said softly.

"You shouldn't make a decision this important based on what's best for Leah and me or Jay and his family."

"And why not?" she asked. "I can't think of a better reason."

"Alanna…I…"

She shook her head. "Please don't say anything. Don't

try to talk me out of it. You have a very special daughter. And this job will be good for me. It's about time I crossed the line for the right reasons. Good night, David."

51

Alanna unpacked her suitcases, took a shower and put on comfortable sweats. She'd made up her mind. She was staying. She had to let Galvin know about her decision. But first she had to clear the uncertainty that was dogging her. It was half past midnight when she called him. Steven himself answered.

"I need to talk to you," she told him. "Can I come over now?"

"Absolutely." There was no hesitation in his answer.

He didn't know that she'd already made up her mind. She was certain David wouldn't have revealed her decision. She wanted to get some honest answers, though, about Ray and the role he'd played in bringing her to this place.

She pulled on a jacket over the sweats and went out. The rest of the cottages were dark. From somewhere, she could smell a cigar, but she didn't know where the aroma was coming from. Ground lights lit up every pathway. She couldn't see the ocean, but she could hear it. A guard had a dog on a leash and was walking on one of the pathways to her left. He lifted a hand and gave her a silent greeting. Alanna returned the gesture.

After leaving David and Leah tonight, she'd had a little time to do some research on Galvin. Online, she'd read some of the news stories that she'd missed last year. His son's death had been a major headline. None of the reports, though, mentioned anything about a kidnapping. There was nothing about foul play being involved at all. The papers called Nathan's death accidental and said that it had happened in Istanbul, Turkey. A traffic accident, it said. Alanna wondered if it was the family's choice not to get in the middle of a political situation. As far as Kei's death, there was only the obituary. She had died suddenly at home. And that was the extent of it.

Alanna respected the privacy that Steven must have been after, especially after the back-to-back loss of two loved ones.

Steven met her at the entrance to the main building. He had the look of a man who never slept. He seemed as alert now as he'd been when she'd met him for the first time this afternoon.

She stepped inside the building. The reception room was lit but no one else was around.

"I'm afraid my staff insists on keeping civilized working hours," he said. "I can offer you coffee or tea, or a drink if you want."

"Tea would be great."

"Do you mind if we go back to my part of the house? They don't trust me touching any of their appliances around here."

Although he knew perfectly well why she was here, he didn't press her with questions. Instead, as they walked through the house, he chatted about the people who kept his estate running here on Grand Bahama Island. In the course of the afternoon and evening, Alanna had probably run into most of them—except for the kitchen staff. He seemed to know all of them personally.

She was impressed that a man with his level of wealth, power and intelligence was so adept at putting a stranger at ease. She remembered reading in some of the articles about him how well he was liked and respected in the business. She could see why he had that reputation.

"This is the lived-in part of the house," he said, taking Alanna past the library and the area where they'd dined.

"Kei loved lots of windows. When she was working with the architect, she was determined to have a view of the water wherever she was in the house," he explained. "So the three connecting structures were built in a U shape, hugging the marina."

"Front office, work area and the private residence," she commented.

"Exactly. It's an ideal design. A few friends keep boats in the marina, too."

"Did she spend much time here?" Alanna asked.

"After I retired, we tried to spend at least a couple of months a year here. We both enjoyed sailing. We'd usually fit a long weekend in here and there during other months, too." He stopped at a double set of French doors. "I think she wanted us to really retire here. Living here year-round and having our son and his family…if he ever got around to having one—come out and visit us…that would have been great. I guess it's the kind of dream any parent would have."

Alanna had only met Steven today. She'd never known Kei. But she had no trouble understanding how deep his love for her must have been. What she herself had with Ray was different. It was infatuation, passion… but it was nothing like this.

He opened the door and ushered her through. A beautiful living area decorated and furnished in white and teal blue greeted them. There were lots of windows with window seats. She couldn't see outside, but she imagined watching the sun rise through one set of windows and watching it set through the opposite. A stylish, well-designed kitchen and a cozy dining area opened into the living area. Beyond, there was another set of doors.

"That leads to the two bedroom suites," he explained. "This was where we spent most of our time when we were here."

He walked to the kitchen. Alanna took her jacket off and placed it on one of the chairs. There were family photos everywhere—all of Nathan and Kei. Most of them were from the time Nathan had been really young. They were gone, but their memories were preserved here.

"Caffeinated, decaffeinated, herbal?" he asked.

He was pouring boiling water from a tap into two cups. She went to the kitchen and he slid a box of tea bags with a dozen choices in front of her. Alanna chose one.

"Honey, sugar, lemon?"

She shook her head to all of them.

"I came to tell you that I've made my decision," she said flatly, knowing that he wouldn't bring up the topic. "But before I tell you what it is, I would like to ask you some questions."

He chose a tea bag himself. "Which means that my answers have no effect on the outcome?"

"That's right," she said. "In fact, my decision is independent of what you choose to tell me."

"I'll tell you the truth," he said.

She believed him. "I think it'd be better if we sit down."

Alanna discarded the tea bag and took her cup. He led her to the fireplace where small flames flickered around some logs. Two chairs and a coffee table were arranged in front of it. She sat down.

"Ray Savoy," she said.

He leaned forward and put his cup down on the table. "I'm sorry…he left this afternoon. I had hoped that he'd change his mind. But he didn't."

She'd already learned from David that Ray had left. Already a strange tautness had taken over the section of her heart that her love for him had occupied.

"He wasn't one of the people you had Diarte and Lyons find for you, was he?" she asked, already knowing the answer.

He sat back in the chair. His feet crossed, fingers laced on his stomach. "No, he wasn't. He was the connection we needed to convince you to just consider this project."

"And I was chosen…?"

"After Kei died. As soon as I knew how I could get revenge on the people who'd killed my son," he told her. "From the beginning. I realized you were the key to the plan. Nothing else could work unless you agreed to be part of it."

"Why didn't you contact me then and just ask?"

He shook his head and reached for his cup. He took a sip. "I don't think you know yourself very well, if you ask that. At least, you don't know the kind of dedicated, driven person you were a year ago. Your work has been your life. Any deviation from established protocol—any argument to deviate from procedure—would have been futile. No matter where that request came from."

Alanna wanted to argue and tell him that wasn't the truth, but she knew it was. This is who she'd been. "What makes you think I'm not still that person?"

"You're here. You listened to my plea. That's all I could ask for. A year ago, I wouldn't have gotten you to come this far."

"So, Ray—his relationship with me…everything that happened—was a setup, from day one?" It hurt to ask, but she had to know.

He shifted in his seat. He drank some of his tea, avoiding eye contact.

"I'm not proud of that," he said finally. "He was already involved with you when we ran into him, though. All I can say is that he may never have really been the man you thought he was."

Alanna kept her voice strong. "How so?"

"In a lot of the details, he is who he says he is. He does have an engineering degree and has been a contractor for most of his working life. As far as how we should convince you to come here so many months later…that was all his own doing…his own planning."

"You mean he faked his own death," she said, still not believing how far Ray had gone.

"That's right," Steven admitted. "We didn't suggest

that. But he was in trouble before we got involved with him. Gambling debts. Some rather tough gentlemen that he owed money to. That story about the witness protection program, that was all a lie, too. He told Diarte and Lyons exactly what to tell you. He scripted the meeting you had with them in Sonoma Valley."

For a long moment Alanna sat, speechless. She'd been played for a fool for a long time. She'd never really known the real Ray at all.

"Wow," she finally managed to say.

He stared down at his hands. "We went along with how he wanted to play it. He'd agreed on a lump sum amount, and he was doing his part."

"How much money did he get?" she asked.

He looked at her.

She shook her head. "Never mind, I don't want to know. I can't be any angrier than I am now."

Alanna grabbed the teacup and stared down into the dark liquid. Everything she'd told Ray on the flight here had been too close to the truth. That was why he couldn't take it anymore.

"So he's legally dead as far as the real world is concerned?" She had to know.

"I believe so. He wanted it that way."

"Where did he go yesterday, when he left here?"

He again looked at her as if it wasn't wise to know.

"I'm not going to follow him," she told him. "And I'm not planning any revenge. I just need to know for my own peace of mind. I never want to see him or run into him."

"He went back to where he was living during the period when you thought he was dead," Steven said. "He lives with a girlfriend in Amsterdam. He's established a new life and identity there."

She didn't want it to hurt, but it did. She wanted to pretend that she hadn't been a victim. But she had been. She took another sip of her tea. She couldn't taste it. The tears burned the back of her throat, but she refused to let them loose. She looked up at Galvin.

"You don't know what my answer is right now. I might tell you no. After all these months of planning, after all the money and expense you've gone through, I might walk away. Was this worth it?"

There was no hesitation in his answer. "Absolutely. I had to take the risk."

She stood up abruptly and carried the cup to the kitchen. She came back and grabbed her jacket. "I can find my way out."

"Alanna," he called to her as she walked away. "Your decision?"

"I'm staying," she said, stopping at the French doors. "I'll help."

52

Taking out Refik Omer was one of the easiest hits Finn could remember making in the past decade. Dikmen Valley Towers provided the perfect shooter's perch, and the shopping area beneath was busy enough that Finn had eased the sliding door closed and drawn the shades before anyone on the ground even realized the reason Omer had fallen into the reflecting pool.

Finn packed away the rifle and went back to the computer, where he'd been reading today's *Belfast Telegraph* online.

He picked up his mobile and speed-dialed Kelly. She answered.

"One hundred," he told her.

"One more?" she asked, questioning as much as telling him.

"Just one," he told her. "But there's been a bloody change of plan. I have to go to Washington."

"Why?" she asked, sounding totally unhappy.

Finn looked at the article. The headline read that the

presidential hopeful's daughter was cutting her book tour across Ireland short. She was returning to the United States today.

"The job has relocated," he said.

"I don't like it," she told him. "Maybe you should stop now."

"No, I'm too close. It has to be done," he said. "How are the twins?"

"They're fine," she answered.

"How about Mick?" he asked.

"He's right here. Do you want to talk to him?" Kelly asked.

They hadn't had much to say to each other for a few weeks now. At least, he'd listened to him and was staying at the house. "No, just tell him I was asking for him."

"Are you sure you don't want to tell him yourself?" she asked.

"Na," he said. Any mending they needed to do had to be done face-to-face.

"Hurry back. I miss you," she said quietly.

"You'll be sick of me real soon, love. I'll be around all the time," he promised her.

"Can't wait."

Finn ended the call and read the article again. He hated when situations became complicated. Now he would need to do some more research, decide on a new location, a new time. And Washington had surveillance cameras everywhere. He'd done only one hit there in the past and he hadn't counted on doing another.

One good thing, his jobber would have no trouble arranging for his rifle. America was even easier to find a

safe gun in than Beirut. Still, there were extra expenses
that he would have to charge to the account.

"Last one," he told himself.

Putting it that way, Finn was almost looking forward
to the trip.

53

Belfast

Kelly ended the call and grabbed the milk off the table to put in the refrigerator.

"What was that about?" Mick asked, finishing up his breakfast at the kitchen table.

Kelly thought it was nice to see her nephew up and around this early in the morning. He was the most sociable she'd seen him in months. He'd played with the twins in their room this morning before coming down.

"It was himself on the phone," she told him.

"When's he coming back?" Mick asked.

She put water on for a new pot of tea. "I don't know. He's not sure."

"What do you mean, you don't know?"

Kelly looked over her shoulder at him, surprised at the sharp tone. "Do you need something, Mick? I can help."

"Where is Finn now?" he asked.

She'd never thought it made much difference to him where Finn was. "I don't see how it matters where he is. Likely he'll be back by the week's end."

"Kelly, please." The young man pushed his plate away from him.

"You two don't say three words to each other when he's around," she said shortly, facing the young man. "Now, you're all in a dither over where he is and when he is getting back?"

He planted both fists on the table, leaning toward her. "This matters. Will you tell me where he is?"

She decided there wasn't any harm in telling him. "He's in Turkey, if you must know."

"And where is he off to next?" he asked.

Kelly almost laughed. He was using that sweet tone of voice that was a signature mark of charm in the boys in their family. They were sure women had no chance when they put that on.

"He's off to America. He'll be coming home right after that, I'm guessing."

Leaving his breakfast half eaten, Mick charged out of the kitchen. Kelly watched him go down the front hall, scoop up his jacket off the bench and go out the door.

"And what in the devil has gotten into the boy now?"

54

Grand Bahama Island

Since Alanna had decided to stay, there was no reason to stretch the schedule any longer than they needed.

The test cycles for the STEREO mission ran once a month but not on any preset timetable. Alanna could schedule it from anywhere. Everything was programmed. She was the one with the passwords.

Once she'd set the time, the wheels would turn on their own.

Two days after their arrival on the island, the nine other people who would be involved in the project met with Galvin. At that meeting, Alanna found out that the center of their operation was a small building on the north end of the property. The setup reminded her of one of NASA's control centers. Each of them had a number of computers that were dedicated to their end of the project.

With the exception of Jay and David, the others appeared to be employees of Galvin's foundations. She wasn't sure if any of those people knew the exact details of what they were going to do or the reasons behind it.

She had an idea that at least some of them would be involved with diverting funds to charities listed among their foundation recipients.

It didn't seem likely that Alanna was going to be involved with them, which suited her perfectly. On the other hand, a feeling of camaraderie quickly formed between her and David and Jay. They didn't have to say it, but Alanna knew that both men greatly appreciated her final decision.

At the meeting, the support personnel were divvied up.

"This will be your group, Jay," Steven said, introducing the four people assigned to work with him. "They'll show you the files, the systems, the mock-ups we've come up with. They'll bring you up to speed."

Jay seemed satisfied with that. Alanna already could see a difference in the young man. He appeared much more confident and comfortable with a computer in front of him.

"David, these are the accounts that we will be transferring funds out of." Steven passed on a report to the banker. "They're all Dubai accounts."

Steven then introduced David to two people who would help him become familiar with the systems.

"And these are the accounts the funds are getting transferred into." Steven passed on a report much thicker than the first one. "Any of you are welcome to add any nonprofit organization you want to this report. The lists include many non–U.S. accounts, as well. And don't be concerned about traceability. By the time we're done, there will be no way to find out how the money reached those accounts."

Alanna noticed David delving into the reports right away. She'd lost another chess game to Leah last night. That little girl was all heart, and Alanna looked forward to her wisecracking comments. Looking at her father now, she figured an organization supporting kidney disease or cloning would soon be there, if it wasn't already.

"Dr. Mendes," Steven turned to her. "You'll be working on your own until the day of the test. Jay's group will assist you with any communications issues once the trigger is set."

This meant that she had nothing to do until then. Alanna would call Phil just to tell him about the schedule, but that was essentially a courtesy call. And it wasn't unusual for her to plan the test at the oddest hours of the day or night. In fact, the whole point was to make sure everyone was on guard twenty-four hours a day, seven days a week. She also had to call her *abuela*. Alanna had made up a story about going on a business trip. After all, that was exactly what she was doing. Alanna knew her grandmother would be happy to hear her voice. She was glad that she'd never let her *abuela* know about Ray's fake death and return. He didn't deserve to be mourned twice by a woman so good as her grandmother.

"When is the earliest time we can schedule the test?" Galvin asked her.

"I need twelve hours' advance notice. That's it."

"How about if we go in two days," Galvin told her.

Alanna nodded. He looked around at everyone else. She couldn't believe it, but she was going with it. It was practically a done deal.

55

Amber used the excuse of jet lag to mope around her father's house for two days. She didn't call any of her friends. She didn't contact her adviser at the graduate school to let him know that she was back, and she made no arrangements to catch up with her work. She didn't let her mother know that she was back from Europe. She didn't even bother to tell her publisher that she'd cut her trip short by a week. She let the bookstores know that she wasn't showing up. That was enough.

Thankfully, her father let her be, and the housekeeper stayed out of her path.

That was good for one day. The attitude wasn't enough to get her through the second day without everyone insisting on interfering with her wallowing. The housekeeper told her that the senator's secretary was on the phone and that she wasn't hanging up until Amber spoke to her.

Susan was quiet, efficient. Amber couldn't imagine what had riled the young woman enough that she was actually issuing a challenge. Actually, there had been two calls from her this morning that Amber hadn't returned. She took this call.

Susan wasn't much for small talk, and this always suited Amber…and especially now. She had no desire to chitchat about her trip. Susan got to the point.

"In the past twenty-four hours, I've received five calls from a man who insists he needs to get in touch with you."

Their phone number at the house was, of course, unlisted. And Amber didn't give out her cell-phone number to too many people.

"Did he give his name?" she asked.

"Let me see, I have it right here. He's got a very hunky Irish brogue. Did I actually just say hunky? Honestly, he sounds like he just got off the boat…although he actually isn't off the boat yet. It was an international call," Susan told her.

Amber leaned against the nearest wall. This was too much to hope. Her heart started beating so fast that she feared Susan would be able to hear it at the other end.

"Was it Mick?"

"Yes, it was Mick. He wouldn't leave a last name," Susan told her. "He kept saying you'd know."

Amber knew. "Did he leave a number where I can call him back?" She kept her fingers crossed, hoping.

"No, he kept saying he wanted your number. But I couldn't give it to him before I talked to you."

Susan continued with a detailed explanation of the conversations. On her end, Amber felt like a two-year-old. She wanted to jump around the room.

"He said he'd call back before the end of the day," Susan told her.

Amber glanced at the clock on the mantel. It was already four-thirty in the afternoon.

"Did you tell him how late you were staying tonight?" Amber asked, needing to know.

"I have a lot of work to do tonight. So most likely I'll be around until six or seven," Susan told her. "But I told him five."

Amber was relieved. "Listen, Susan. Please give him my number. My cell-phone number," she added as an afterthought.

Susan laughed at the other end. "So is he anywhere as good looking as he sounds?"

"Even better," Amber said, feeling a sliver of warmth slip through her.

"Where did you meet him?" the secretary asked.

"At a book signing."

"Was he buying a children's book?"

"Kind of...well, not really."

Amber was glad she wasn't the only one who got rubbery-kneed at hearing Mick's accent. Susan, as solid a person as they come, was hooked. And she hadn't even seen him in person.

She wrapped up their conversation and ran to take a shower. But she stopped. She didn't want to miss his call. She paced through the house. She couldn't sit still. She tried to pick up a book she'd started on the flight back from Ireland. It was no use. She couldn't concentrate. Her gaze kept going to the clock every couple of minutes. Her mind was full of memories of what they'd done. How great she'd felt.

She didn't want to think about why he'd left without

leaving a number or address. She didn't know why he was trying to reach her. Maybe he wanted to return the money he'd taken out of her wallet. She would only accept the money if she could see him in person. She'd read him the riot act…and then she'd jump him.

Her cell phone rang at two minutes to five. The hello was enough to know it was Mick.

He talked for a couple of minutes as if he'd never left that hotel suite without so much as a goodbye. She responded to his questions, hiding how messed up these past few days had been. He asked her about cutting her trip short. She lied about some appointments she had back home.

"Listen, I'm flying over there for a short visit, and I was wondering if I might bunk in with you," he finally asked.

Amber couldn't believe it. She was ecstatic. But she needed to clear the air about the way he'd left.

"Before I say yes, Mick, I need to ask you about something."

"I know what it is. You want to know about the money."

"Okay? So?"

"It wasn't that I needed it. I just wanted to, well…" He was searching for words halfway around the globe. "It's difficult to explain over the phone. But I will explain. And I know you'll forgive me."

"Oh, you know that?"

"I'm certain of it. In fact—" his tone became much lighter "—I'm thinking you've already forgiven me."

"Really…?" she asked.

"If you hadn't, we wouldn't be talking now, would we?" His voice was like a caress.

Amber smiled. This guy was too much.

"So, what is it?" he continued. "Can I stay with you for a few days?"

"Absolutely," she said. "Count on it."

She knew her father might mind, but it didn't matter. She was old enough to make decisions like that herself. She'd lived on her own since she was eighteen. Just because she'd moved back to the house, it didn't mean that he had any power to object to her personal choices.

She realized she was having this argument prematurely. She hadn't even spoken to her father yet. In a worst-case scenario, she'd stay at a hotel with him if she had to.

"Can I pick you up at the airport?" she offered.

"Sure, sure thing. I'll call you back as soon as I've made my flight arrangements."

"That's great," she said.

"By the by, I'm thinking it might be a good thing for you to catch up on your sleep before I get there."

Her insides twisted deliciously. She felt her face burn. She was actually blushing. "I'll do that…and you'd better, too."

"Don't you be worrying about me, darling."

"Mick, I don't know your last name."

"That's true. But it doesn't matter, does it?" he asked.

It didn't. She stared at the cell phone for the longest time after they ended the call. At least she had his return number.

She was acting on impulse again. The same way she'd hooked up with him in Dundalk. The same way she'd left Ireland and come back home. She wondered if he was acting on impulse coming here to see her…or if it was how he was feeling about her that was making him do this.

Amber snapped her cell phone closed. It had to be something more than impulse. She hoped.

56

David Collier looked at his guests with real pleasure.

After the first night, they'd made a point of having dinner together. Because of Leah's dialysis, David's cottage was the natural place for everyone to gather. And, of course, Leah treated them all as if they were her long-lost uncles and aunts. She was having the best time she'd had in years, David thought.

Taken together, they were the most unlikely group of individuals to form such a close bond. But it had happened.

Jay Alexei was twenty-one. His wife was eighteen. New parents and a hell of a lot younger than he was. Their baby was absolutely the perfect infant, though. He never cried…but of course, Padma almost never put him down, either. Jay had to nearly tear the infant out of her arms. David remembered Nicole being the same way the first month after Leah was born.

Outside, David could see him sitting on the patio with the baby. Alanna was out there, too, looking at the moon on the water and chatting comfortably.

Alanna Mendes was the dictionary definition of "married to the job." Or, at least, this was the way she described herself. She felt comfortable enough to joke about it—willing to admit the television shows she'd missed out on and the movies she'd never seen and the places she'd never gone because of her dedication to her work. She'd never seen a single episode of *Friends* or *Seinfeld,* for God's sake! Here on the island, though, she couldn't have taken more time being nice to Leah. David could see his daughter really getting attached to her.

This group's cheerful camaraderie was one reason David felt uncertain about sharing what he'd discovered with Alanna and Jay. But he owed them the truth. They were all connected. They were all in this together. And each had their own reason to be concerned about taking part in this project.

Tonight, after dinner, Padma was taking her turn playing chess with Leah in the living room. The young mother was the best of all of them at the game, and she and Leah never stopped arguing as they played. David figured that was because of their closeness in age.

David got up and went outside. It was a good opportunity to mention his concerns. Harsha, as everyone now called the baby, was draped across his father's chest, sleeping peacefully.

"There's something I'd like to talk to you two about," he said, sitting on one of the cushioned patio chairs.

He could see Alanna's face immediately grow serious.

"Okay," Jay said. "What's up?"

"I've gone over all the accounts that money will be transferred from," he told the other two. "All together, the balances today put the amount we'll be moving at nearly five hundred million dollars."

"And you checked to make sure all the accounts are listed under the name Osama bin Laden, I hope."

Jay's crack made them laugh. It had been a running joke that Galvin might also be cleaning out Bill Gates's personal checking account.

"We're taking Galvin's word that these are the right accounts," David said, getting serious again.

"We're taking his word for a lot," Alanna admitted. "This late in the game, though, the only thing we can do is to trust him and let the dice roll."

"You always surprise me," David said to her. "But I guess that's right."

"That's what I'm doing," Jay agreed.

"But there's something else," David continued, "about the accounts that the funds are going to."

"Is there a problem?" Alanna's black eyes shone in the moonlight.

"As far as I can tell, they're all nonprofits and U.S. and international charities, as he says…except one."

David saw he had their attention. "Ten million dollars is getting transferred to Senator Paul Hersey of Pennsylvania."

"Hersey?" Alanna repeated. David nodded.

"Wait a minute. Isn't he running for the White House?" Jay asked.

"At this point he's hoping for his party's nomination," Alanna commented.

"I don't know what this guy stands for," Jay told them. "But is a campaign-fund donation a charitable contribution?"

"No," David answered. "But there's more than that.

This is just a few zeros more than the allowable twenty-three hundred for a candidate. Also, this is a transfer, not to the campaign fund, but to a personal account of Hersey's. And another thing. The account is in the U.S., meaning it will be investigated and traced back to its source. This could not only destroy the guy's political career but put him personally at risk of being charged with all kinds of fraud and conspiracy and any number of other things…especially if the word got out that some terrorist organization was the source of the money."

The two sat still, wordlessly staring at him. He finally broke the silence.

"I've been in a position like that. I know what it's like to be set up. It can destroy you. It will destroy him."

"Galvin has something against Hersey," Jay responded.

"That's what it looks like to me," David agreed.

Alanna shook her head. "Maybe we should ask him about it."

"Listen," Jay suggested. "Let me do some poking around—my way—and see if I can find out what the connections are between Galvin and Hersey."

"I like both ideas," David told them.

57

Washington, D.C.

Mick was arriving tomorrow, and Amber still hadn't been able to get two minutes alone with her father to tell him about their Irish guest. Campaign business was swallowing up all his time.

He was speaking at a fund-raising dinner for some organization tonight. She'd been invited, as well, but she'd passed. She was too wound up for tomorrow to put up with the speeches and smiling. She heard her father come in a few minutes after ten. Unfortunately, his good friend Matt Lane arrived immediately after.

Amber decided to interrupt them for a minute to let him know. This was his house and she'd respect his decision, if he preferred to have them stay at a hotel. She went downstairs.

Her father's study was a comfortable room off the library in the front of the house. She walked into the library. The door to the study was open only a fraction of an inch, but she could hear their voices clearly. It sounded as if they were already in the middle of an argument. Amber decided to wait.

Matt Lane and her father had known each other for decades. They'd gone to law school together. They'd started their careers in Washington at the same time. Matt didn't have the charisma or the looks for politics, so he'd pursued a successful career in the law. Amber knew he was smart. He'd also held a couple of low-level cabinet positions under one or two presidents. Lately, though, Amber knew Matt Lane was the person working the lights for her dad. He was the eyes and ears for him, smoothing the way. Her father trusted Matt Lane's counsel like no one else's.

And Amber had never heard them argue like this. As she turned to go, she couldn't help hearing bits and pieces that made her stop dead.

"…two deaths…couple of days apart…"

"Overreacting…" her father was saying.

Amber moved to a leather chair near the senator's office door. She turned on the light next to her and grabbed today's newspaper off the ottoman.

"…It's not over. You're letting down your guard…" Matt warned.

She could hear their discussion clearly. Amber felt no embarrassment listening in on what was being said. Her father always treated her as a confidante in his political dealings. They'd become especially close since she'd moved back home.

"…Amber is home safe. All I care…"

Her father lowered his voice behind the door, but she was starting to think that perhaps the security bulletin her father had received when she was in Ireland hadn't been complete nonsense.

Matt Lane's voice suddenly came through, his tone angry and accusatory. "But you let Nathan die."

Hearing the name, Amber felt her spine stiffen. There was only one Nathan that she knew was dead. Nathan Galvin. He'd died this past year, traveling in Turkey.

"Steven is over it. He's retired."

They *were* talking about Nathan Galvin, Amber realized.

"For God's sake, Paul. He lost his son, his wife. Kei killed herself because of what *you* allowed to happen to Nathan. Don't you think he's holding a grudge?" Matt asked.

The newspaper slid through Amber's fingers. She stood up and walked toward the study door.

"I'm telling you, he doesn't blame me," Paul Hersey said. "He still thinks I did everything I could. Shit happens. People die. You're wrong, Matt. We just got a donation from Steven. He wouldn't still be supporting my campaign if he was holding a grudge."

Amber pushed open the study door. Her father looked up with a start. Matt was standing with his hands on Paul's desk, leaning over. He turned around quickly.

"Amber," Paul said, sounding as if there was nothing wrong. "Come in, honey. You missed a great party tonight."

"I need to talk to you," she told him.

"Matt and I are done here, anyway." He looked meaningfully up at his friend.

"Not quite."

"But we can talk about this tomorrow," Paul stressed.

"I'll be by to see you early," Matt told him.

"I'll tell Susan to call your secretary with my schedule."

Matt Lane gave Amber a quick pat on the shoulder as he charged out of the room. A few seconds later, they heard the front door open and shut.

"So what's up, honey?" he asked, putting on a campaign smile.

Amber felt as if she was looking at a stranger. She remembered Nathan's funeral. She recalled the years that she and Nathan had gone to the same summer camps. The sailing classes they'd taken together. The get-togethers of the two families. All of them had been great friends for as long as she could remember.

"Nathan," she said. "How did he die?"

"Oh, forget you heard that, sweetie. Matt's getting paranoid in his old age," he said, brushing her off. "What is this thing Susan was telling me, though, about some Irish charmer who's been calling—"

"How did Nathan die, Dad?" she asked forcefully, interrupting him.

He leaned back in his chair. He tugged at the bow tie of his tuxedo, loosening the knot. "I really don't want to talk about it."

"But I do," she persisted. "Tell me."

Her father took a deep breath and frowned.

"Nathan was kidnapped by a group of terrorists. They killed him before we could negotiate anything for him. Are you happy now?"

She remembered the vagueness at the time of the funeral. Someone said he'd died in a car accident. It wasn't exactly a question you could ask his parents. Everyone was shocked.

"Did Steven and Kei know about it?" she asked.

"Yes…they knew," he told her.

"Why all the secrecy? Why the rumors about an accident?"

"Because he was working for the CIA. That's why."

She sat down in the chair across from her father. That didn't make any sense. She just couldn't see Nathan doing that. He was too normal to get involved with spies.

"Why did Matt say that you let Nathan die?" she asked.

"He was being melodramatic." He turned his chair and booted up his laptop.

"Dad, why would Steven Galvin blame you for Nathan's death?"

"He doesn't."

"Why, Dad?" she asked again.

"That's history, Amber," he snapped at her, whirling around and facing her. "Let it go."

"I can't. You're my father. Nathan was my friend. I need to know the truth."

"And you've decided I'm not telling you the truth?" he asked. "Look, honey. That's enough talk about Nathan. I told you, it's history. Now, I have work to do."

He turned his chair again, dismissing her.

Amber stared at him. She didn't recognize the man. He wasn't her father. There were no emotions in him, no compassion. He didn't care about the truth.

"I don't get it," she said, standing up. She moved toward the door. "You're a different person. I don't understand you."

58

Getting up early, Alanna went looking for Steven. At the main building, she was told she could find him working in the stone gardens.

Alanna knew where that was. Walking around the property a couple of days ago, she'd spotted the area. It was a twenty-by-forty-foot garden of exotic flowers near the sandy beach. The plants were protected by a handmade stone wall four feet high. When she got there, she found him down on his knees, weeding around some of the flowers. The colors were vibrant. The bed of soil and greens was well cared for.

"I never would have taken you for a gardener," she admitted.

"Another project that Kei started. She loved to work the soil, bring beauty to life." He straightened his back and looked down at the flower bed. "I think she'd be happy to know I'm taking care of them. Considering how much I teased her about my hating gardening."

Alanna sat down on a stone bench right outside of the enclosure and stretched her arm out along the wall. The stones were warm and smooth to her touch. The sky was blue. The weather forecast promised a sunny day on the island. The wind never stopped.

"This afternoon, the countdown starts." He glanced at her, resting an elbow on a raised knee. "Are you ready?"

She nodded. "There's an important question that I'd like to ask you, though. It's actually a question from all of us—Jay, David and me."

If he was nervous about what the question might be, his expression gave nothing away. He shrugged. "Fire away."

"Why Senator Paul Hersey?" she asked.

He stared at her for a minute, and then he nodded. "I knew David would find it. Actually, I was counting on it."

"But you haven't answered my question," she pressed.

He pushed himself to his feet. The old jeans he was wearing were covered with dirt at the knees. The sneakers on his feet had holes in them. He dropped the clippers in a basket sitting on the ground and took off his work gloves, dropping them on top.

"Paul Hersey, one of my oldest friends, was responsible for Nathan's death." The anger was barely concealed in his tone.

"I thought you said terrorists killed your son."

"They did. But that was because they thought he was someone else, a more experienced CIA operative, the real target of the kidnapping," he told her.

"So how does Senator Hersey come into this?" she asked.

"I went to Paul. I begged for his help. I begged him to let me be involved…" His voice rose with the morning breeze. "I told him to offer any amount of money.

He patted me on the back and lied to me about helping Nathan. But when I walked out of his office, he never passed on my offer to the people who mattered. And when the time came to let Nathan be sacrificed—to be killed so that they could protect the more valuable agent—he let it happen. He said nothing. He turned his back on a friend. He did nothing to save a boy that he claimed to love like his own."

Alanna watched him pick up the basket of tools. His back was bent with the weight of his grief. His hair seemed more gray this morning. The lines on his face were deeper, more pronounced. For a man who was only in his fifties, he looked so much older.

"Is that why none of the public reports mentioned anything about the kidnapping?" Alanna asked.

"Yes." He looked up at her. "Our government and those in charge at Langley didn't want to blow the cover of the agent my son was to die for."

"How do you know Paul Hersey was responsible for any of this?"

"In this great country of ours, everything is for sale. Actually, the same goes for anywhere around the world. You can buy information for the right price. I have my connections, Alanna. I know who did what during the situation with my son, and I know who did nothing. I know who is responsible for my son's death…both at home and in the Middle East."

He came out of the stone enclosure, and she stood up. The two of them started walking back toward the main building.

"When that money gets transferred to his account," she said, "his political career is over."

"I know. I have not formed my plans without careful thought. I want to take away from him what he values most."

59

Washington, D.C.

Paul Hersey tried to kid himself that what his daughter thought of him didn't matter. But that was a lie. Her opinion mattered greatly.

He waited some fifteen minutes, busying himself with checking his e-mail, his schedule for tomorrow. It was pointless. Shutting off his laptop, he trudged upstairs. All the lights were on. At the top of the stairs, he found a suitcase already packed. Amber's bedroom door was open. She was going back and forth between the closet and the bed, dropping armloads of clothes into an open suitcase.

"What are you doing?" he asked, standing in the doorway.

"Moving out," she said quietly, but not pausing.

"Why?"

She didn't bother to answer.

"Amber," he said sharply. "I deserve an explanation."

She whirled on him. "And I don't?"

Their glares locked.

He looked away first. He couldn't let her go. He wouldn't admit it to her right now, but she mattered more to him than any political career, more than his wealth, more than anything else he held dear. The renewed relationship between them made Paul feel as if he'd finally done something right in his life. She was the flower who'd blossomed, despite how badly he'd screwed up his marriage. She was part of him.

She was too much like him.

"I don't think it's right to dredge up the past," he said in a reasonable voice.

"How are you responsible for Nathan's death?"

"I didn't take a gun to his head and shoot him," he told her.

"What was it that you did or didn't do?" she asked, slowly enunciating each word.

"You've grown up with politics all around your whole life. You know that things can't be black and white. We can't feed everyone. Some have to go hungry."

"Don't give me a campaign speech, Dad," she told him. "Just tell me the truth about Nathan."

He could refuse to tell her, but she would walk out. Paul thought he *could* tell her the truth, but she'd probably still walk out. Still, she was a smart kid. Maybe he could make her understand.

"I wasn't the mastermind behind some grand scheme, if that's what you're thinking. No one was. It just happened. Nathan was kidnapped because some wires got crossed out there. He was mistaken for one of our other agents who had been operating in southern Iraq and had been recently moved to Istanbul."

He looked at her. She was listening.

"Then there were decisions that had to be made."

"What kind of decisions?" she asked.

"The agent Nathan was mistaken for was undercover in a very sensitive situation. The best thing that could have happened was to have his name wiped off the slate." He leaned against the doorway. He felt tired. Old. He was sick of lying. "I'm not proud of what happened."

"What happened, Dad?"

Paul sat down on a straight chair just inside her door. He leaned his arms wearily on his knees. "The decision was made…to confirm to the kidnappers that they had captured the experienced agent. We came up with enough false data to fool them."

"What did that mean for Nathan? Would they want more money? A prisoner exchange?"

He shook his head. "No. They wanted revenge for something that other agent had done in Iraq."

"And you knew that."

"Yes," he said quietly.

"What did they do to him?" she asked flatly.

"You know what they did. They executed him. He gave his life for his…"

Paul's voice trailed off. He might as well have punched her. Tears streamed down her face. She didn't move for a long time. She didn't wipe away the tears. She just stared at him.

Paul wanted to go to her, gather her in his arms and say how those decisions had haunted him. But something in her look told him that she wouldn't accept his embrace.

"You knew what they were going to do?"

He could still lie, but he decided on truth. "Yes. I was included in every one of those briefings, but it was complicated. There are times, politically, when a man cannot be soft…cannot *look* soft." He looked down at his shoes. They had gotten scuffed somewhere tonight. "I knew everything, Amber. I knew they would kill him."

"And you let it happen."

She didn't wait for an answer. She didn't bother to close the other suitcase. She simply walked past him and down the stairs.

60

Jay sat on the edge of the bed and stared lovingly at Padma. He'd brought Harsha to her when he'd gotten up a half hour ago to shower and shave. Now, both of them, facing each other on the mattress, were sound sleep. He put his pillow behind the baby on the bed. Not that he was old enough to roll over, but Jay was a fussy father. He leaned down and brushed a kiss on his wife's hair.

Her eyes opened. She reached for his hand. "Going already?"

"I'm supposed to meet with Galvin before we start work today," he told her.

"Is this the day he tells us?"

"I think so." Steven Galvin and Jay hadn't had a one-on-one talk since he'd arrived. There hadn't been any problems with communication, though. The group that was assigned to work with him had all the answers. One thing that they couldn't help him with, though, was what would happen when they were done with this project on the island.

Galvin had told Jay yesterday that he wanted to see

him this morning, before the project countdown began. He hoped this was when he'd find out.

"These past few days have been wonderful. And I'm grateful for that," Padma told him. "And just so you know, it doesn't matter where we go from here. We have each other. We'll be fine."

He kissed her lips. Through thick or thin, she would stick by him. "I'm a lucky man," he whispered, getting up to make the appointment.

Every morning since arriving here, Jay enjoyed his commute to work. Blue ocean, soft warm sea breeze, manicured landscape everywhere he looked—so much like his commute in Boston. Right.

This morning, however, he was to meet with Galvin at the main building, so he had a shorter commute. Approaching the building, Jay saw him walking with Alanna up from the direction of the beach. He was dressed in old jeans and a faded polo shirt. He was carrying a wooden basket with gardening tools in it. Jay wondered if she'd asked him about the senator.

Alanna waved and took the walkway toward her own cottage before they reached him. Galvin waited for him.

"You've been working already," Jay said in a way of greeting.

"I don't have a baby to keep me up all night, so I'm an early riser."

Jay sensed a touch of longing in the other man's tone. "Harsha is a good sleeper. I can't complain at all."

"Nathan was always a good sleeper, too," he said. "He was a happy boy—like yours."

Jay thought how crazy he was about his one-month-old son. He couldn't imagine loving and raising a child for all those years and then losing him. He felt terrible for the older man.

One of the landscapers approached and took the tool basket from Galvin.

"Have you had breakfast yet?" Steven asked.

"No, but I'm fine," Jay said politely.

"Well, I'm not. I need three meals a day."

Jay smiled and followed the other man through the building to a glassed-in porch facing the marina. Steven gestured to one of a handful of tables and they sat down. A member of the kitchen staff came out and took Jay's order for breakfast before turning to her boss.

"And the usual for you?"

"That'd be great. Thanks."

Steven turned to Jay as soon as the two of them were alone.

"Well, are we on schedule?"

"I believe so, sir. We'll be tapping into the backup system during the eighty-three-second shutdown using a long-range antenna. We can get right in through their wi-fi networks. Once we are in, David can do his thing."

"Encryption? Passwords? Anything that might slow us down?"

"I'm all set for whatever they throw at us, but I don't think we'll face any surprises. I've been surfing through their networks and hardware for days now."

"What about Alanna's requirements, as far as the communication?" he asked.

"It's all set. Everything is synchronized, timewise. The botnets attacks have already started this morning.

Their e-mail system should be shut down for at least eight hours, so when the signal hits them, it should be accepted as the real McCoy."

"Excellent. Good work."

Jay was pleased to see Steven's reaction. He seemed satisfied. The same woman who'd taken their order came back with two cups of coffee before leaving them again. Jay took a sip.

"And what are you doing poking around in my accounts?" Steven asked calmly.

Jay almost spewed the coffee all over himself. He had been doing exactly that since last night, when David told them about Senator Hersey's name being on the list of recipients.

"I only hacked into your PC," he said, deciding on honesty.

"Did you find anything interesting?" Steven asked.

"No, not really. But the security system on your personal files isn't too good at all. You should be using—" He caught himself short. "I realize I shouldn't have done that."

"But you did it," he said.

Jay cursed inwardly. If this messed up their future, he wouldn't forgive himself. "What I was trying to do… to find out…I don't know if Alanna mentioned to you about seeing Senator—"

"Yes, she did," Steven told him. "And I told her exactly why Paul Hersey's name is on the list. Now, before the three of you get started today, you need to get together and decide how, as a group, you feel about this. We need to get it out of the way before the real fun starts."

Jay nodded. Their breakfast arrived, but his appetite was totally gone. Steven hadn't mentioned anything about the future.

"Have you ever been to Oregon?" Galvin asked suddenly, diving into his poached eggs.

"No," Jay admitted.

"Do you think your wife would mind living there?"

"No. Both of us will be happy wherever I can work and provide for us. We both…we're game for anything, sir."

"Eugene, Oregon. I'll move your family there. You'll take courses at the university, get your degree. While you're doing that, you can work part-time at one of my offices. You'll work enough hours to keep you out of trouble, and I'll pay you a comfortable salary."

"That's incredible, sir. I can't…there's no way we can thank you enough."

"Yes, there is. You can set up a solid security system for my home office. Then, you can do it for my satellite offices. After that, we'll go from there."

The hostess from the party appeared at the door and came across to the table. There was an urgent call for Steven.

61

Mick's flight had just landed, but Amber knew it would take another ten or fifteen minutes before he cleared customs. She dug through her bag and found the phone number for Steven Galvin.

She had to make this call. Since leaving her father's house in the middle of the night, she hadn't stopped thinking about Nathan and his funeral. Nathan's parents had been in so much pain, and Amber hadn't known the extent of her own father's responsibility in the matter. She'd stood beside her father, next to the family, shaking hands with those who came to offer their condolences. And she hadn't known.

She knew Steven Galvin spent a couple of months in the winter in the Bahamas. She'd also heard her father talk about it a couple of weeks ago. Making the call, Amber was put on hold, and that was a good thing, she realized. In truth, she didn't know what she was going to say. She didn't know how much Galvin already knew of what her father had admitted to her.

She wanted to help Uncle Steven, if she could. More so, she wanted to help herself. She needed to shed some of the guilt that was clinging to her, and the only person who was able to help peel it away would be Steven Galvin.

Then his voice came through the phone.

"Uncle Steven," she started.

"Who is this?"

The airport was so loud. There was so much background noise. She moved over to one of the windows. She looked out at the passing traffic and people. She had the feeling of being a fish in a bowl. "Uncle Steven, this is Amber."

"Amber…where are you? *How* are you?" He seemed more than surprised by the call.

The last time she'd spoken to him was at Kei's funeral. That was so many months ago. "I'm in Washington, at the airport, picking up a friend. But I had to call you." She wasn't able to hold back anymore. The tears rushed down. "Uncle Steven…I'm so sorry."

"About what, honey?"

"I'm so sorry about Nathan. I didn't know. I was stupid. I thought he died in an accident. I never knew what you were going through…what really happened to him."

She slid down until she was sitting on the floor in a corner, her back to glass and polished granite.

"And Kei. You were so happy. And you had to go through all of that pain. All alone."

People walking by stared at her. She didn't care anymore.

"Amber…why now? How did you find out?"

"It doesn't matter. But please believe me when I say

I didn't know. It's just so painful, and I…I don't know what to do for you… You've lost so much. Nathan. Kei. I feel…I don't know…responsible. And you have all been like family to me." The words poured out.

"Is your father with you, Amber?"

"No…no. I left home. I'm too old to live there, anyway. It was a mistake." An idea came to her. "Uncle Steven. Could I come and see you…stay with you… perhaps bring a friend?"

"Of course. Anytime. When…when can you come?"

"I don't know. Maybe toward the end of the week," she told him.

"Why don't you come right now. You're in an airport, you said. Get on the next flight. I'll call and buy your ticket." There was a sense of urgency in his voice. He cared. He was happy that she'd called.

"No, thank you," she said. She was already feeling better. "There are some loose ends that I need to take care of. Some appointments I can't cancel. But I'll be there. I promise. I need to see you."

"And I need to see you. Amber, please, come today. Now."

"End of the week. I promise." Looking across at the crowd of people coming into the Arrivals lobby, she saw Mick.

"I have to go now. My friend is here. I'll call you," she said. "Love you, Uncle Steven."

62

They were all gathered in the operations center. Steven was the only one absent.

Alanna, Jay and David had gotten together to discuss Paul Hersey. None of them felt strongly opposed to Steven's plans for the senator once Alanna told them what she'd learned. They'd all made up their minds that they were going through with this. They called and let Galvin know before they came here.

David was the most anxious to be done with the project. He and Leah would be going off to the clinic in Germany right away. His daughter was doing great, but David knew how quickly her condition could turn. He didn't want to test their luck.

Steven had told David he was keeping him on salary, even though he couldn't officially start working at any of his offices until Leah was finished with the transplant. He said David could collect his benefits up front.

This was another reason why David couldn't bring himself to question Galvin's decision regarding Hersey. The man's generosity was abundant. And considering everything David himself had gone through with his family, he understood the frustration the other man had to be feeling. If he were in Galvin's shoes, he would get his revenge, and he'd do it in more ways than one.

David saw Alanna hang up the phone. She'd been speaking with one of her coworkers in California. Her role in the project was finished. It was all up to him and Jay now.

Jay was wearing a headset and he said something into the mouthpiece. He turned to the other two. "Galvin says not to wait for him. We're to start."

David and Alanna exchanged a look. He wondered if she was thinking the same thing that he was thinking. Why develop all these elaborate plans and not be here to enjoy the outcome?

Maybe, he thought, Galvin had already realized that no matter what he did—no matter who he made to suffer—his wife and son were not coming back.

63

Steven Galvin was frantic. He had to call off the hit man. But he couldn't find a way to contact him.

The entire setup of the contract—the payment, the instructions, everything—had been accomplished through a very complicated web of people. He'd done it to protect himself. He wanted no trail leading back to him. Steven didn't know who was at the killing end of the line, and he'd wanted to keep it that way. The only thing he did know about the man he'd hired was that he'd never failed at delivering on a contract.

He called his contacts. They assured him that they would reach their contacts, but they didn't hold out much hope that they could stop the end result before it happened.

Meanwhile, he paced. He waited. He contemplated making other calls and hiring protection for Amber. But he knew it didn't make a difference. She was already guarded by Secret Service because of Paul's campaign. But they wouldn't be able to stop the person he'd hired.

The only communication he'd had since contracting with the killer had come a couple of days ago. Two were down. One required a change of location. There would be additional expense. And that was it. Again, the message had traveled through a maze of carriers, and Steven didn't know who'd originated it.

Amber was back in Washington. That was the meaning of the change of location.

Steven sat down at his desk. He didn't know what he'd been thinking. Killing the two Turks was justified in his mind. They'd killed his son. The third one had figured out Nathan's real identity through the cell phone. But he'd been too late. They'd already killed Nathan. He'd contacted Galvin, anyway. He'd accepted two hundred thousand dollars to hand over the names of his associates. They were killers, terrorists.

He wanted to have Paul feel the pain as deeply as he had. But Amber? How could he do that to someone who was totally innocent of her father's transgressions?

He touched his face. It was wet. He was crying. There was no end to the pain. He was responsible for this. Amber couldn't die. He couldn't take a life as callously as Paul had taken Nathan's life. He had to put a stop to it.

But he didn't know how.

64

"Are you not glad to see me, woman?" Mick asked, gathering her in his arms. He spun her away from the glass and pressed her back to the granite.

Amber held on to him. She should have felt better after talking to Steven, but the sadness in his voice stayed with her. She couldn't shake it. She had a mother that she fought with anytime they were together for more than a day. She had a father that she now hated.

And Steven had no one. She would try to make that up to him. She would be family to him—if he'd let her.

"What's wrong?" Mick asked. "Who were you speaking with on the mobile?"

She looked up into his handsome face. He was wearing a Washington Nationals baseball cap. The tag still dangled from the side.

"Nice hat," she said, trying to smile as she dashed away a stray tear.

"Thanks. I just bought it, coming down from the gate." He gave her a profile. "Does it suit me, then?"

"Very…handsome. But I don't think you need to leave the price tag on."

They'd only been together for one night, a few hours, but she felt as if she'd known him forever. He grinned and yanked the tag off.

"Thanks. And who did you say you were speaking with just now?"

"A man. A friend. He's closer to me than my father."

"And is he dying, now?"

"No," she asked, surprised. "Why would you say that?"

"You were crying so hard, I thought he must be dying."

She couldn't help but laugh, in spite of everything, and he pulled her again into his arms. It felt so right for him to be here.

"My friend lives in the Bahamas for part of the winter. I didn't know how long you were staying, but maybe this coming weekend, if you're still around, we could go and see him."

"We can go now," he said, showing her his bag. "I'm ready."

She laughed. This was the second time in an hour that she was being encouraged to hop on the next plane. "No…I can't. I just got back from Ireland. I have things to do before I go away again."

"Ireland?" he asked. "The country?"

"You've heard of it."

"Nasty place, by all accounts. How did you find it?"

"I liked the sights."

"That's all?" he asked, glaring at her.

"Okay. The men aren't too bad."

"I'll show you 'aren't too bad'." He kissed her greedily

right there in public. She gasped in surprise when she felt his hand under her jacket, cupping her breast.

"You can get arrested in this country doing that in public," she whispered against his lips. He was way too tempting. She looped an arm into his, pulling him toward the door.

"Is the car considered public?" he asked.

"Yes. Now, stop it." She felt like a teenager when she was with him. Her Secret Service agents were standing by the door. She'd ditched them last night when she walked out of her father's house and checked into a hotel. But they'd been waiting for her outside this morning.

"We have the car waiting," one of them told her.

"I'm not going back to the house," she told him.

"We'll take you back to the hotel," the other one told her.

She was going to argue with them, but Mick interfered. "Don't be so difficult. They're only doing their job."

Amber didn't think this was the right time to tell him she'd had a blowout with her father. He didn't know anything about her personal life, other than what he'd read in some Irish newspaper or online. She thought it was best to keep it that way, for now.

The black SUV pulled up in front. They got into the backseat with the two agents sitting up front.

Mick looked around the car. He rapped his knuckles on the smoked-glass window. "Is this bulletproof?" he asked one of the agents in front.

The man nodded.

"Good," he whispered.

Amber smiled at his reaction, and he caught her.

"I might be from Belfast," he joked, "but I've seen movies."

"I see," she replied. "Never been to D.C. before?"

"No." His hand moved to the hem of her skirt and slid up the inside of her thigh. She pushed his hand away and with her look tried to make him understand that the two agents were right there, in the front seat. There were no glass dividers. Nothing.

"Then we'll have to plan some sightseeing," she said.

"Why?" he asked.

"Because that's what tourists do when they come to Washington. They go and see the monuments and—"

"Are you daft? We have monuments in Ireland four thousand years old, and I don't go to see them. What makes you think I'm going to play the tourist here?"

"Then why are you here?" she asked in a lower voice.

"I'm here to see you, of course…as if you didn't know it."

Her heart melted. She didn't think he knew what he was doing to her. She rubbed her cheek affectionately against his shoulder, holding on to his arm. She couldn't wait to get to the hotel.

He reached into his pocket and took out his wallet. She saw him reach in and take out some euros. He handed them to her.

"What is this?" she asked.

"I took it when we were in Dundalk." His blue eyes met hers. "I took it to be sure I'd see you again—to return it."

"And you expect me to buy that?"

"And are you buying?"

She didn't care about the agents in the front seat. She took his face in her hands and kissed him.

65

The accounts they were tapping into were in Dubai. As expected, ahead of the anticipated blackout, the Dubai bank shut down their banking services worldwide. During the eighty-three-second switch over to the backup system, a local wi-fi network was activated. The long-range antennas on Grand Bahama did their job. They got in. That was when the room went crazy.

Alanna was glad that she was only an observer during this part of the operation. Everyone else was involved. David was in charge. Fingers flew over keyboards. The target accounts were emptied, transfers were made. Someone was keeping track of the time. Before the final countdown had started, Alanna had asked whether the Dubai bank could be held responsible for the breach in security. The answer was that there would be no evidence that anyone but the account holders had made the transfers. There would be no trace of a security meltdown. Jay had engineered that entirely.

She was amazed that Steven wasn't here to witness this. The group finished the transfers with two seconds to spare, and as the cheers rang out in the room, the boss finally walked in. Alanna thought he didn't look like a man who had achieved his goal.

He shook hands with a few and congratulated David before joining Alanna.

"Didn't you get the end result that you expected?" she asked. "You made the reallocation of wealth look pretty easy."

He didn't smile.

"Oh, yes. Here…in this place…" He looked around the room. "I did. Everyone did an incredible job."

Alanna decided to be serious. "This might be a setback, but whoever the contributors were to those accounts, they'll continue to build them up."

He nodded. "That's true. But at least we created an obstacle. We have successfully disrupted the smooth commerce of terror for the moment. Perhaps created questions about credibility. Maybe we'll have them pointing fingers at one other and venting their bile on each other's head. Perhaps we will save a few lives."

"And what happens now with Senator Hersey?" she asked.

"The arrangements pertaining to him were made long in advance of this moment." He glanced down at his watch. "Over the next hour, a handful of major newspapers and television and radio stations will get an anonymous tip, putting them on the scent of Senator Hersey's questionable and rather sizable accounts."

"Once he's questioned in the public eye, then he's lost."

"Confidence lost is rarely regained."

She saw Galvin look at his watch again. He seemed restless, upset. "Is there something else?"

"I have to get back to my office. I'm waiting for a phone call," he said vaguely, turning on his heel and walking out.

66

Paul Hersey showed up at his office an hour earlier than usual. None of his staff was in. That was fine with him. Most of them had burned the candle at both ends yesterday. He hadn't been able to sleep at all last night. The argument he'd had with Amber kept playing again and again in his head.

He couldn't understand how they'd gotten to the point where she'd walked out. There was no reason for her to know, in the first place. It was Matt's fault for bringing up all the crap. And what was Matt thinking, believing all that bullshit about Steven Galvin going off the deep end and having everyone executed who had anything to do with Nathan's death? Matt Lane didn't know Steven Galvin the way Paul did. Steven was the original gentle soul. The guy who wouldn't slap at a mosquito even if it was sucking his blood. He was the behind-the-desk geek who'd gotten lucky and made a fortune off the start of the Internet.

When Paul thought about it, of course, his one regret was that he hadn't talked Nathan out of joining the CIA.

The young man had come to him, consulted with him. The problem was that Nathan was too much like his father. He couldn't survive in that world of deception and murder.

He somehow had to explain all of this to Amber, and do a better job than he'd done last night. He didn't want to lose his daughter. Not again. She knew how cutthroat this politics business was. What happened to Nathan wasn't personal. Someone had to die. They lost agents in the field every year. Unfortunately, Nathan was the prime candidate on that specific date.

When the phone started ringing, he realized he was still standing by his secretary's desk. There was no one in the office to answer it. He decided to let the message system handle it. He'd barely unbuttoned his coat when his cell phone started ringing. He pulled it out of his breast pocket, just in case it was Amber calling.

It was Matt Lane—absolutely the last person he was in the mood to talk to right now.

"Are you near a TV?" he asked. Matt's voice sounded borderline crazed.

"I'm at my office."

"So, turn on the TV," he said.

His office phone started ringing again.

"What the hell?" He went into his office, carrying the cell phone.

No sooner had the message system picked up one call than the office phone was ringing again. He glanced back at the display on Susan's desk. Every line was lit up.

He held the cell phone to his ear. "Just tell me what's going on, Matt," he said shortly.

"You won't believe me unless you see it yourself."

"I don't have time for this," he snapped. But he switched on the light and opened the cabinet housing the television. The phones were still ringing in the outer office.

Paul turned on the television. Some cartoon came on. "What channel?"

"Any news channel. You won't miss it."

"What's going on? Was the president shot or something?" he asked.

He didn't have to wait for an answer. He saw it. The reporter on CNN had Paul's picture on the left corner of the screen. A red bar reading Breaking News ran across the bottom of the screen. Paul turned up the volume.

"…from unidentified sources that one of the largest contributors to Senator Paul Hersey's campaign has been a terrorist group associated with al…"

"What the hell is this?" Paul snapped. "Is this a joke? Where are they getting crap like this?"

"I warned you, Paul," Matt said at the other end. "It wasn't the president who was gunned down. It was you. He got you. The campaign is over."

67

Technology had helped make him a fortune. For many in the world, it was the foundation of education, the basis for everyday sustenance. Water, air, food, Internet, cell phones.

At this particular moment, however, Steven Galvin found technology totally useless. Amber wasn't answering her cell phone. Paul's housekeeper didn't know where she was, except that it looked as if she'd left with a suitcase. Galvin called the two airports in the D.C. area, having her paged. There had been lengthy holds, but no answer.

He couldn't call the police. He couldn't tell them that a faceless, nameless assassin was about to kill a U.S. senator's daughter. He couldn't tell them where or when. And by the way, Steven Galvin was the one who'd paid this assassin to make the hit.

They wouldn't be able to stop the killer anyway.

In a moment of desperation, Steven had even tried Paul's number. He didn't know what he would say to his old friend. Perhaps that he was looking for Amber. Paul's office phones were busy. Paul's cell sent his call directly to voice mail. Galvin didn't bother to leave a message.

There was a knock on his library door. He knew it could be any number of his people. This was the time when he should be with them—celebrating a project perfectly executed. Alanna and David and Jay would leave some time next week. Jay's and David's paths would cross with his again. They were both remaining on Steven's payroll. Alanna's case, however, was more complicated.

The soft knock came again. He knew who it was before opening the door.

"Can you use some company?" Alanna asked.

He left the door open and walked back across the room. He moved to the wall of windows behind his desk. He looked out at the overcast sky.

"I think you should see this," she said to his back.

He didn't have to turn around. He heard her turn on the television and switch to a news channel.

"Senator Paul Hersey…"

She switched the channel again.

"The five-term senator from Pennsylvania…"

She changed the station again.

"We haven't been able to contact Senator…"

She muted the sound when Steven turned around. "Why aren't you enjoying this?"

He walked closer to the television and stared at Paul's picture on the screen. This should have been enough. He should have ended it at this. He didn't know what madness had made him add Amber's name to the list of those who must suffer. Of those who must die.

"There's something else, isn't there?" she asked softly. "Something else you're waiting for."

He sat down on a nearby chair. Kei would have never forgiven him for what he had planned. He picked up the phone and dialed Amber's number again. As before, it went directly to her cell-phone message. This time he decided on leaving a message.

"Please call me, Amber. Please. This is Steven. It's urgent. Call me."

She put the remote on the table and sat on the chair next to him.

"Who's Amber?"

"Paul's daughter," he told her.

"Are you worried about how she'd be affected by all this news?"

He buried his face in his hands. He couldn't admit to the truth. Kei wouldn't have wanted this. Alanna would never forgive him. He realized the two women's judgment had somehow gotten woven together into a single conscience. He couldn't face them.

"Yes," he lied. "I'm worried about her."

68

Washington, D.C.

Amber was starved. She'd had no dinner last night, no breakfast this morning. She knew once they got to the hotel room, they wouldn't come up for air for hours. Of course, that was what Mick would call a "good problem."

She asked the agent driving the car to drop them off at a breakfast place a block away from their hotel. She was staying at the Ritz-Carlton in Georgetown. She loved the quaint, historic neighborhoods here...much better than the hectic pace of downtown D.C.

The agents dropped them at the door.

"Sit anywhere you want," the hostess told them as they walked in.

Amber headed for one of the booths by the window. Mick pulled his baseball cap off his head as he grabbed her elbow and directed her to a busy corner near the kitchen door. She let him have his way.

Mick hadn't mentioned anything about being hungry, but he ordered about three times more food than she did.

As a result, she licked her plate clean before he was halfway through his breakfast.

She ordered a cappuccino, keeping him company as he ate.

"You won't tell me your last name, which is perfectly okay," she teased him as he poured half a bottle of syrup onto the pancake left on his plate. "At least, tell me how old you are."

"Nineteen."

Her jaw almost hit the table. "Oh my God. I'm robbing the cradle. You're five years younger than I am. I'm…I'm…Mrs. Robinson."

"Who's Mrs. Robinson?"

"Did you see *The Graduate?*" she asked.

"Is it a movie?" he asked between mouthfuls of food.

"Yes, but never mind…it's definitely before your time. You probably haven't seen it. "'Mrs. Robinson' was a song, too, by Simon and Garfunkel."

"I've heard of them," he said.

She was relieved. She still couldn't believe, though, that she was having an affair with a nineteen-year-old. "Aren't you too young to be traveling without your parents?" she asked.

"They're both dead."

She looked at him, checking to make sure he wasn't pulling her leg. She couldn't tell. He hadn't slowed down. "Are you serious?"

He nodded. "My mother passed away when I was a year old. My father died when I was seven."

"That's so sad," she told him, reaching out and touching his hand. She was the product of a broken family.

But despite the problems she'd had over the years with both of her parents, they were still part of her life. "Who raised you then?"

"An uncle and his wife."

"They must be very special people," she said.

"She's great, he's okay."

Amber took another sip of her coffee, watching him. He was almost done with the food. "So were you telling the truth when you said you were a college student?"

"Yes…unfortunately."

"Why unfortunately?" she asked.

"Because I don't belong there," he said.

She watched him stab at the last bite of food with his fork but then drop it back on the plate.

"Why do you say that?" she asked gently.

"No one in my family ever went to the university."

"That shouldn't matter, should it?" she asked. "We don't have to follow in our parents' footsteps."

"You are."

Amber felt annoyed by that comment. "You don't know my parents. Why do you say that?"

He shrugged. "Your father is a senator. He's handsome, talks well with the reporters. He looks good in front of people. You have the same qualities. Someday, you could be a senator if you wanted, I'm thinking."

She thought about the argument she'd had with her father. She would never make the choices that he had made.

"I think I'll pass," she told him. "So, do you want to order another course, or are you ready?"

"Depends on where we're going from here," he asked, his gaze moving down the front of her sweater.

Amber told herself she didn't care if he was nineteen. "How does my hotel sound?"

"Fine with me."

She tried to pay for their breakfast, but he wouldn't listen to her and paid instead.

At the door he paused, pulling his baseball hat on. "So, are the fellows going to pick us up here?"

"No. I told them we'd be fine. We're practically across the street from the hotel."

"Let's take a cab."

"Don't be ridiculous." She slipped her arm into his. "Come on. We can walk."

"No, I'm dog tired, lass."

His reluctance made her more determined. They stepped out on the street.

"And I don't care what you said about not wanting to do any sightseeing," she told him. "You and I are going to fit in a couple of places tomorrow…at least the Smithsonian Aerospace Museum. It's awesome."

The cars were crawling down the street. She didn't wait for the intersection and tugged on his hand, crossing.

"So am I the only one staying at this hotel?" he asked.

"No, we both are. I moved here last night."

"You don't have your own place?" he asked.

"I moved back into my father's house about a year ago."

"And he doesn't want you to bring your lads home?" he asked, putting his arm around her shoulders and pulling her against his body. Their steps matched in stride.

"That's not it," she said. She wasn't ready to tell him more. But she didn't think he really cared anyway. He was totally preoccupied with looking at the buildings on the street.

"Who knows that you are staying here?" he asked.

"You mean at the hotel?"

He nodded.

"Nobody." She shrugged. "It's not like I check into places under a false name. I'm not some celebrity. No one cares where I go."

"Shouldn't those agents be here now, watching you?" he asked, looking around him.

"They're sort of escorting me as a favor to my father. He's a major candidate, but I'm not really on their list of people needing protection. So they listen to me when I tell them to give me space," she admitted.

"That does not seem right to me, lass. Someone could swipe you, then, right off the street."

"You are the nervous kind. I don't think Washington is anywhere near as dangerous as Belfast."

She motioned to the hotel entrance a hundred feet ahead of them. There was a news van parked in front of it. As they approached, she saw a person with a mike and another holding a camera jump out of the van and rush toward them.

"What the hell?" Mick said, tugging his hat down on his face and shoving her behind him.

"Ms. Hersey…Amber. Do you have anything to say about the report on your father?"

"What report?" she said, stepping up to the reporter.

She didn't know how it happened or why. But the

next thing she felt was Mick's hand shoving her to the ground. She landed on the sidewalk with Mick's body following with a loud thud.

The breath was knocked out of her. Mick was lying diagonally on top of her, his head pressed against her throat. Reporters were swarming around above them, and then there was shouting and complete chaos.

Amber couldn't figure out what was wrong, why he pushed her down, why he wasn't moving. Then she felt the warm wetness seeping onto her throat.

69

Alanna could tell he was becoming increasingly upset.

"I think I should leave."

"No, don't," he said, sitting back straight in the chair. "We need to discuss some kind of arrangement. I owe you a great deal."

She knew what he was talking about. Her deal with him had been Ray's return to her life. But that had all been a lie. Alanna realized that this week had helped readjust her life. She didn't resent him at all for what had happened. She was grateful. She was a smarter person for it. She recognized what was wrong before and what she had to change in future.

"I don't want anything," she told him.

"But there has to be something. Perhaps some financial compensation for your time. A consultation fee," he suggested.

She shook her head. "I have all I need."

He seemed unsettled about her decision. She realized he was a man who didn't like owing anyone anything. And here, he felt indebted to her.

Another breaking news story flashed across the screen. A street scene. People were shouting. A frantic reporter was saying something into the microphone. He reached immediately for the remote and turned up the volume.

"…police are everywhere. The sniper had to fire the shot from the top of one of the buildings…"

"No. Please, don't be…" Alanna heard him whisper.

"Our camera crew captured this footage minutes ago. They were standing a foot away from the victim in front of the Ritz-Carlton hotel in Georgetown."

Alanna stared at the television screen in disbelief. A young, good-looking man wearing a Washington Nationals baseball hat stepped in front of the camera.

A reporter shoved a microphone past him to someone who was standing behind. "Amber…Ms. Hersey. Do you have anything to say about the report on your father?"

"What report?" A beautiful young woman appeared beside him.

And then everything went crazy. She was down. The young man was down on top of her. Everyone ducked, including the cameraman, who was obviously on the ground as well. The camera panned around. People were taking shelter against a news van. There was screaming. Sirens. Two men who looked like plainclothes policemen were running toward the camera. The cameraman swept his camera around, stopping at the two people on the ground next to him. There was blood on the sidewalk.

Steven jumped to his feet in panic. He moved to the front of the television. "No! Who's hurt? Tell me…tell me it's not her."

"The initial reports are that Amber Hersey, the daughter of Senator Paul Hersey, who has been in the news this morning, was unhurt in the incident. I repeat, the daughter of Senator Hersey was unhurt after an attack on a Washington street. The condition of her companion is unknown at this time."

Alanna looked up at Galvin. There were tears on his face.

"Did you plan this, too?" she asked.

He turned up the volume and said nothing.

Alanna stared at him for a moment and then left the room. At the reception area in the main building, she stopped and asked one of the people working in the office to make flight arrangements for her for tonight.

She was ready to go home.

BOOK 3

*There's a special
providence in the fall of a sparrow. If it be now,
'tis not to come; if it be not to come, it will be
now; if it be not now, yet it will come: the
readiness is all...*

—Hamlet

70

Belfast, Ireland

Hundreds of people were expected to attend the funeral service at Saint Brigid's church this morning. Monsignor Cluny had called the house last night. He was worried that, with the large number of mourners, there might not be enough room inside the church for everyone.

Kelly was left to do everything by herself. She first had to make the call to the funeral parlor. She had to pick a casket, arrange for Mick's body to be sent back to Belfast from America, plan the wake, order flowers, buy food for the get-together at the house later.

Finn hadn't said a word since he came back. Even though she couldn't count on him putting himself back together, she wasn't about to speak at the funeral service about Mick. That, she couldn't do.

He didn't want to talk about it. She didn't ask. She knew there had been a mix-up, some serious problem, as all kinds of people had been trying to get hold of her husband the morning that everything had happened. His mobile had been off. There'd been no way to reach him.

When he arrived back home, he'd spent hours locked up in his office. He came out for meals, but said nothing. He didn't go out.

Finn might be retired now, but Kelly didn't know if her husband would ever recover from this tragedy.

The twins ran into the kitchen screaming something. Kelly envied their innocence. They knew Mick was gone, but they didn't understand that it was forever. She supposed, come Easter, all the questions of where he was would start up again. And they'd repeat everything again at Christmas.

Kelly poured Finn a cup of coffee. He'd not even gone to the wake. Kelly had to face everyone herself. There was no option this morning, though, and she'd told him so. He was leaving the house and coming to the funeral. He was going to mourn his brother's son like the man he was.

"Someone is at the curb, Mum," Liam said, tugging on her hand.

No one was supposed to come to the house. She left the cup on the counter and peered out the window down their driveway. A car had pulled up in front, on the street. A woman was getting out of the car.

"Who's that?" she found herself asking.

"She's pretty," Liam said to his brother. "Maybe you can marry her."

The next second the two boys were rolling on the floor in a fight.

"Conor! Liam!" she shouted, trying to pull the two apart. Their shirts were pressed. Their ties straight. She'd have to dress them up all over again if they continued with this. She yelled up the stairs. "Finn, I need you down here." The sound of the doorbell was more effective than a bucket of ice water. The two let go of each other and ran for the door. They didn't wait for Kelly to catch up to them, and opened the front door.

By the time Kelly arrived in the front hall, she found her husband had reached the bottom of the stairs. She was relieved to see him wearing his black suit. They both looked at the open door and the woman who was standing on their doorstep.

"Hello. You don't know me, but I'm Amber Hersey," she said, her voice breaking up. She had an American accent. "I…Mick was with me…when he was…I thought I would come here to the funeral…but I thought I should see you…and say how sorry I am about what happened. I want to tell you…for as short a time as we knew each other…how much he meant to me. I—"

The tears cut short her words. Kelly looked at Finn. He walked toward her.

"I know about you, Miss Hersey," he told her. "You meant a great deal to him."

He opened his arms and Amber moved in against him, her sobs muffled against his suit.

Kelly stepped behind her and closed the front door. Perhaps there was a chance, she thought. Maybe they would all recover from this, yet.

71

Eugene, Oregon
Seven Months later

Harsha enjoyed the lectures the best.

One hundred to two hundred students, sitting in a huge hall, listening to the drone of some professor talking about economics, or history, or psychology. It was deadly, and the baby was sure to be sound asleep in no time. There were times when Jay wished he could grab a pillow and curl up in the baby carrier next to his son. But he wasn't cutting any corners. He refused to break any rules.

The abrupt sound of students closing books and notebooks and banging to their feet at the end of the class always woke up the eight-month-old. He didn't cry, though. He never cried.

"I hope you took lots of notes in this class," Jay told him. "It's your turn to write the paper."

Harsha gave him a wide grin, showing his two bottom teeth as he kicked his chubby legs.

"That's my boy."

Padma was waiting right outside the conference hall. She took the carrier from him.

"What's next?" he asked.

"Done with my lab. I'm heading home," she told Jay, kissing him quickly. "See you for dinner?"

"You can count on it," Jay said, looking after his wife and son.

They lived about ten minutes away. The restored two-bedroom, hundred-year-old house with the large yard in the quiet neighborhood had been an incredible find. Especially when, with the help of Steven Galvin, they'd been able to pay cash for the property and buy it outright.

As a result both of them had decided to go back to school. Padma was taking two courses this semester, one in chemistry and one in accounting. She was officially applying to engineering school midyear. Jay was very proud of her.

The University of Oregon didn't charge any extra tuition for bringing Harsha with them to the halls, so they saved plenty of money not paying babysitters. School was going well. Jay was taking two courses as well, both in the humanities. He was trying to get them out of the way.

His job was going even better.

He liked the people he worked with. There were fourteen of them that worked in his office. Everyone operated pretty independently. A quirky bunch, each of them had a unique story. They were kind of a tech-support group for the rest of the company. Jay had been told there would be some travel involved, but so far he hadn't had to do any, and that was good. He set his own hours, and he was pretty much his own boss.

The best news of all, Padma was on speaking terms with her parents again. In fact, they were coming to stay with them for Thanksgiving and to see their grandson for the first time.

And Jay wasn't nervous at all. Life was good.

72

San Francisco, California

Seven months had passed since Leah's kidney transplant and there'd been no complications. All the test results were still normal. Her body had accepted the new organ as if it belonged there. She was even being weaned off the antirejection medications.

David was too cautious to think their troubles were over. At the same time, he knew they needed to go on with their lives.

Steven Galvin's wealth was managed by his foundations, and it ran extremely well on its own. David thought the people at the foundation had been extremely generous to him during all the months he'd stayed with his daughter in Germany. There'd been some consulting jobs he could work on long-distance for them, but that was the extent of it. They'd kept him on salary, and the benefits had been fully paid. David owed a serious debt of gratitude to Steven Galvin and the arrangements he'd made.

With Leah leaving the hospital, there were a number of openings in Galvin's organization that David could choose from. They were scattered all over the world. The one he'd decided on happened to be in San Francisco.

Leah and David needed a change, new surroundings, a fresh start. Leah had been out of school for months and had been working with tutors to keep up with other kids her age. Now she was well enough to actually go to school, sit in classes, play sports. She could finally live like other healthy nine-year-olds.

They were arriving on the West Coast two weeks before Christmas, but the time of the move wasn't much of a concern to David. Leah was a pro at making friends whenever and wherever she was. And she'd been a great sport about the decisions that David had made for both of them.

"So what is this surprise?" she asked him for the hundredth time in six hours. Their flight from New York had one stop in Phoenix. David realized five minutes after takeoff that he should have stayed quiet about his surprise until they'd arrived at their destination.

They were standing in San Francisco airport with the others who'd come off their plane and were waiting, as they were, for their luggage.

"A surprise isn't a surprise if you know what it is," he told her just as he had the other hundred times. "Wait and see."

"This isn't fair, Daddy," she complained. "It's like handing me a box at Thanksgiving and saying, 'Here's your Christmas present, but you can't open it until Christmas Day.'"

He pulled a midsize suitcase off the conveyer belt. He put it in front of her. "All your Christmas presents are in this bag…but you can't open them for two weeks."

She stared down in disbelief at the bag. "You've gotten *so* mean."

He laughed and pulled two more suitcases off the belt. The rest of their things would be brought in by movers, hopefully by the end of the week. David was anxious to have everything settled so that he could have a happy and normal Christmas for his daughter.

She held on with both hands to the alleged bag with gifts. "I'm pulling this one. You can handle the other two."

His initial reaction was to stop her from lifting anything or pulling things. It was so hard to let go and believe she was fine, even though her doctors had given her permission to do all of those things.

Resigned, he nodded. The two of them started for the door.

"So this place we're moving into…you said it has a pool?"

"Yes." After years of not being allowed to go swimming, pools were her biggest fascination.

They stepped out onto the sidewalk. Taxis and various vans and buses were lined up at the doors.

"This way, miss," he told her.

Leah looked around her as she followed. "Do you know if there are any kids living around us?"

"I assume there are. I really don't know," he told her.

"How far away is my school from where we'll be living?" she asked.

"Maybe a ten-minute drive."

"Do I take a bus to school?" she wanted to know.

"I think so," he answered.

"Sweet."

"We'll find out all the details when we go check it out tomorrow."

They stopped at a crosswalk.

"Actually," she said, "this is pretty scary, moving into a new city. Not knowing anyone. Not having any idea—"

"Think of the positives," a woman said beside her. "Now you'll have someone to play chess with."

Leah turned to the person who'd spoken the words, the bag of gifts forgotten. She wrapped her arms around Alanna's neck.

"I was hoping that we'd see you…that we'd be near you. Daddy wouldn't tell me, though." She looked over her shoulder at David. "Is Alanna my surprise?"

He nodded. Alanna and David gave each other a high five.

The light at the crosswalk turned green. David shook his head as Leah forgot the bag of gifts and started crossing arm in arm with Alanna. He juggled the third bag and followed them.

He'd been in touch with Alanna during the months that they'd been in Germany. She had as much to do with making Leah's kidney a reality as he did. When he was looking for a job, it seemed natural to look at the West Coast, somewhere close to the friend he and Leah had made on the island. She'd been instrumental in helping him find a place to live and a school for Leah and make their move go smoothly.

David watched them walking ahead of him.

"Are we going to live in the same building as you?" Leah was asking hopefully.

"In the same complex," Alanna told her.

"Can I come and visit anytime I want?" she asked.

"Anytime you want." Alanna put an arm around Leah's waist. "You know, you've gotten taller."

Leah started walking on tiptoe. "Pretty soon, I'll be taller than you."

"It doesn't matter. I can always beat you in chess."

A couple minutes of trash-talking followed about who was the better player. Alanna told David which level she'd parked her car, and they headed for the elevators.

"So is there any other person in the picture?" the nine-year-old asked.

"My grandmother comes and visits a couple of times a week."

"I don't have a grandmother. Do you think she'd mind if I called her grandma?" Leah asked.

"Actually, I call her *abuela*."

"Can I call her *abuela?*" Leah asked.

"She'd be delighted. I've talked so much about you that she can't wait to actually meet you."

Leah looked over her shoulder and cast a beaming smile at her father.

"So…Alanna. You didn't answer my other question."

"What question?"

"Is there a *boyfriend* in your picture?" Leah asked.

"What are you, nine going on twenty-nine?"

"Answer the question," Leah ordered.

"No boyfriend," she finally admitted.

Leah turned around and gave him the thumbs-up sign. She turned to Alanna again.

"Can my dad come and visit anytime, too?"

73

Erie, Pennsylvania

It didn't matter that Paul Hersey claimed he didn't know where the funds came from. The money was in his account, and it hadn't come in one lump sum, either. After that first horrible day, the money had continued to pour in over time from what the newspapers were claiming to be "'terrorist organizations.'"

The whole thing was totally a lie. But they kept saying that computers don't lie.

There were allegations of campaign fraud, commercial bribery and embezzlement. The trips he'd taken to the Middle East in his official capacity as a member of the Intelligence Oversight Committee were being scrutinized. The gifts, the dinners, everything he'd done, everywhere he'd gone. They'd tried to stick him with a hundred and one other charges, too. Most of them were thrown out of court. One that Paul Hersey was still struggling with, however, was explaining campaign contributions that were not under the name of an actual contributor. There were a number of them, it seemed.

It was all a setup. He knew it. But it didn't matter. It was too late. If you're explaining, then you've already lost.

In March, he'd announced that he was ending the run for the presidency. His goal was no longer to get into the White House, but to avoid going to jail. Last month, he'd officially resigned his seat in the Senate. He'd used health issues as an excuse, but no one was fooled.

During this mess, Amber had stayed away. It wasn't until last month, when he'd started chemo for prostate cancer, that she'd come to visit him in Erie. Even during that visit, it was obvious she was fulfilling an obligation. Her heart wasn't in the visit.

Matt had come up from Washington this past weekend to see him, too. He was Paul's only defender, his only friend left in a city of cutthroats. He came up to see him at least once a month. Paul appreciated that.

Paul had been born and raised in Erie, but there weren't too many people willing to associate with a disgraced politician, even an unindicted one.

He'd moved back into the same house that his parents built back in the fifties. To him, it was home. The city was a place where he would get healthy again. Where he would begin to rebuild his life.

He heard Matt's car pull into the driveway. A housekeeper came three days a week and took care of things, but on weekends especially, Paul was left on his own. Matt had gone to the drugstore to pick up some of his prescriptions for him. Chemo was not easy. He'd lost most of his hair. He looked as if he was in his eighties and not in his fifties these days. He didn't go out unless he absolutely had to.

He closed his book and lowered the foot of the easy chair. Matt had a set of keys. He walked in, a couple of minutes later, through the backdoor.

"Have you been listening to the news?" Matt asked.

The television was on in the background all the time just to keep him company. But Paul didn't pay much attention to it. He looked over at the screen. They were showing weather.

"America is obsessed with weather," he told Matt, turning up the volume slightly.

"It's Al Gore's doing," Matt commented. "Global warming."

Paul laughed. It was still fun to blame everything on the Democrats. "So, what did you hear on the news?"

"Steven Galvin."

The simple name was enough to push his blood pressure to stroke level. They hadn't seen each other since the crisis started. They hadn't spoken. But Paul knew there was only one person who was capable of working this kind of revenge. Another tragic thing was that Amber had become very close to Galvin. Paul had the idea that she visited him quite often.

"So what?" he growled.

"He's missing," Matt continued.

"How?"

"He left on his sailboat six days ago from Grand Bahama Island for Florida," Matt explained. "There's been no sign of him. No contact at all. He just disappeared."

"Was anyone else with him?" Paul asked.

"They don't think so." Matt dropped the prescriptions on the coffee table. "What I heard around Washington was that he's been acting pretty strange. He stayed on the island even through the summer. Nobody has seen him in public in quite some time."

"Amber still goes to the island to see him, doesn't she?"

"She does. She's one of very few people he's in touch with," Matt told him. "The word is that Kei's death finally caught up to him. You knew him pretty well. Do you think this would be his way of finishing it all?"

Paul stared at his friend. "What do you mean?"

"I mean ending it. Taking his life like his wife did—except doing it his own way."

Paul looked at the screen, into the face of the man who had once been his friend. Before it all went bad.

"I don't know. I thought I knew him. But I was wrong, Matt." Paul shrugged again and looked away. "I was dead wrong."

Authors' Note

Once again, thank you for allowing us to entertain you with this story.

Many people write to us and ask where we get our ideas for our stories. To answer a difficult question simply, our novels are all about characters. And the characters in our stories come to us from real life. A headline from the news, a whisper from some forgotten history, a face in an airport or train station, a name from a gravestone. We weave and twist together qualities and flaws and hopes and fears until a new character is formed. And then another. We put them on the page, and they begin to breathe. And a story is born. That's all there is.

The idea for *The Puppet Master* came to us from characters who exist in a moment of desperation. Most of us have been there at one time or another. A sickness in the family. A financial hardship. A love lost. A mistake in life that could ruin an entire future. And then, of course, the desperation of one of those characters evolves into a desire for revenge. How many of us are capable of going through with a scheme calculated to exact so terrible a vengeance? And if we are, how many of us would find any sense of satisfaction in the end?

This question is for you to answer. It might be the birth of *your* story.

In writing this book, there were many organizations and people who helped along the way. There are two people, though, to whom credit is particularly due. To our son Cyrus McGoldrick…thank you for the detailed account of your travels. We hope we did justice to some of those places in our descriptions. Also, to our son Sam McGoldrick…thank you for your creative input; thank you for your imagination and talent. We love you both. And may your dreams always come true.

As always, we love hearing from our readers:

Jan Coffey
c/o Nikoo & Jim McGoldrick
P.O. Box 665
Watertown, CT 06795
or
JanCoffey@JanCoffey.com
www.JanCoffey.com

A novel that could only be written by

RICK MOFINA

A VENGEFUL WOMAN WHO ACHES FOR HER
PLACE IN PARADISE...

AN ANGUISHED MOTHER DESPERATE TO FIND HER CHILD...

A DETECTIVE WHO NEEDS TO REDEEM HIMSELF...

THREE STRANGERS ENTANGLED IN A PLOT THAT COULD
CHANGE THE WORLD IN ONLY SIX SECONDS...

"Six Seconds...moves like a tornado."
—James Patterson,
New York Times bestselling author

*Available the first week of January 2009
wherever books are sold!*

MIRA®

www.MIRABooks.com

MRM2612

ANOTHER SHOCKING THRILLER BY
J.T. ELLISON

It was a murder made for TV: A trail of tiny, bloody footprints. An innocent toddler playing beside her mother's bludgeoned body. Pretty young Corinne Wolff, seven months pregnant, brutally murdered in her own home.

Cameras and questions don't usually phase Nashville Homicide lieutenant Taylor Jackson, but the media frenzy surrounding the Wolff case is particularly nasty...and thorough. When the seemingly model mommy is linked to an amateur porn Web site with underage actresses and unwitting players, the sharks begin to circle....

JUDAS KISS

*Available the first week of January 2009
wherever books are sold!*

MIRA®

www.MIRABooks.com   MJTE2629

REQUEST YOUR FREE BOOKS!

2 FREE NOVELS
FROM THE ROMANCE/SUSPENSE
COLLECTION PLUS 2 FREE GIFTS!

YES! Please send me 2 FREE novels from the Romance/Suspense Collection and my 2 FREE gifts (gifts are worth about $10). After receiving them, if I don't wish to receive any more books, I can return the shipping statement marked "cancel." If I don't cancel, I will receive 4 brand-new novels every month and be billed just $5.49 per book in the U.S. or $5.99 per book in Canada, plus 25¢ shipping and handling per book plus applicable taxes, if any*. That's a savings of at least 20% off the cover price! I understand that accepting the 2 free books and gifts places me under no obligation to buy anything. I can always return a shipment and cancel at any time. Even if I never buy another book from the Reader Service, the two free books and gifts are mine to keep forever.

185 MDN EF5Y   385 MDN EF6C

Name _____ (PLEASE PRINT) _____

Address _____ Apt. # _____

City _____ State/Prov. _____ Zip/Postal Code _____

Signature (if under 18, a parent or guardian must sign)

Mail to **The Reader Service:**
IN U.S.A.: P.O. Box 1867, Buffalo, NY 14240-1867
IN CANADA: P.O. Box 609, Fort Erie, Ontario L2A 5X3

Not valid to current subscribers to the Romance Collection,
the Suspense Collection or the Romance/Suspense Collection.

Want to try two free books from another line?
Call 1-800-873-8635 or visit www.morefreebooks.com.

* Terms and prices subject to change without notice. N.Y. residents add applicable sales tax. Canadian residents will be charged applicable provincial taxes and GST. Offer not valid in Quebec. This offer is limited to one order per household. All orders subject to approval. Credit or debit balances in a customer's account(s) may be offset by any other outstanding balance owed by or to the customer. Please allow 4 to 6 weeks for delivery. Offer available while quantities last.

Your Privacy: Harlequin is committed to protecting your privacy. Our Privacy Policy is available online at www.eHarlequin.com or upon request from the Reader Service. From time to time we make our lists of customers available to reputable third parties who may have a product or service of interest to you. If you would prefer we not share your name and address, please check here. ☐

BOB08R

A new thriller from the author of *Body Count*

P.D. MARTIN

Increasingly haunted by her ability to experience the minds of killers in the throes of heinous crimes, FBI Profiler Sophie Anderson's talent is uncontrollable and unpredictable. When bodies start showing up on a university campus, she and Tucson police detective Darren Carter are pulled into the case. However, Sophie's puzzled by the fact that certain signature elements are different in each killing. The FBI database has a record of many of the signatures—but they have been used by different serial killers.

As the bodies continue to appear, Sophie must hone her terrifying skills to try and track down the killer—or killers.

THE MURDERERS' CLUB

"Enough twists and turns to keep forensics fans turning the pages."
—*Publishers Weekly* on *Body Count*

Jan Coffey

32458 THE DEADLIEST STRAIN	___ $6.99 U.S.	___ $8.50 CAN.
32192 FIVE IN A ROW	___ $6.99 U.S.	___ $8.50 CAN.
66919 TWICE BURNED	___ $6.50 U.S.	___ $7.99 CAN.

(limited quantities available)

TOTAL AMOUNT	$ _____
POSTAGE & HANDLING	$ _____
($1.00 FOR 1 BOOK, 50¢ for each additional)	
APPLICABLE TAXES*	$ _____
TOTAL PAYABLE	$ _____

(check or money order—please do not send cash)

To order, complete this form and send it, along with a check or money order for the total above, payable to MIRA Books, to: **In the U.S.:** 3010 Walden Avenue, P.O. Box 9077, Buffalo, NY 14269-9077; **In Canada:** P.O. Box 636, Fort Erie, Ontario, L2A 5X3.

Name: _____

Address: _____ City: _____

State/Prov.: _____ Zip/Postal Code: _____

Account Number (if applicable): _____

075 CSAS

*New York residents remit applicable sales taxes.
*Canadian residents remit applicable GST and provincial taxes.

MIRA®

www.MIRABooks.com

MJC0109BL